D1234573

The frail woman struggled to catch her breath. She fought to right herself in the bed but could not, so I offered soothing words to encourage stillness. The dear one gazed over at me, eyes so filled with pain that my heart twisted inside of me.

"Tomorrow," she whispered, "I shall keep on. Tell my boys to sleep well and await the morning light when we shall set to flight once more toward freedom."

A fit of coughing followed, and I spoke the only words that came to mind in the moment. "Father, be merciful to this, Thy daughter."

I reached my hand to soothe her, as if the comfort of my palm might somehow breathe life back into a worn-down body not long for this world. The older woman seemed to melt under my touch, much as yesterday's batch of butter had done when I left it sitting in the afternoon sun. The wrinkles around her eyes smoothed as she drifted off to sleep. I prayed as I kept a watchful eye on her breaths, which came and went like gentle whispers of wind through an open doorway.

I stroked her tight gray curls, their texture familiar. In that moment, I was a child once more, seated at my grandmother's bedside, watching her breathe her last.

I pulled my hand away, grief snatching my heart like fingers around a chicken's neck before the kill. Had my own precious grandmammy not passed from this life on that horrible morning all those years ago, I would have sworn I was staring into her beautiful face, even now.

April 3, 1860

SECRETS OF
WAYFARERS INN

The Bucket List

JANICE THOMPSON

Guideposts

Danbury, Connecticut

Published by Guideposts Books & Inspirational Media
100 Reserve Road, Suite E200
Danbury, CT 06810
Guideposts.org

Cover and interior design by Müllerhaus
Cover illustration by Bob Kayganich, represented by Deborah Wolfe, LTD.
Typeset by Aptara, Inc.

Printed and bound in the United States of America
10 9 8 7 6 5 4 3 2 1

The Bucket List

DEDICATION

In loving memory of my mother, Shirley Moseley, whose bucket list included as many Caribbean cruises as she could squeeze in.

Just as each day brims with your beauty, my mouth brims
with praise. But don't turn me out to pasture when I'm old or
put me on the shelf when I can't pull my weight. My enemies are
talking behind my back, watching for their chance to knife me.
The gossip is: "God has abandoned him.
Pounce on him now; no one will help him."

Psalm 71:8–11 MSG

CHAPTER ONE

Where do we stand, ladies?" Tess Wallace paced from table to table in the Wayfarers Inn café and surveyed the scene. Everywhere she looked, she saw bright pink, yellow, blue, and green Easter eggs, waiting to be filled, and far too many bags of sugary candies to count.

Tess's good friend and business partner, Janice Eastman, looked up from her work at the table nearest the window. "I've stuffed two hundred and fifty plastic eggs with candy so far. Winnie's going to help me with the next two hundred and fifty, aren't you, Winnie?"

"Mm-hmm." Winnie Washington, the inn's very own Top Chef, wiped her hands on her apron and then glanced at her watch. "I just got the bread in the oven, so don't let me forget to check on it in a while."

"I have four hundred eggs completed," LuAnn Sherrill Grimes added from her table. "If my helper would stop distracting me, I'd have even more." With the tip of her head, she acknowledged her husband, Brad.

He shrugged and offered a sheepish grin. "Hey, no one told me I couldn't eat the candy. So, I've helped myself to a piece or two."

"A piece or *four* would be more like it." LuAnn laughed and then stuffed another egg. "But we're getting it done. How many did you say we need, in total, Tess?"

"I purchased two thousand plastic eggs and enough candy to fill them." Tess surveyed the chaos at the table where she sat. "But that doesn't include the prize eggs. When the business owners show up early tomorrow, we'll let them stuff their own prizes into eggs and then I'll fill the golden egg with the cash they provide." Tess could envision the whole thing now. Tomorrow morning, the front lawn of Wayfarers Inn would be teeming with children on the hunt, especially for the golden egg, the one filled with three hundred dollars cash.

"It's a lot of work, but I think this whole thing is so much fun." Janice glanced up once again. "A community-wide Easter egg hunt at Wayfarers is just the ticket. Maybe this can become a tradition, you know?"

"I love that idea," Tess responded. "Good promotion for the inn too."

"Yes." A warm smile turned up the edges of Janice's lips. "Now, let's hope the weather cooperates."

"We're expecting a high of sixty-nine, light breezes, sunny skies. That's what the weather forecast predicted for Saturday, anyway." Tess rested easy in the knowledge that tomorrow would be a lovely day.

"Perfect." Janice went back to work.

Tess turned her focus to a new bag of candy, a combination of sweet and sour delights. Her mouth watered just looking at them.

Just as she reached for the bag, a cheerful voice sounded. "What do we have here, ladies? You're throwing a party and didn't invite us?"

Tess turned to discover one of the inn's guests, Daisy Carmichael, standing at the entrance of the café alongside her granddaughter, Miranda.

The petite senior clasped her hands together in obvious delight. "I didn't see any of this when I came down for breakfast earlier."

"We had them in the office," Tess explained. "We're filling plastic eggs for tomorrow morning's Easter egg hunt on the front lawn."

"Oh, yes, I saw a sign about that when we checked in." Miranda tucked a loose hair behind her ear. "Sounds like a lot of fun."

"We're expecting around two hundred and fifty kids, if all goes as planned," LuAnn explained.

"Which is why we've got so many eggs." Tess gestured to the tables.

"And so much candy." Brad held up a handful.

Daisy squealed. "Mmm, looks yummy. Can we help?" Her eyes sparkled with merriment. "I haven't prepared Easter eggs since my children were little. Do you mind?"

"Of course not. And thank you." Tess pointed to an empty café table, happy for the additional helpers. "If you want to have a seat, I'll give you some candy and empty eggs."

As she prepared a work station for Daisy and Miranda, Tess couldn't help but give them a closer look. These two were quite a pair, the older woman all giggles and smiles and the younger, more studious and quiet. And did they ever differ in clothing taste. Miranda's conservative attire looked almost matronly next to the vivacious flowery colors in her grandmother's wardrobe.

Tess found the elderly woman completely mesmerizing, from her hot-pink pants and wild floral top to her oversized black round glasses. She reminded Tess of a famous fashion designer she'd seen on TV once, a quirky older gal with tight gray ringlets and vivacious personality.

But despite their differences in age and style, the two resembled each other. Tess could almost picture Daisy looking like Miranda as a younger woman. They had a similar build and the same contagious laugh and piercing blue eyes.

As Daisy settled in, she glanced Tess's way and grinned. "I must thank you all for placing me in that lovely room with my name in it."

"Oh, that's right. You're in Sunshine and Daisies," Tess said. "I'm so glad you like it."

"Like it? I love it! You ladies seemed to know exactly what I needed."

"I can promise you, it was only a coincidence," Tess said with a smile.

"Well, a lovely coincidence, then. I just love the decor. That stained-glass piece hanging in the window makes my heart want to sing. Every morning when I wake up, streams of sunlight come bursting through and I just want to throw my arms up in the air and say, 'Thank You, Lord, for another day.'" An egg shot out of Daisy's hand and flew across the room. "Oops!"

The woman's childish squeal warmed Tess's heart.

Daisy fetched the egg and then sat back down. "I have to ask, is that bed topper hand crocheted?"

"It is." Tess smiled. "I think it's gorgeous, don't you?"

"Oh, yes! All those sunny yellow and white flowers on such a lovely blue background. It's like a walk through the garden in springtime! If I didn't think you'd miss it, I'd slip it into my bag when I leave." Daisy winked. "But seriously, it matches my name so beautifully." She turned her attention to the eggs in front of her.

"So, how will the Easter egg hunt work?" Miranda asked after she started filling eggs. "Are all the kids going at once?"

"No." Tess shook her head. "That wouldn't be fair to the little ones. We're dividing the lawn into three sections—one for the preschoolers, one for the five- to seven-year-olds, and another for the bigger kids. There will be prize eggs in every section with a golden money-filled egg for one of the bigger kids to find."

"Three hundred dollars in cash," LuAnn threw in. "Several local businesses are pitching in."

"Oh my." Daisy fingered a sour candy. "That sounds like a lot of fun."

"It's very generous of you to give money away like that," Miranda said as she snapped open an egg.

"Local business owners are donating most of the other high-dollar eggs too. They're coming early tomorrow morning." Tess pointed to a bag of extra-large plastic Easter eggs. "They're stuffing these bigger eggs with coupons for free merchandise from their restaurants and stores. Along with candy, of course. But the grand prize winner will be the one who finds that golden egg."

"What a lovely idea." Daisy nearly dropped the egg in her hand. "The kids will love it."

"We're offering a free night's stay at the inn in one of the bigger eggs," Janice added, "as well as free lunch at the café."

"Speaking of lunch…" Daisy looked around the room. "Are you not serving lunch today?"

"Oh, we are." Tess glanced down at her watch. "It's only nine thirty. We've got plenty of time."

Winnie glanced up from her spot next to Janice. "It's soup and salad today. Chicken salad, to be precise. And chicken and wild rice soup."

"I just love a good chicken salad." Daisy held up one of the eggs, as if to show it off. "And isn't it ironic?"

"Ironic?" Tess gave her a curious glance. "How so?"

"Eggs. Chicken." Daisy giggled and set the egg back down.

Tess loved the woman's vivacious smile and carefree laugh. She could almost imagine that Daisy Carmichael was a bit of a handful, not unlike herself.

"Remember when we used to boil eggs and dip them in dye to make them colorful?" Daisy asked. "I still remember how messy my fingers got. And I ruined more than one egg, for sure. One time I played a prank on my brother and gave him a rotten egg on purpose."

"You sound just like Tess," LuAnn said. "She's our resident prankster."

As Daisy carried on, Tess couldn't help but think she would be like her when she reached her older years. To have so much life and energy was a contagious thing.

Not that she really knew much about these guests. In the few days they'd been at Wayfarers, she couldn't exactly pick up on their story, except that they were grandmother and granddaughter. Daisy was as eccentric as they came, and Miranda seemed content to care for her grandmother's every need.

"It's a shame I'm too old to look for eggs." Miranda's lips curled up in a smile. "That free night's stay at the inn sounds good."

"Oh? Would you like to extend your visit?" Tess asked. "I think that would be wonderful."

"Maybe?" Miranda glanced at Daisy. "But I'm letting Mimi call the shots. This is her trip, after all."

"And what a wonderful traveling companion you've been, sweet girl." Daisy rested her hand on Miranda's arm. "Have I mentioned how grateful I am for this little adventure?"

"Only a thousand times." Mirada's broad smile spoke of her love for the older woman. "Though, truth be told, I'm probably not quite as adventurous as you. I can hardly keep up with you, Mimi."

"Mimi." Tess offered a smile. "That's a coincidence. My grandchildren call me that, as well."

"How wonderful! This sweet girl right here holds a special place in my heart. Always has, always will."

"I feel the same about you, Mimi," Miranda responded.

"That's why my very favorite piece of jewelry is going to be yours one day." Daisy unpinned a lovely brooch from her blouse and held it up. "This was my great-great-grandmother's."

"What a lovely fleur-de-lis," Tess observed.

"Yes, it's beautiful. Very French, my ancestors. Anyway, my great-great-grandmother has ties to this area. That's why we've come. I want to get to know the place where she once lived."

"But Mimi..." Miranda looked perplexed. "Shouldn't you pass it down to Aunt Victoria?"

"No ma'am." Daisy shook her head. "That daughter of mine might think it's coming to her, but it's not. I had always planned to pass it to your mother, sweetheart, but since she passed away...well..."

A somber silence followed as everyone seemed to process this news.

"Anyway, it's going to you, not to Victoria. And I don't care how much she fusses about it." Daisy lit into a lengthy story about the history of the piece and its value, both monetary and sentimental.

Tess drew near and gave the piece a closer look. Whoa. Were those real diamonds? And pearls too? With so many of them forming the lovely fleur-de-lis shape, this thing had to be worth a fortune.

"Well, please don't plan on passing it to me anytime soon." Miranda continued to stuff eggs with candy. "I'd much rather have you than a brooch, lovely as it is."

Daisy gave her granddaughter a wink and pinned the brooch back on. "I'll do my best to stick around a bit longer, sweetie. I've still got adventures aplenty to share with you. They're all written down on my bucket list."

"Bucket list?" Janice echoed.

"Mm-hmm." Daisy grinned. "One day, I'll tell you all about it." The brooch slipped off her blouse and hit the table below.

"Are you sure you don't want me to hold on to that for you, Mimi?" Miranda asked.

"Hold on to my brooch?" Daisy shook her head. "Oh, no thank you, child."

"I wouldn't mind a bit." Miranda's words seemed strained, as if she meant to press the issue.

"No, that's okay. I'll be careful with it, sweet girl. No worries."

Things grew quiet after that as everyone continued to work on the eggs. After several minutes Winnie rose. "Time to check on that bread. It sure smells good."

"Sure does," Daisy agreed. "My stomach is rumbling, just thinking about it."

Winnie buzzed into the kitchen, still talking about all the things she had yet to do today.

"Sometimes I worry about her." Janice started loading some of her filled eggs into a plastic bag. "She works so hard."

"Well..." Tess put a finger to her lips. "Don't tell anyone, but I've been putting away a little money for a special gift, just to bless her."

"Oh?" LuAnn shot her a curious glance.

"Remember how she told us that the stand mixer she uses at home went out on her?"

"I believe she said she burned it up, using it so much," Janice said.

"Easy to do," LuAnn chimed in. "I've overworked a mixer or two in my day."

"Well, anyway, I've been setting aside some money for a new one for her. A really nice one with lots of attachments. I thought it would be a fun surprise."

"That's so sweet, Tess." LuAnn gave her an admiring look. "She'll be tickled pink."

"I hope so." Tess turned back to her work stuffing eggs. She wanted to ask a couple of questions about Daisy's bucket list but was distracted by a phone call. She didn't recognize the number coming through on her cell but took the call anyway, just in case it happened to be one of the business owners participating in the Easter egg hunt.

It turned out the call was from someone altogether different, their new yard guy. She chatted with him for a bit, and then he asked if he could come over to mow the lawn this afternoon instead of early morning.

"Sure, that's great. Come on over," Tess said. "I think that's a perfect idea." She ended the call and dove back into her work, now stuffing filled eggs into large plastic bags. Afterward, she started counting the still-empty eggs but got flustered when she lost count.

LuAnn approached with a full bag which she set on a chair. She leaned in close to Tess and lowered her voice to ask, "You doing okay over here?"

"Hmm?" Tess stopped counting and glanced her way. "Oh, yes. I'm just distracted by that call. It was Griffin Patterson. But you made me lose count again."

"Sorry."

Tess began again. As far as she could tell, they still had about three hundred and fifty to fill, not counting the ones at Daisy and Miranda's table.

LuAnn pulled up an empty chair and sat down. "So, that was the new yard guy on the phone?"

"Yes. He's coming by in an hour or so to mow the lawn and get it ready for tomorrow morning. We want everything to be perfect."

Brad looked up from his eggs. "Is that the guy you just hired, the one who…" His words hung in the air.

Tess nodded. No point in talking about Griffin Patterson's recent release from prison in front of their guests.

"I heard he's been mowing the church lawn for free since he got out," Janice said. "I think that's admirable."

"Got out of where?" Daisy looked up from the egg she was stuffing.

"Oh, he was just…away for a while," LuAnn said.

"But now he's back, mowing lawns." Brad reached for another piece of chocolate.

LuAnn slapped his hand. "Enough already."

"Okay, okay." He laughed.

Janice glanced toward the stairs that led up to their apartment on the fourth floor. "I'll be right back. I need to head upstairs for a bit."

"Sure." Tess shrugged.

Janice disappeared and came back minutes later, camera in hand. "This old thing's giving me fits, but I hope I can still get some good photos tomorrow."

"Why not use the one on your phone?" Tess suggested. "These newer phones have amazing cameras, right?"

"Yeah, but I still love the feel of a real one in my hand."

"I just heard about a wonderful new camera that's got the sharpest images ever. And the speed is incredible." Miranda flashed Janice a warm smile. "You should look into that." She gave her the specs, and Janice agreed to check it out.

"Should I just leave the eggs here?" Janice asked. "I've bagged up the filled ones."

"Yes, leave them." Tess took a look at her own stash and realized she was nearly done with the stuffing process.

Janice walked out of the café, then turned back. "I might test out my camera by taking some pictures of the flowers blooming in the front garden. I saw the honeysuckles are in bloom. They're my favorite. And the daffodils are gorgeous this year."

"You might want to do that before Griffin gets here," Tess reminded her. "It won't be a very peaceful photo shoot if there's a big mower going in the background."

"True."

Several minutes later, Daisy and Miranda finished filling their eggs. LuAnn and Brad finished up their batch too. Tess dumped all of them into bags, along with the others. Soon, all two thousand eggs were filled, bagged, and ready to go. Tess could hardly wait for tomorrow morning.

But first, to tidy up this café before lunch. Cellophane bags that once held the plastic eggs were strewn about, along with empty candy bags and leftover pieces of candy that had landed on tables, chairs, and the floor. What a fiasco.

They worked hard to bring some order to the room. By ten forty-five the place was looking spick-and-span. Tess carried the bags of eggs into the office and deposited them on the floor behind the desk. They wouldn't bother anyone in here.

She walked back into the café to give it one last spot check and saw that Daisy appeared to be distressed about something. She clutched a hand to her chest and repeated the words, "Oh dear, oh dear!"

"What is it, Mimi?" Miranda asked. "What's happened?"

"My brooch!" Daisy patted the spot where she'd pinned it onto her blouse. "It's gone missing."

"Did you put it back on after it fell on the table?" LuAnn asked.

"I honestly can't remember." Tears filled Daisy's eyes. "Oh dear. What have I done? That brooch is supposed to be yours one day, Mandy. I can't believe I've lost it."

"Surely you didn't lose it. I mean, you didn't leave the room." Tess joined them at their table. "It has to be here somewhere. We just have to search."

They all spent the next couple of minutes peering under the tables and chairs. Brad even moved the serving table and searched behind it. There was no brooch to be found.

"There's really only one place it could be," Tess said after they'd given up. "It's got to be in one of those eggs." Her heart sank at the very notion.

"Oh dear." Daisy sniffled. "I can't imagine how that could have happened without me noticing. How will we ever find it?"

With over two thousand stuffed eggs in those bags, Tess couldn't help but ask herself the same question. How, indeed?

CHAPTER TWO

That afternoon after the lunch crowd left the innkeepers spent two hours opening and searching every single one of those two thousand eggs...with no luck. Everyone went on about their day, hoping the brooch would turn up, but Daisy was quite distraught, and so was Tess. Late that night, she had a hard time sleeping. Hopefully the brooch was hiding in one of Daisy's pockets or even inside her clothing, as Miranda had suggested. The idea that they had somehow overlooked it while tearing those eggs apart was baffling.

Tess finally fell asleep and dreamed about eggs. She awoke early and rolled over in her bed, anxious to see if the sun was up. The weather forecast had predicted a clear, temperate day. To her great relief, the morning had dawned bright and sunny, with barely a cloud in the sky. Tess peered out of her bedroom window, pausing long enough to thank the Lord for the beautiful weather. Off in the distance a tugboat chugged its way along the Ohio River, headed north. She watched until it disappeared from view.

Tess made quick work out of getting ready for the day. She helped Winnie and Janice prepare breakfast for the guests then rushed back up to her room to make sure her hair and makeup looked all right.

LuAnn and Brad arrived just after she made her way back downstairs. Brad passed off some cash for the golden egg, and Tess thanked him. She then put the couple to work dividing the lawn into three sections for the various ages of children. Before they started, the two of them carried the bags of eggs outside onto the front stoop in anticipation of scattering them around the lawn.

The shop owners started arriving at nine, as anticipated. Tess ushered them inside the café, and before long the whole room hummed with excitement as they stuffed their various offerings into the larger colored eggs. There was a coupon for a hot fudge sundae from the ice cream shop, one for a dozen hand-painted cookies from the bakery, and even one for a bucket of chicken from a local restaurant chain. The children might not appreciate the coupons as much as cash or candy, but their parents would certainly love the freebies.

Finally, it came time to load the golden egg. Tess pulled it out of the bag and pried it open, then waited as several of the local business owners contributed cash to go toward the grand prize. She took their money with a smile, imagining how happy the lucky winner would be.

At the end of the line was Rankin Smith, owner of ASAP Insurance. He passed off a twenty and a five. The well-put-together man looked a little out of place dressed in a business suit and tie on a Saturday morning. And the clip-on name tag with the name of his business was a bit much. On the other hand, he probably saw this as a good way to promote himself to the community—and why not? She would probably do the same thing in his position.

"I can't thank you enough for this," Tess said, as she took his cash and added it to the rest. "I know whoever finds this golden egg will be thrilled."

"I sure hope so. And I'm happy to be of service. It's been great getting to know my new neighbors in Marietta."

Tess smiled at him then remembered the money in her pocket. After adding Brad's fifty to the mix, she stuffed three hundred dollars in cash into the golden egg and snapped it shut.

Tess glanced at her watch. "If you'll excuse me, I need to head outside."

"Surely you're not hiding all those eggs by yourself."

"Oh no," she said. "Anyone can help. We've just got to hope the kids don't show up while we're working. But I'm going to ask Brad to act as security guard, just in case. If any kids do show up, he'll hold them at bay on the side of the inn until the time is right."

"Sounds like you've got this all planned out. Good for you."

She smiled again. "Thank you."

"Hide that golden egg in a tricky place."

"You bet. I'm excited to see who finds it."

Tess noticed her friend Sandie Ballard from the local bakery, the Better Batter. Tess walked up to her just as Sandie put a coupon inside of a large egg.

"Hey, Tess." Sandie snapped the egg together. "I just put a coupon for a free birthday cake in this egg. Two tier."

"Perfect. That's very generous of you."

Sandie shrugged. "Actually, it's good promotion and a lot cheaper than an ad in the paper."

"True."

"Hey, wait till you see what Maggie from the art store put in hers."

She pointed, and Tess took a few steps in Maggie's direction.

"I thought this would be fun." Maggie popped open her egg to show Tess a coupon for a free painting class.

"Oh, that's clever. I know the kids will love it."

"They're going to love all of this," Maggie said. "I can't wait to see their faces."

"Yes." Tess checked her watch again then raised her voice to reach the vendors scattered around. "Brad and LuAnn already brought out the bags with the candy-filled eggs. They're just waiting on me to give the go-ahead to start hiding them as soon as all of you are ready to help."

The shop owners confirmed that they were all raring to go, and they joined her on the front walkway moments later. Tess was relieved to see the families hadn't started arriving yet.

Janice approached, camera in hand. "This is going to be so much fun." She lifted it and snapped a shot of the bags of eggs, which Brad and LuAnn had stacked along the front walkway.

"Yes, I'd say so. I'm still so worried about that brooch, though."

"Nothing we can do about that today. Maybe tell folks to be on the lookout for it, just in case we overlooked it?"

Tess shrugged. "I guess. We'll see what Daisy wants us to do. It just feels like an odd kink in our overall plan."

LuAnn walked their way. "Hey, I just sent Brad for a look-see around the far edge of the property. He's worried people are going to start arriving soon."

"Yes, we need to get going hiding these eggs." Tess called everyone together to give them instructions.

"We've divided the yard into three sections, as you can see," Tess explained. "To my right is the section for the youngest ones." She gestured. "Just beyond that is the area for the early elementary-aged kids. And beyond that is the biggest area of all, for the older kids. All three sections will get the smaller eggs and the larger eggs. Meanwhile, I'm going to hide the golden egg in the section where the oldest kids can hunt for it." She held up the egg. "But no peeking, folks."

Tess gave the okay and within seconds, bags of eggs were unloaded across the freshly mowed lawn. Janice snapped pictures of it all, pausing on occasion to grumble about the condition of her older-model camera. While they worked, the song sparrows sang out their morning tune overhead, clearly oblivious to the incoming crowd.

As Tess crossed the lawn, headed for the daffodil bushes near the front window, she couldn't help but notice that the grass looked particularly green this morning. It also had that lovely fresh-cut scent she loved so much. She located the perfect spot under the bushes and set the golden egg in place, then smiled as she thought about how excited the winner would be once he or she located it.

After placing the egg, Tess noticed the yard man walking toward her. She smiled when she saw his button-up khaki-colored shirt with THE LAWN RANGER patch above the pocket.

"Griffin, you're back. And I love the new shirt."

"Thanks. Thought it might make me look more official."

"Definitely. But why are you here? I thought you finished up the yard yesterday. It looks great, by the way."

"Thanks." His nose wrinkled as he glanced toward the front of the inn. "Yes, I mowed, but I got to thinking about these bushes to the right of the daffodils." He gestured to the cedar bushes. "They're pretty overgrown, and the needles are sharp. I don't want a child to get jabbed."

"Oh, sure. Whatever you think. But you'd better hurry, okay? The kids should be arriving any moment."

"I will. I've brought my hedge clippers." He reached into his large bag and came out with a pair.

"Won't take a minute." He sprinted toward the front of the inn, nearly colliding with Rankin Smith, who somehow managed to dodge the hit.

Tess headed toward the front walkway and noticed someone she didn't recognize coming toward her. The handsome young man with the sandy-colored hair had a tablet tucked under his arm and was snapping photos with his phone. The stranger walked right toward her and gave her a look of curiosity. "You the one in charge of this event?"

"One of many." She put her hand over her eyes to shield the sunlight, which threatened to blind her. "Tess Wallace. I don't think we've met before."

"Corey Sampson. I work for the paper."

"Nice to meet you. I don't recall seeing you around before. Which column do you write?"

"I'm more of a roving reporter right now." His gaze shifted to Rankin Smith, and his expression immediately morphed to one of concern. "Looking for a story."

"At our Easter egg hunt?" She laughed. "Are you pulling my leg?"

"No."

"Ah. I thought maybe you might have a child attending."

He lifted his phone as if to take a picture and pointed it directly at Griffin Patterson, who was clipping the cedar bushes.

"Hey, that guy cutting your bushes...I know him."

"You do?"

"Yeah." Corey put the camera down and lifted his hand above his eyes as if to shade them from the sun. "That's Griffin Patterson, right?"

"That's right."

"I thought so." He pursed his lips and reached for his tablet.

"Where do you know him from?" Tess asked.

"Prison."

"Ah."

"Yeah. Kind of a long story. Maybe he can fill you in on the rest."

Interesting. Had this guy done prison time too?

Corey's brow wrinkled as he glanced Griffin's way again. "Excuse me, but I've got a little unfinished business with him that won't wait."

Before she could say, "Don't go onto the lawn until the kids arrive," Corey was sprinting across the yard, headed straight for Griffin. Oh boy. She could hardly wait to see how this panned out.

Unfortunately, Tess found herself distracted by Daisy and Miranda, who bounded out the front door of the inn, headed right for her.

"Good morning, world!" Daisy called out. "I'm here now! The party can begin!"

Tess smiled as they approached. Daisy looked very fetching this morning in her lime-green pedal pushers and hot-pink sweater with white fleur-de-lis.

"I just love this!" Daisy clasped her hands together and looked around the yard. "It takes me back to my younger days, when my children were little."

Tess couldn't help but notice the soft wrinkles on the backs of Daisy's hands. But what really caught her eye—along with the expensive oversized jewelry—were the knotty, misshapen fingers. Those hands had seen a lot of years and now bore the twists and turns of a life well lived.

Tess didn't spend much time gazing at Daisy's hands, however—not with such a sparkle in those soft blue eyes and joy-crinkles around her painted lips. Tess was drawn to this woman for much the same reason she'd been drawn to candy as a child. Daisy was sweet and delightful, a bona fide treasure of a woman.

Daisy's broad smile diminished, and a cloud seemed to settle over her. "Memories are funny things. They can hurt almost as much as they can bring joy."

"So true," Tess said. "Any luck finding the brooch?"

Daisy's frown deepened. "No. We searched everywhere. I don't know what I could have done with it."

"We were thinking about making an announcement for people to be on the lookout for it," Tess said.

Miranda shook her head. "I, well, I just don't think that's a good idea."

"Why not?" Daisy asked.

"What if the brooch isn't even out here, Mimi? Then what? We've worried the children and their parents for nothing."

"But I want to find my brooch." Fine creases formed between Daisy's brows. "It's important, Mandy."

"I know, Mimi." Miranda gave her a sympathetic look. "And we will." Under her breath she muttered, "We always do."

Interesting. Was Daisy prone to losing things, perhaps? Maybe they had nothing to worry about after all. In any case, Tess would continue to keep an eye out for it.

Janice came up the walk, camera in hand. "I got some good shots of the lawn." She turned her attention to their guests. "You look wonderful this morning, Daisy. That outfit is divine."

"Why, thank you. I pride myself on being colorful. As soon as the egg hunt is over, Mandy and I are headed off on an adventure. We're doing a steam rudder tour."

"Oh, I've been many times," Tess said. "You're going to love it."

"Can I get a picture of you and Miranda together before we begin?" Janice lifted her camera.

"Oh, is that that new camera Mandy told you about?" Daisy asked. "It's perfect!"

Janice's nose wrinkled. "No, I'm afraid this is my old one. Maybe one day I'll get something fancy. But hopefully I can still get some good pictures with this one in the meantime. So, how do you feel about a photo op to test that theory?"

"Why yes, dear. Of course. That would be lovely. But where?"

"We have the prettiest flowers at the front of the house," Janice said. "The daffodils are in full bloom. I think it would make a nice backdrop for the photo."

"Perfect! I just love daffodils." Daisy lit into a story about how her husband used to bring her a single yellow daffodil every Sunday morning at breakfast when they were in bloom.

"Griffin is trimming back the cedar bushes right now," Tess told her. "But he said it wouldn't take long at all."

"We'll find the perfect spot." Janice took off across the lawn with the ladies behind her.

Tess gave her watch another glance and realized they only had about fifteen minutes until the event was set to begin.

Off in the distance, the sounds of children's voices rang out. Tess could see a crowd gathering on the edge of the property where Brad held them at bay. She waved at him to let them come up the walkway, and they rushed her way.

"While you wait, feel free to have some lemonade!" Tess gestured to the table where Winnie and LuAnn served up cups of the cool refreshment.

Before long, the whole place was awash with people. The chatter of children's voices filled the air. Oh, what a delightful sound that was. Tess was flung back in time to her days as a young mom, to the first time she'd taken her children to an Easter egg hunt, husband Jeffrey at her side.

Out of the corner of her eye she caught a glimpse of Rankin Smith on the edge of the property. He kept a watchful eye on Daisy and Miranda, who had planted themselves directly in front of the daffodils for photos.

Corey returned from his conversation with Griffin, still snapping photos, this time aiming his phone in Rankin's direction.

"Did you get to connect with your friend?" she asked him.

"What?" He lowered his phone and glanced her way. "I'm sorry. What did you say?"

"Just asking if you talked to your friend."

"We had a few words, but I'm distracted today. I'm waiting for someone."

"Oh, that's nice."

"Yes. My best friend's wife is coming with their little girl."

"I hope she has a great time."

"I'm sure she will." With his free hand Corey wiped the sweat from his bald head and then rubbed his palm against his slacks. "It's unusually warm out here."

"Yes, maybe the forecast was off by a few degrees. Feels warmer than sixty-nine, for sure." Tess paused as an awkward silence rose up between them.

A lovely young woman approached with a girl who looked to be about ten or eleven at her side.

"Uncle Corey!" The girl ran to him and reached up for a hug. "I knew you'd come! I told Mom you would!"

"Well, of course. Have I ever let you down?"

For a moment, Tess thought she saw a hint of sadness in the mother's eyes but didn't ask any questions.

"Hey, Brianna, Uncle Corey has a secret to tell you." He leaned down and whispered something in her ear. Her eyes widened, and she nodded in response to whatever he was saying. Corey gave Brianna a wink. "Glad you could come, Bri."

"Me too."

They headed off toward the lemonade table together.

Janice walked toward Tess, fussing with her camera. "Who was that?"

"Corey something-or-other. Works for the paper."

"Oh." Janice squinted off in the distance. "Weird, I thought I knew most everyone at the paper."

"Me too." Tess shrugged. "Maybe he's new. Anyway, he's hoping for a story."

"Here?" Janice laughed. "At an Easter egg hunt?"

"That's what I said. Hardly the place to go looking for a juicy tale, but he seems pretty focused."

"So is Brad. He says it's time to start the hunt for the little ones. Their area is ready, and they are too."

"Perfect. Tell him to kick things into gear, then. He knows what to do."

Finally, the moment arrived. Brad approached the microphone he'd set up earlier that morning and faced the crowd.

"Ladies and gentlemen, boys and girls, thank you for coming!" He sounded a bit like a carousel barker, the sound of his voice quite animated. He spent the next several minutes giving directions for dividing into groups by age.

They started with the little ones, ages two to four. Their section was smaller and had more visible eggs. As soon as Brad gave the word, they were off across the lawn, snatching up the colorful eggs and pressing them into their baskets with squeals and obvious delight.

Next came the early elementary kids. It didn't take them long to take off running in search of eggs. Tess found one of the little girls particularly adorable. When she located her first egg she popped it open, took the candy out, and started eating it.

"Look for more, Katie!" the child's mother yelled from the sidelines. "Keep searching!"

Unfortunately, the little one didn't quite catch on to the fact that she would end up with more candy if she just kept going. Instead she stood there, frozen in place, until she finished the piece in her hand.

Finally, the big moment arrived. Brad had the oldest children take their places, and the countdown started.

"On your mark, get set…," Brad hollered. He blew a whistle, and the kids took off across the largest section of the lawn in search of eggs.

Tess looked on with Janice at her side snapping picture after picture. On and on the kids ran, picking up egg after egg. But no one happened upon the golden egg until a couple of minutes had passed. Finally, a giddy voice rang out.

"I found it, I found it!"

Tess was surprised when she realized it was the same girl Corey had whispered to.

Brianna sprinted toward her mother, basket in hand, and then pulled out the golden egg and shoved it in her mother's direction. "Look, Mom! I won!"

"You won, honey," her mother said. A crowd gathered around as the youngster opened the egg.

Tess looked on, excited for this special moment. The reporter looked on too. He held his phone perched, ready to take pictures. So did Janice, who lifted her camera to capture the moment.

The egg cracked open and Brianna's smile flipped upside down. She glanced at her mother, confusion registering in her eyes.

"What is it?" LuAnn asked as she nudged her way into the spot beside Tess. "Can you see?"

"No."

Brianna's mother held the now-opened egg up, one piece in each hand.

"There's nothing in here," she said as wrinkles formed between her thinly groomed brows. "This egg is completely empty."

CHAPTER THREE

The egg is empty?" Tess made her way through the crowd until she stood next to Brianna's mother.

"Goodness gracious goat!" Janice clamped a hand over her mouth then pulled it away. "Really?"

"Maybe this is the wrong egg?" The woman seemed perplexed as she examined it. "It's gold, but there's no candy or anything inside."

"That's the right egg," Tess said, feeling perplexed herself.

Brianna dove into a rant about how unfair the whole thing was. Tess could hardly believe the scene she was making, and in front of such a crowd.

Tess turned to LuAnn and Janice, who asked, "What should we do?"

"There's really only one thing we can do," Tess answered. "I'll be right back."

Tess sprinted toward the inn. She raced inside and went straight to the office, then pulled open the top drawer of the desk. Inside, she found an envelope, one she'd tucked away for a completely different reason. She pulled out three crisp one-hundred-dollar bills then reached into a small candy jar to grab several chocolates. She headed back outside and found the news reporter questioning Brianna's mother. Great. Just what they needed. Negative publicity.

Tess slipped into the spot next to the woman and spoke in lowered tones, so as not to alert Brianna. "Could I have that egg, please?"

"Sure." The mother passed it her way.

Tess pressed the chocolates and the bills inside the egg, closed it, and held it out to Brianna.

"Yeah, right. Like I want an empty egg." Brianna rolled her eyes.

"I think you'd better check again, honey," Tess said. "I think you'll find something special."

Brianna cracked the egg open, and a smile lit her face when she saw the money inside. "Whoa. It's there."

"It's there!" Tess said. "Congratulations on finding the golden egg, Brianna. You're our grand prize winner."

"Thank you." She beamed as she showed off the money to her mother.

"Hey, Bri, I want to get your picture for the paper." Corey snapped a photo just as the girl plastered on another wide smile.

"And one with me, please." Rankin Smith pressed himself between Corey and the little girl and held up his business card as the photo was being snapped.

"Well, there's a story for you," Brianna's mother said to Corey after he finished taking the picture. "And you thought this day was going to be boring."

Tess asked Brad if he would make an announcement that the café would be offering an egg-themed brunch for a reasonable price, and before long a handful of the guests were drifting inside the inn.

Janice stepped into the spot to Tess's right. "All's well that ends well. But I'd like to know where you happened to find three one-hundred-dollar bills inside the inn."

"I'll explain that later. But God always provides."

"Yes, He does." Janice offered her a warm smile and rested her palm on Tess's shoulder. "And I know He'll bless you for blessing that little girl."

Instead of sharing her suspicions about Corey tipping off Brianna, Tess kept them to herself. What good would it do at this point?

The crowd thinned, and Tess's stomach grumbled. Only then did she realize she'd skipped right over breakfast. Oh well. It was almost time for their special brunch.

Brad and LuAnn approached, all smiles.

"What a great morning!" LuAnn looked almost giddy.

"Yes, but what a mess." Tess looked over the yard, littered with candy wrappers and broken plastic eggs.

"You ladies go inside," Brad said. "I've got to pull down the tape we used to section off the areas of the yard. I don't mind picking up the trash."

"Are you sure?" Tess asked.

He nodded. "Yes, I'm sure. Thorn just got here, and he'll help."

Tess glanced across the yard to discover their resident handyman was already hard at work, pulling stakes from the ground.

"I'll just need a trash bag, is all." Brad leaned down and scooped up several candy wrappers.

"Done!" LuAnn sprinted toward the front door of the inn and disappeared inside.

Brad turned his attention to Tess. "You've all worked hard to make this day special. Go inside and rest."

"You won't have to tell me twice." Tess turned toward the inn, then turned back to thank him.

He offered a smile then went to work gathering up the tape and stakes.

Tess and Janice walked toward the inn, still chatting about what a great turnout they'd had. Daisy and Miranda joined them.

"We were just admiring those beautiful daffodils one more time before leaving on our little steam rudder experience," Daisy explained. "So lovely. But I do believe I need a little pit stop before we head off on our adventure, if you know what I mean."

As they drew near the front door of the inn, they came across a little girl seated on the sidewalk with a woman standing at her side. She was a beautiful youngster, probably four or five, with tight curls and bright blue eyes that sparkled with joy as she looked up at them. Just as quickly, she shifted her gaze back to her basket of goodies, oohing and aahing over the various candies inside.

"Did you have a good time?" Tess asked as she approached the little girl.

"Yes! And I got lots of candy!" She grabbed a piece and started to unwrap it, but her mother stopped her.

"You've had enough, Aubree. Time to go home now. Thank the ladies for the Easter egg hunt."

"Thank you!"

"You're so welcome, sweetheart. I'm glad you could come." Tess gave her a warm smile and then led the way to the inn entrance. "I can't believe we still have to serve brunch, after all of that." She paused as a realization hit. "Oh! The lemonade stand. We still need to break it down."

Janice reached to open the door. "Brad said not to worry about it, that he and Thorn would break it down and bring everything inside."

"Awesome. I'm so glad Thorn stopped by," Tess said.

"Me too. Now, I want to see if Winnie needs anything."

When they got inside, Daisy and Miranda seated themselves in the café, but Tess and Janice went into the kitchen, where they found Winnie up to her eyeballs in egg salad, deviled eggs, breakfast casserole, and fruit.

Tess dove right into the preparations. With the help of the servers, food reached the tables in record time.

A short while later, Brad popped his head in the kitchen. "Hey, Winnie. Where do you want me to put the leftover lemonade?"

"Bring the container in here," she said. "If you don't mind."

"Don't mind a bit." A couple of minutes later he entered the kitchen with the bright orange drink cooler and set it on the counter.

"You hungry, Brad?" LuAnn asked.

"Always."

She gestured for him to sit at the kitchen table then scooped up a serving of the casserole and a generous portion of fruit salad. She set the plate on the table in front of him. "There you go."

When the crowd thinned, Tess, Janice, and LuAnn helped Winnie with the dishes.

"You need to go home and rest, Winnie," Tess said, as she noticed the exhaustion on their friend's face. "You've gone above and beyond this week."

"You won't have to tell me twice." Winnie slipped out of her apron, grabbed her purse, and headed for the door.

"You too, Taylor," Tess said to the server. "We'll finish up."

"Are you sure?" He didn't look convinced.

"Very sure. Go. Rest."

The young man shot out the kitchen door into the café, doors swinging behind him.

Tess leaned back in her chair, completely exhausted. "What a morning."

"I think it went pretty well, though, don't you?" LuAnn asked.

"If you don't count the part where someone absconded with three hundred dollars."

"That's so strange," Brad said. "I can't figure out who would've taken off with that money. I say you walk us back through everything that happened."

"Okay." Tess led them back into the café. "I was standing here with all of the business owners around me stuffing their individual eggs with coupons and such. Then they formed a line and handed me their donations—some gave fifty, others gave twenty-five."

"Then what?" LuAnn asked.

"Then I remembered I'd put the fifty-dollar bill from Brad into my pocket, so I pulled it out and added it to the rest. I stuffed it all into the egg and snapped it shut."

"Was anyone watching you do this?" Brad asked.

She nodded. "I mean, I guess. The room was pretty full. And I still had the egg in my hand when I got caught up in a conversation with Sandie."

Brad's forehead creased. "And you're absolutely sure no one else laid a hand on that egg other than you."

"I'm sure."

"Then what did you do?" LuAnn asked.

"I walked outside...." She gestured to the front door.

"Let's go out and see if maybe the money fell out along the way without you realizing it," Janice suggested.

"I don't see how that's even a possibility. The egg was snapped shut when I put it on the ground." Still, what would it hurt to retrace her steps?

Tess led them outside and followed the same path she'd taken earlier to the daffodils. When she reached the flowers she knelt down to give the ground a closer look. "I don't see a thing."

"If the cash fell out, the wind could've blown it." Janice took a few paces and started looking under the cedar bushes while LuAnn moved in the opposite direction. After some intense searching, they came up with no clues whatsoever.

"I guess it's really gone, not just missing." Tess rose and brushed the dirt off her slacks, then noticed the cedar bushes.

Griffin had done a wonderful job trimming them back. She would have to thank him later.

"This is such a bummer." LuAnn sighed. "But I guess when you have a crowd with this many people, anything is possible."

"But no one knew where that egg was, except you, right?" Janice asked.

Tess paused, not wanting to tell them that Griffin could have noticed it while trimming the cedar bushes next to the daffodils. But surely he wouldn't have taken off with the money, right?

She deliberately neglected to mention his name. But who else might have known where the egg was? "I saw that reporter, Corey, headed that way right before the kids arrived," Janice said. "I didn't think anything of it at the time, but now, knowing the egg was right here…" She pointed to the spot beneath the daffodils.

"Yes." Tess agreed. "He came this way."

"Why was a reporter looking at flowers?" Brad asked. "That makes no sense."

"He wasn't looking at the flowers. He wanted to talk to Griffin, who was pruning the cedar bushes."

"Wait, the reporter knows the lawn guy?" LuAnn appeared confused by this.

"From prison." There. She'd said it.

"What?" Brad and LuAnn spoke in unison.

"I know, I know. He didn't say how he knew him, but Corey mentioned that he knew Griffin from prison. Next thing you know, he's racing over there to talk to him. But I got distracted looking at Daisy's new outfit."

"It was very colorful," LuAnn agreed.

"Wait. Let's go back to the prison part," Brad said.

Tess looked Brad's way. "I have no idea how Corey knows him, just that they met in prison. That could mean any number of things."

"I guess." Brad shrugged.

Tess paused, overcome by a memory. "I just thought of someone else who was in this spot before the egg hunt," she said. "Janice brought Miranda and Daisy over here to take their picture. But I have no idea if they noticed the egg."

"What are you getting at?" LuAnn asked.

"I'm not saying Daisy did it," Tess countered. "Just mentioning that she and Miranda were also over there, along with the others."

LuAnn pursed her lips. "That sounds pretty innocent."

"Right. They're great. And I'm not blaming either of them. I'm not blaming anyone, in fact."

"Are we sure Daisy wasn't the one who stuffed that egg?" LuAnn chuckled. "She seems to misplace things."

"No, she wasn't. I did it myself."

"The kids still had a great time, and so did the parents." Brad reached for his phone and started scrolling then paused to turn it toward them. "See? Pictures are already going up on social media. The event was a hit."

Tess gave a couple of the pictures a closer look and smiled. "I'm glad. And Rankin got his moment in the sun, so I guess he's happy."

"I just remembered I left my camera at the front desk. I don't want it to go missing." Janice took several quick steps toward the front entrance of the inn, and they followed on her heels.

Once inside, Janice located it. "Whew! It's still here, thank goodness." She took a seat in the lobby on the sofa. "I think I got some good pictures of today's event, in spite of the quirks with my camera. A few videos too."

"That's great."

"Daisy really fussed at me this morning to get a new one, but I told her I'm better off waiting. Just because you want something doesn't mean you need it." She fidgeted with her camera and then pointed it toward Tess to show off a picture of Rankin Smith in his stiff business attire. "I didn't know quite what to make of this guy. Found him easy to photograph, though."

"What do you mean, you didn't know what to make of him?" Brad asked.

Janice shrugged and kept scrolling through her photos. "He's just like a game show host, hyped up, dressed nice, over the top. Big booming voice."

"That hair, though." LuAnn chuckled. "I think he uses more product than I do. It reminded me of the Ken doll I had when I was a kid. Very...stiff. I guess that's the word."

"Yeah, that hair wasn't going anywhere, even in a strong breeze," Tess agreed. "But it looked formal. Very nicely styled."

"Toupee," Brad chimed in. "The man wears a toupee."

Tess gasped aloud as she glanced Brad's way. "You think?"

"I know. I saw him adjust it as he was leaving." Brad gave her a knowing look. "I suspect he's as bald as a billiard ball underneath that thing."

"Between the hair and the suit, I'd say he's putting his best foot forward to impress the town." Janice shrugged. "I just got the impression he's trying too hard."

LuAnn nodded. "Which reminds me, did you see his shoes? I'm pretty sure they were Armani. But they looked nice with the suit. I think he's just new in town and wants to spread the word about his business. If you're generous and present yourself well, then others might be drawn to you. That's probably his goal, wouldn't you think?"

"I guess." Tess paused to think through Janice's description of the man. "But I still think he was a little overdressed for an Easter egg hunt."

"And extremely happy to let everyone know that his company contributed to the goose that laid the golden egg," Brad said.

"The egg that flopped," LuAnn added.

"Yeah, that stinks." Tess shrugged. "But look on the bright side. I had the cash to spare. Although…" She sighed and then looked around to make sure Winnie was really gone. "Remember that new stand mixer I was saving up for?"

"The one for Winnie?" LuAnn asked.

"Yeah." Tess sighed. "I guess it'll have to wait."

"Tell you what…I'll buy Winnie a mixer," Brad said. "It will be my gift to her, and to all of you, to make up for what happened today."

"It's not your fault, Brad."

He messed with his phone and then looked up. "I don't mind. I feel bad that you all had to make up the difference with the egg, so it's the least I can do. Consider it my offering to further the cause of good eating at Wayfarers Inn."

"Winnie will be so surprised!"

"Just send me the link, and I'll order it online and have it delivered here."

"I'll do that."

He tapped his phone with his index finger. "No, I mean right now, before we forget. Show me the link, Tess. I'll buy it right now."

He handed Tess his phone. She quickly pulled up a link to the mixer she'd had her eye on.

Brad pointed at it and nodded. "Lookee there, folks. It mixes, it mashes, and it even raises your firstborn child for you."

"Very funny." Tess chuckled at his joke. "But it really does have a lot of great features. Winnie will be thrilled."

"If she can figure out how to use it." LuAnn peered over Tess's shoulder. "Look at all of those attachments. Wow."

"Winnie's a whiz. She'll figure it out." Brad reached for his wallet and handed LuAnn a credit card. "Go ahead and get it now. But let it be a surprise. Promise?"

They all agreed to keep it a secret.

Still, as they finalized the purchase, Tess couldn't help but think of all that had happened. Someone had stolen that cash. And because the cash was stolen, Wayfarers had to cover the difference. Because Wayfarers had to cover the difference, Brad chose to cover the cost of the stand mixer.

Still, gauging from the look on his face, he didn't seem upset at all by it. In fact, he looked rather content.

She should learn from him, perhaps. But Tess still couldn't get past the fact that someone had taken off with that money from the golden egg. Who would do such a thing...and why?

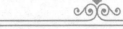

CHAPTER FOUR

April 3, 1860

Prudence Willard stepped outside of her tiny cabin into the afternoon sunlight, wet rag in hand. She released a slow breath as she thought about what she'd just witnessed inside. The elderly woman she was tending to wasn't long for this life, not from the looks of things. Even in her weakened condition, dear old Lolly, as her grandsons called her, had been nothing but kind to Prudence and her husband, Jason.

She leaned against the cabin and sighed as memories of the soft wrinkles on Lolly's face entered her mind once more. A heaviness settled over Prudence and she could not seem to shake it off, try as she may.

"Pru? Is thee well?" Jason approached and rested his palm on her shoulder, forehead creased with concern.

"I am fine, but Lolly is very weak, Jason." Prudence wrung out the rag, then hung it over the porch rail. "I don't know how much longer she has." In spite of the warmth of the sun, a shiver wriggled its way down her back underneath her thin calico dress.

"I just got her grandsons bedded down in the barn in the stall next to Charity."

"She will keep them awake, stomping and snorting and such."

Jason shook his head. "Not even the whinnies of a cantankerous horse could rouse these boys. The whole family is in need of rest. They are so grateful for our care."

"I cannot believe they have journeyed this far. How did those boys lead such a frail one across these many miles?"

He shook his head. "I do not know how any man or woman could garner the strength or courage. And yet they have, and would do it again, if their words to me just now are true."

"An elderly woman like that? She's too frail to take another step, even one that might lead to freedom."

"Thee is wrong about the steps, Pru."

"What do you mean?"

He pulled off his hat and raked his hands across his tight spirals of hair. "The oldest grandson—Caleb—he said they carried her much of the way."

"Carried her? From Tennessee?"

Jason adjusted his hat on his head and nodded. "They crafted a makeshift gurney out of cloth. It's nothing but rags now, Pru. We'll have to find something else before they head back out."

"But Jason, she is in no condition to leave. I cannot abide the idea." Prudence's eyes filled with tears at the notion that Lolly might be forced to journey on. In so many ways, the gentle elderly woman reminded Prudence of her own grandmother. Those large brown eyes. Those tight curls. As she pondered the similarities, memories overtook her. Prudence was a little girl once more, seated at Grandmammy's side on the front porch of their cabin, snapping beans.

"The boys said it's her dying wish to make it to Syracuse before she dies. Her oldest son is already there. From what they said, he owns his own home, has a beautiful wife and children. Lolly hasn't seen him in over thirty years. This is her dying wish, love."

"But..." She could not find the strength to argue the point. Surely Jason could see that this was an impossible task. Short of a miracle, Lolly would not see New York. Prudence was not sure she would live to see morning.

"We are called by God to give bread to the hungry and a place of rest to the weary, Pru. That is all He asks of us. If they choose to carry on with the journey—"

"But surely, thee must agree, Jason. It is a foolhardy venture. She won't make it another five miles, let alone all the way to Syracuse."

"Let her rest, sweet Pru. And trust God. He knows the desires of our hearts, does He not?"

"Of course, but..." Her words drifted off as she heard cries from inside the cabin. For a moment, she thought they came from Lolly. Just as quickly, Prudence realized her young son must have awakened from his nap and realized she was gone.

"'Tis Moses. I must tend to him before he wakes her."

"The cries of the boy will do her good." Jason reached for the bag of grain leaning against the porch and tossed a handful to Patience, their pet goose. "They will give her hope that life goes on."

"Perhaps." Prudence took several steps into the house and fetched Moses from his mat, then tiptoed to Lolly's bedside. She kept a watchful eye on the woman's breathing, each breath reminding her of that awful day, so many years ago, when she watched Grandmammy die.

Prudence ushered up a prayer that Lolly's story would not end in similar fashion. "God, be merciful," she prayed, resting her palm against the sleeping woman's cheek.

CHAPTER FIVE

As they walked into Christ Fellowship on Easter Sunday morning, Tess turned to Janice and smiled. "This is one of my favorite days of the year."

"Mine too. The services are amazing." Janice paused and seemed to lose herself in her thoughts.

Tess realized she must be remembering what Easter Sunday services were like when her husband was pastor of Christ Fellowship. She decided to keep the conversation moving forward. "Everyone always looks so nice on Easter."

Tess looked around the room to check out the attire of her fellow parishioners. To be honest, they didn't look that much different today than any normal Sunday. Still, the altar looked beautiful, all decked out with Easter lilies.

Tess's eye was drawn to the large "He is Risen!" banner above the baptistery. Lovely.

"Remember when we were kids?" Janice's voice roused her back to the conversation. "Back then everyone wore brand-new clothes on Easter Sunday."

"And the women wore hats!" A familiar voice sounded from their right.

Tess turned to see LuAnn and Brad had joined them.

"My mother had the most fabulous wide-brimmed hat with flowers on it," LuAnn said. "I always wanted to wear it. It's funny, I haven't thought about that hat in years."

"I think we all had Easter bonnets as kids. At least I did."

"Me too," LuAnn agreed.

"I remember new white stockings that I got when I was, maybe, seven?" Janice sighed. "And Mary Janes. We always wore Mary Janes."

"Man, what I wouldn't give for a pair of Mary Janes right now." Tess gestured to her feet. "Am I the only one with aching feet after yesterday?"

"No, I'm hurting too," Janice said. "But it's mostly my back, from bending down so much."

"Who knew that putting Easter eggs on the ground could be so painful?" Brad rubbed his back and laughed. "Will you listen to us? We sound like a group of old people."

"We *are* a group of old people," LuAnn countered, then laughed too.

"I'm definitely not a whippersnapper anymore," Tess said. "When I was young enough to wear Mary Janes, bending down didn't make my back hurt." She stretched from side to side. "I'm not sure why I'm feeling my age more lately, but I seem to be."

"Hey, at least they haven't put us out to pasture yet," LuAnn said. "I suspect they never will, not with three workhorses like us."

"Three?" Brad's eyebrows shot up.

"Four." LuAnn slipped her arm around his waist. "Don't want to you leave you out. You're part of the Inn Crowd too."

He had certainly earned the right to bear that name, Tess decided.

Janice headed off to greet the pastor and Tess noticed her friend, Maybelline Rector across the sanctuary. The petite woman bounded her way, clearly on a mission.

"I guess you saw the paper?" The lines on Maybelline's face grew deeper than usual as she spoke, and that was really saying something.

"Paper?" Tess shook her head. "I didn't open it this morning. Why?"

"That reporter..." Maybelline clucked her tongue. "He could've done a nicer job of describing your Easter egg hunt. Instead of focusing on the fun everyone had or the smiles on the children's faces, he had to go and write about the missing money?"

"Did he?" Tess groaned. "Really? Why did he have to focus on that? I made good on the money, and the kids had a great time. Why didn't he mention all of that?"

"He did." Maybelline fussed with her dark red hair, finally shoving a loose piece behind her ear. "You'll have to read the article. Other than the part where the money went missing, what's your take on how the day went?"

"Great. We had a terrific turnout, and everyone had a wonderful time."

"Well, there you go. Then who cares what anyone thinks? That's what I always say, anyway." Maybelline gave her a curt nod and took off toward her favorite pew on the left.

Tess did her best not to sigh aloud as she thought about the fact that the reporter had written about the missing money.

Sure, he had a connection to the little girl who won. And yes, she'd definitely been upset. But did he have to go there? Tess had made good on it, after all.

Oh well. She wouldn't let it ruin a perfectly good Easter service.

After greeting a handful of friends, Tess settled into a pew. A few minutes later, Janice joined her.

"Everything okay?" Janice asked. "You look like someone asked you to swallow worms."

"Remember that big Easter hat we were just talking about?"

"Yes."

"I'd like to have one right about now so I could hide my face."

Janice looked flabbergasted by this comment. "Why, Tess? Because of what happened yesterday?"

"Yes. Maybelline just told me there was a write-up in the paper, and it wasn't very flattering."

"I read it. I thought he did an okay job of covering the event...except for that one part." Janice tucked her purse next to her hip.

"You read it and didn't tell me?"

"I didn't want to upset you, Tess, and I knew it would. You wanted everything to be perfect."

"Not perfect, but...memorable."

"It was memorable. It made the papers."

"For the wrong reasons. We made a really big deal out of hosting that egg hunt for the kids, and in the end the golden egg was a bit of a letdown."

"Not true!" Janice shrugged off her sweater. "Maybe she had to wait five minutes or so for her money, but that girl walked away with her prize."

"Maybe people think we did it to get free promotion for the inn. You know what I mean? Maybe it looked to some like we set the whole thing up."

"Just to make ourselves look like fools?" Janice laughed. "That's just plain silly."

"What's silly?" LuAnn plopped into the pew in front of them and glanced their way. "What did I miss?"

"Maybelline told Tess about the article in the paper."

"Oh, that." LuAnn shrugged. "It wasn't so bad. But I don't pay any attention to negative chatter. Wayfarers has a wonderful reputation, and that Easter egg hunt was divine." LuAnn waved her hand and appeared to dismiss Tess's concerns.

"I got lots of great pictures," Janice said. "That's one good thing that came out of it. Absolutely adorable images of some of the kids, if I do say so myself. I even captured a few minutes of video beforehand, as we were setting things up. We'll have to look at it later. I think you'll see that it was a truly delightful day."

Tess gave her an admiring look as the musicians took their places on the stage. "You've been on quite a kick with this photography hobby, Janice."

"I love it. There's something amazing about catching a glimpse of something through the lens of a camera. It's almost like time stops."

The music began, and Tess turned her full attention to the service. She loved every moment of it, from the songs, to the prayers, to the message. Pastor Ben was on a roll today, really hitting her in the heart with every word.

After Ben's wonderful sermon about the empty tomb, the worship pastor came forward and led the congregation in a traditional version of "Just as I Am." Tess felt shivers go up her spine as she sang the old familiar song. How many Sundays had she sung those words as a child?

At the end of the service Pastor Ben prepared to say the benediction.

"Now, I know on a day like this you've got big plans with family," he said. "I can almost smell the Easter ham from here." He rubbed his stomach, which got a chuckle out of the congregation. "Can almost taste it too. But I want us to linger just a few moments longer, and I'd love to open the altars to anyone who might need prayer. Feel free to come on up. The rest of you, don't worry about slipping out, if need be. I know those kids and grandkids are waiting."

Tess was tempted to leave at first, but as the pianist continued to play the familiar melody to "Just as I Am" she felt inclined to sit still and enjoy the moment. Lingering in God's presence was always the better choice, no matter what yummy food one had waiting at home.

As the music finally drew to a close minutes later, Janice slipped out of her spot and whispered, "I have to make a pit stop before we head home."

Tess nodded, then settled back in the pew. Out of the corner of her eye she caught a glimpse of someone familiar coming up the aisle, headed straight toward the pastor. Griffin Patterson.

She watched in silence as he made his way to the pastor and leaned in to share something privately. Moments later, the pastor rested his hand on Griffin's shoulder and began to pray in hushed tones. Tess shifted her gaze to the stained-glass window, not wanting to intrude. Afterward, Griffin shook the pastor's hand and turned around. He noticed her and smiled.

"Good to see you, Tess."

"You too."

"I'm glad you ladies attend church here. It's good to see familiar faces."

"I'm glad too. I don't know if you realize it, but Janice's husband used to be the pastor."

"Her husband?"

"Yes." Tess had better offer an explanation. "He passed away years ago, but he was the pastor before Ben came on staff."

"Oh, I see. I'm sorry for her loss."

Strange, as he spoke the word "loss" she could almost see the evidence of pain in his eyes.

"Well, I'm glad you were able to come today," Tess said. "If you come back, please feel free to sit with us."

"I would like that. I really would." He offered a bright smile. "I might just take you up on that."

"Please do."

Janice showed up moments later. She looked Griffin's way and smiled. He offered a "great to see you" and then turned to leave.

"I had no idea he was here," Janice said.

"I knew he's been coming. Ben told me on the same day he asked if we might be willing to use him at the inn."

"How come I didn't know that Ben had recommended him?"

Tess shrugged. "Guess I forgot to tell you that part."

"Yes, I guess you did."

"Anyway, Griffin went up for prayer after you slipped out."

Pastor Ben approached after praying with another parishioner. He paused to shake their hands.

"That was a wonderful Easter message," Janice said. "Just what I needed, as always."

"Thank you." He paused. "I saw you talking with Griffin Patterson just now, Tess. I just wanted to thank you again for taking him on at the inn."

"Of course. He's done a fine job so far. Goes above and beyond what we ask him to do."

"He still won't take any money for his work on the church lawn." Ben shook his head. He directed the next words at Janice, as if to explain. "He's been cutting our grass for free ever since he got out."

"Yes, that's what I heard."

"I appreciate you giving him the benefit of the doubt," Ben said. "All of you."

Janice's lips turned up in a smile. "We're happy to help."

"He seems to have made a real turnaround in his life," Tess chimed in. "Not that I'm one to pry. I haven't asked for any details. But he's easygoing, which is nice. And a hard worker, to boot."

"I have to agree with that analysis." Ben rested his hand on hers. "Tess, in case others don't say it often enough, you're remarkably welcoming. I had a feeling you would be just the right ointment for Griffin's wounds."

"Ointment?"

"Yes. His story isn't mine to share but he's had plenty of hurts along the way. You're positive and upbeat. I can see that he's probably got a lot of similar qualities, but life has squeezed them out of him."

"Prison has squeezed them out of him too, I'm sure," Tess said. "I'll be as welcoming as I can, and I'm happy to give him a chance. We all are."

Pastor Ben smiled. "I appreciate that more than you know. Not everyone is open to giving second chances for folks who've done prison time. I understand that. I really do. But when I see someone who's willing, I find it very comforting."

"Yes. Well, thanks for the referral. He's doing a great job so far."

Tess thought about Pastor Ben's words as she headed toward the back of the sanctuary. God *was* in the business of offering second chances, wasn't He? And how happy she was to do the same.

Chapter Six

On Monday morning Daisy and Miranda ate a quick breakfast and then gathered their things to go on one of their little adventures, as Daisy called it.

Tess looked up from bussing a table to see Thorn come into the inn. He nodded at her as he came through the lobby, headed toward the kitchen. "Sorry to come in the front, Tess. I wanted to check the hinges on that front door before I check the sink. They've been sticking."

"Thanks so much." She flashed him a warm smile.

After he shot out of the room, Daisy approached with a wrinkled brow.

"And who, might I ask, is that man with the long gray ponytail? A love interest for one of you, perhaps?"

Tess couldn't help but laugh at that notion. "I'm sure his wife would be opposed to the idea. That's Thorn. He's our handyman."

"Well, he certainly came in handy when I locked myself out of my room a couple of days back. He let me back in. I discovered my key right there where I'd left it...on the bureau."

Hmm. More confirmation of Daisy's memory issues, perhaps?

The older woman paused and appeared to be sniffing the air.

"Do my nostrils deceive me, or is someone baking lemon cake?" Daisy asked.

"I do think Winnie's baking today, yes."

"Oh, how I remember that smell from childhood." Daisy seemed to lose herself to her thoughts. "Our cook would do her baking on Saturday for the week ahead. I could smell her lemon cake from outside and would come running in. I've always loved the smell of citrus."

"Me too," Tess agreed.

Daisy's eyes twinkled as she said, "It's enough to rouse a dead man from his slumber."

"That's some pretty powerful cake, Mimi." Miranda laughed.

Daisy refused to budge. Instead, she stood with her nose in the air and eyes closed for some time. "I like to capture things like photographs in my memory. Snapshots."

"But you can't capture a smell in a picture, Mimi."

"Oh yes I can. It's heaven, come down to earth."

Tess walked them in the direction of the door, chatting all the way about the day's weather forecast. As they stepped outside, she got a closer look at Daisy's soft face in the early morning light. It was covered in fine crinkles, the kind that moved and changed shape as she laughed, which Daisy did often. And that hair! Wisps of winter-white framed the woman's delicate face.

But what she lacked in color with her hair and skin, Daisy more than made up for with her makeup. This gal had spent years learning the craft at expensive makeup counters, no doubt about that. Either she had a skillful hand or Miranda helped her out with the finer points, like that perfectly applied eyeliner and those painted-on brows. This morning she looked particularly fetching in a bright yellow-and-white daisy-themed ensemble. She smelled lovely too.

Tess sniffed the air. "Okay, Daisy, I give up. You smell absolutely delicious. What is that you're wearing?"

"Oh, you like it?" A smile tipped up the edges of her lips. "It's tea rose. I've worn it my whole life."

"It's very familiar. I think my mother must have worn that, back in the day. It evokes certain memories of her."

"Probably so. Are you much like her, Tess?"

Tess stopped to think that question through. "I guess we're all like our mothers in some ways, right? I'd like to think I got some of her traits. She was a pretty remarkable woman."

"Then you definitely did." Daisy paused. "Was she a prankster too?"

"Oh no. Not my mother. She was too prim and proper for that."

"I keep thinking about what LuAnn said about you being a practical joker." Daisy's gaze narrowed, and she waggled an arthritic finger in Tess's direction. "Now I've got my eye on you. You can't pull anything over on this old gal."

"Oh, I hadn't planned to try." Tess laughed. "More likely you'd pull one over on us."

"Boy, that's the truth." Miranda laughed. "She's got some doozies up her sleeve most of the time, trust me."

"No, I care too much about you ladies to play any pranks on you." Daisy's eyes filled with tears. "You've been so welcoming, all of you. You've treated us like family." She paused. "My own daughter could learn a few things from you."

Tess wasn't sure what to say in response to that, so she said nothing.

"What I'm trying to say is we love it here. We love you ladies, and we adore this old inn. It's just the cat's meow."

"Thank you for those kind words. We're tickled to get to know you too. And for what it's worth, we're pretty fond of the inn as well. I wish you could have seen it when we first purchased it. Talk about being in a state of disrepair! But we've put some TLC into it."

"It shows." Daisy's eyebrows arched as she repeated the words, "Cat's meow!" She stopped just outside the massive front door and fingered the aging bronze plaque on the front of the building. "This is the reason we chose Wayfarers, you know… because it was a stop on the Underground Railroad."

"Really?" Tess pulled the door closed and gave Daisy an admiring look. "Are you interested in Civil War-era stories? We've got dozens of them in a diary that ties back to the inn all those years ago."

"Yes, please! I would love to see it."

"We have learned so much since moving in," Tess explained. "But new stories are always coming up that surprise me."

"I feel the same about our family's history." Miranda slung her purse strap over her shoulder. "Mimi always makes the stories come alive when she tells them. I get goose bumps." She paused, and a sad look came over her. "It almost makes up for some of the modern-day people in the family when I read about the really wonderful ones, back in the day." She shrugged. "Gives me hope that we can strive toward all that they achieved. You know?"

"I do know," Tess responded. "This place is rich with the history of amazing people. There's a lot more to Wayfarers than what you can see with your eyes. You have to feel it with your heart."

"I do feel it." Daisy rested her hand on her heart. "I thought it was just you ladies, welcoming us and making us feel so comfortable. You're very good at what you do, Tess. Has anyone ever told you that? You were born for hospitality."

A warmth of emotion washed over Tess at such kind words. "Thank you, Daisy. No, I don't hear that very often. But I do know I was born for this, as you say. My husband was the general manager of an exclusive resort in the town of Stow, Ohio. I actually taught courses in hospitality and hotel management back in those days."

"Well, it shows, sweet girl. God has placed you in the perfect place. And He's shown you how to take something that was broken down and nearly lost and give it new life and hope."

"You're sweet."

Daisy's eyes sparkled, and she reached to squeeze Tess's hands. "We really do have a lot in common. We're both Mimis and we both love Wayfarers Inn." She pointed to the old building with its hardy brick exterior. "Now, I know those bricks are originals, and the cobblestone street too. But what about those fabulous windows?" She gestured to the front of the house, very near the spot where the daffodils were in full bloom.

"Handblown," Tess explained. "They are original to the house. We would never replace them unless we had absolutely no choice."

"My goodness. Well, they're lovely."

"Lovely." Tess smiled. "I love that word. It's so…lovely."

"Isn't it, though?" Daisy's warm smile had a hint of merriment to it. "That's the only word I can think of to describe how Wayfarers makes me feel, Tess. There's something more here that one can't take in with the eyes. One has to feel it deep in the soul."

"I totally agree," Miranda said. "This place has something special."

"My great-great-grandmother would have said it has a certain *je ne sais quoi*. That special something you can't quite put your finger on."

Tess nodded. "What you're feeling is generations of men and women who risked their lives to save all. Their courage lives on. That's why we take such wonderful care of the building and preserve its stories. And, Daisy, I commend you for passing down your family stories to Miranda. She'll keep them forever and pass them to her children. You're leaving a very special legacy."

"God bless you for saying that." Daisy's lips tipped up in a smile. "I'm a firm believer in leaving a legacy. I want Mandy and all of my other grandchildren to know that I lived life to its fullest, that nothing was left undone."

"Speaking of which..." Miranda glanced at her watch. "We'd better get started, Mimi, or we'll miss today's adventure. We're on a bit of a tight schedule for this one, remember?"

"Yes, of course."

Daisy and Miranda headed off on their adventures. They weren't specific about today's plans, but from what Tess could make out, they had something to do with a relative who used to live in the area. Maybe the same one Daisy had referred to the other day. Tess wasn't quite sure. Miranda did say they would be back by evening.

Before walking back in, Tess paused to glance up at the inn. She saw it through Daisy's eyes, a building with a welcoming spirit.

She walked back inside just in time to see Thorn come barreling through the lobby maybe in search of something he'd left behind. Tess gave thought to helping Winnie with lunch preparations, but before she could give that much thought, new guests arrived.

Tess checked in the family of four from Alabama—the Martindales. She fell in love with the little curly-haired girl at once. The boy, who couldn't seem to look up from his video game, didn't seem as outgoing. Maybe Winnie could win him over with some of her delicious offerings.

After checking them in, she headed up to the second floor to walk them to their rooms. They were delighted with their new digs and couldn't wait to unpack.

After descending the stairs, Tess finally made it to the kitchen, just in time to see Winnie wrapping up food preparations with Janice and Taylor at her side.

"I peeked into the lobby when I heard voices," Janice said. "New guests?"

"Yes, the Martindales from Alabama."

"Which rooms are they in?" Janice asked.

"The parents are staying in the honeymoon suite and the children are together in Lily and Lace, so they're close by. We don't have anyone else on the second floor right now, so they've pretty much got the run of the place."

"The children are in Lily and Lace?" Janice asked.

"I know, I was a little worried too. All of that tatted lace over the bed. I do hope it's still intact when they leave."

"I agree." Winnie clucked her tongue.

"Yes. By the way, the parents loved the English garden theme in the honeymoon suite. From what I could gather, they went to jolly old England on their honeymoon and found it to be a lovely coincidence." Tess laughed. "I said it again. Lovely."

"What's wrong with lovely?" Winnie asked.

"Oh, nothing. Daisy and I were just talking about what a lovely word it is." She laughed again.

She prayed Lily and Lace would look just as lovely once the children checked out a few days from now.

CHAPTER SEVEN

Around ten Janice walked into the office where Tess was looking over some bills.

"I need to make a run to the store." Janice slung her purse strap over her shoulder. "I promised Winnie I'd pick up some things from her list. LuAnn said she would do it, but she hasn't shown up this morning."

"Maybe she slept in?" Tess suggested.

Janice's nose wrinkled. "I have no idea, but it's not like her to go missing."

"She's a married lady now. I guess she needs her space."

"Hmm. She should have called, then."

"Right. Well, I'll try to call her in a bit, but you go ahead." Tess remembered something she wanted to add to the grocery list. "Oh, and would you mind grabbing some chocolate chips while you're there? I plan to bake some cookies later this week."

"Don't mind a bit. I'll be back in a while. If you think of anything else we need, just text me."

"Will do." Janice took off, leaving Tess to her work.

She wrapped up just in time to see the café open for lunch. Taylor made sure the room was ready, and then he got busy wrapping silverware. Tess joined him just as their first customer arrived. How wonderful to see Sandie Ballard, owner of the Better Batter, Marietta's premiere bakery.

Tess took a few steps in her direction. "Sandie, I'm so glad to see you. What a lovely surprise."

"Thanks." The tall, willowy blond released an exaggerated sigh and ran her palms along her messy hot-pink and lime-green apron. I'm glad to get out of the bakery. I've been at it since four this morning, if you can believe that."

"I can. But I would think you'd be done with all your Easter offerings at this point."

"Oh, I am. But we were running low on everything else. So now it's time to restock the shelves with all the cookies, cupcakes, and pies we're known for. I spent the morning working on snickerdoodle and oatmeal raisin. Oh, and I did the usual cinnamon rolls. They sold out in a hurry, as always."

"You're making me hungry."

"Me too, but I'm ready for some real food, which is why I came here. No one can top Winnie's cooking."

"True, that. Well, we're glad to have you. It's a lovely surprise. But did you shut down the bakery for lunch?"

"No, my assistant is there, taking care of customers. But I've been so preoccupied that I didn't think to bring my lunch to work today. So I decided this was the best option—some of Winnie's good food and a chance to make myself actually sit down for a change."

"Well, come on in and have a seat. We'll be opening in about fifteen minutes. You just rest until then."

"Rest? What is this word you speak of?" Sandie offered a faint smile.

"I know, I know. But try."

As she offered her friend the closest table, Tess wondered if Sandie realized she was still wearing her batter-covered apron and that she had flour on her cheek. Should she tell her? Nah. She'd let that go. Instead, Tess flashed a smile and said, "Winnie will be so excited you're here. She thinks you're the best."

"Girl, Winnie can bake circles around me, as was proven at the baking competition last year. I'm just grateful she shared her winnings with me. I can't tell you how wonderful it's been to have a supply closet filled with flour and baking powder. Quite a gift, one I don't take lightly."

"I'm sure. Well, I'll let her know you're here."

Tess went into the kitchen and found Winnie fighting to lift a hot pan of bowtie pasta over the strainer in the sink below. Tess rushed her way, ready to help. "Here, let me strain that for you, Winnie. You've got a guest."

"A guest?"

"Yes." Tess took the pan out of Winnie's hands. Whoa. It was heavier than it looked. She hefted it up and then tipped it over into the strainer. "Sandie Ballard stopped by for lunch. She's been baking all morning, and she's beat."

"I can relate to that." Winnie gestured toward the refrigerator. "Speaking of baking, I've got a strawberry lemonade cake with fresh whipped cream for dessert today. It's chilling in the fridge. I still have to add dollops of whipped cream on top, along with some fresh berries. But I'm leaving that until the last minute."

"Sounds yummy. I just love lemons and strawberry together. And no one can top your strawberry lemonade cake, not even Sandie." Tess rinsed off the strainer and set it on the drying rack.

"I'm not sure I'm buying those flattering words, but thank you." Winnie grabbed a rag and started drying the strainer. "I was going to make an almond cake from a recipe I found online, but I switched gears and went with the strawberry lemonade."

"Everyone loves your strawberry lemonade cake. Besides, it's spring, and strawberry lemonade is very spring-like."

"True." Winnie put the strainer down, swiped her hands on her apron, and then headed out to visit with Sandie.

Tess took over with the pasta, adding the Alfredo sauce and chunks of chicken Winnie had baked. By the time Winnie got back to the kitchen, Tess had the main dish ready to go.

"I would've finished up that cake for you, but I didn't want to mess it up. You've got such a way with baked goods, Winnie. You're so great with the decorating part."

"Are you trying to butter me up for something?" Winnie's eyes narrowed to slits.

"Not at all. Just explaining why I didn't finish the cake. My version wouldn't have been as pretty." Tess dried her hands.

"And with Sandie here, I figured you'd want everything perfect."

"Nah. I gave up on perfect years ago. Tolerable will do. There's less stress that way."

"True." Tess paused and glanced toward the swinging doors leading to the café. "I'd better head out to check on our guests. Hopefully Janice will be back soon."

"And LuAnn?" Winnie shot her a quick glance.

Tess shrugged. "I have no idea where she is. It's strange that she didn't call. And she's not responding to my texts."

Oh well. She would give LuAnn her space. Tess walked through the swinging doors into the café and was startled to see the place had really filled up. She worked alongside Taylor, taking orders.

Tess was surprised to see Corey show up. After that article he'd written in the paper, she wasn't sure she wanted to see him but offered him a polite hello anyway. He stood just outside the café, waiting to be seated.

She took several steps in his direction. "Welcome to Wayfarers. Is this your first time?"

"No." He shook his head. "I ate brunch here with my friend and her daughter after the Easter egg hunt and we loved the desserts, so I decided to come back for more."

"I'm so glad." She paused. "We're pretty busy right now, so there might be a bit of a wait."

"No problem." He glanced down toward his shoes, then back up at her. "Hey, while I'm here, I wanted to talk to you about that article I wrote."

"Yes?" She wasn't too sure she wanted to talk about it.

"It wasn't my goal to focus so much on the missing money. I wanted to emphasize the kids and the fun they had."

"But you wrote it, right?"

"The first draft, yes." He sighed. "Look, I'm sorry. You know editors. They're always looking for an angle. He told me to find something exciting, and that missing money was about as exciting as an Easter egg hunt can get. My editor did a pretty extensive rewrite of the article, which bummed me out."

"Oh my."

"And by the way, I did mention in the article that you made good on the missing money."

"Did you?" She paused to think that through...and to confess something. "I didn't actually read the article, now that you mention it. A friend told me about it."

"You might want to read it for yourself. It wasn't unflattering, if that's what you're worried about."

"Okay, then. I will. I probably should've read it before drawing any conclusions."

Corey's gaze shot toward the front door of the inn, as if he was expecting someone. "I'm actually working on a much bigger story than the one about the Easter egg hunt."

"Anything you can tell me about?"

He quirked a brow. "Hey, a writer never gives away his secrets until it's time for the story to break. But you might be seeing more of me around the café as I flesh out the story. Is that okay?"

"Always happy for a customer." She gave him a thoughtful look. "That's my way of saying you're welcome to come by for lunch any time you like."

"Thank you. I will."

"Tess! Yoo-hoo!" From across the room, Sandie called out to her.

Tess made her apologies to Corey and headed toward the woman, who looked overly eager.

"Ready to order?" Tess asked as she approached Sandie's table.

"I've already placed my order with Taylor, actually. That bow-tie pasta with Alfredo sauce sounds yummy." Sandie gestured with her head to Corey, who looked around the room for a free table. "He's new in town, isn't he?"

"Corey?" Tess shrugged. "Sort of, I guess. He's been at the paper for a few months now, so not that new."

"Single?" Sandie gave her a hopeful look.

Tess smiled. "To my knowledge, yes. I've never seen him with anyone."

"Good to know. Can you seat him next to me?" Sandie stared down at her attire. "Ack! I'm still in my apron. What kind of goober am I?"

"The kind who works very hard on behalf of others," Tess said. "And trust me, no one cares about the apron or the flour."

"Well, I do. And I doubt any man would give me a second look, dressed like this. Except to roll his eyes, I mean."

Tess couldn't imagine that any woman as breathtaking as Sandie Ballard might actually feel that way about herself, but apparently she did.

"Would it be too obvious if I pulled off the apron?"

From what Tess could gather, folks were busy chatting amongst themselves, not paying a bit of attention, so she said so.

Sandie wriggled out of her apron, folded it, and set it on the empty seat next to her. "There. Much better." She reached into her purse and came out with a compact and a tube of lipstick. When she saw her reflection in the tiny mirror, she gasped. "For pity's sake, my cheeks are covered in flour." She brushed it off, swiped on the lipstick, and then shoved the compact back in her purse. "There. Ready."

Tess glanced over at Corey, who was talking to the server. Then she turned her attention back to Sandie. "Before I seat him, let me just tell you that he—"

"Oh, pooh. That one's taken already." Sandie looked at the table next to hers. "Bummer."

Tess continued to scan the room until she realized every table was full. She left Sandie and headed over to Corey and Taylor.

"Like I said, we're pretty busy, so I'm afraid there's a bit of a wait," she explained. "We've got more people than tables."

"That's too bad." His smile quickly faded. "I'm on a deadline today. I might have to pick up some fast food on the way back to the office. Thanks anyway."

Sandie stood, raised her hand, and gestured to the empty seat across from her. "If you don't mind sharing a table, you're welcome to join me."

"Are you sure?" Corey didn't look convinced.

"Do you mind?" Tess looked back and forth between the two. She couldn't imagine any fellow would mind having lunch with a beauty queen like Sandie, but she would never voice those thoughts aloud.

Corey shrugged. "I don't mind if she doesn't."

"Oh, I don't," Sandie called out with a smile. "I really, really don't."

Tess made introductions, and before long Corey and Sandie were deep in a conversation about a potential article concerning her bakery.

Janice walked into the café and headed straight for Tess, who was holding a tea pitcher and hovering near the door leading to the lobby.

"Hey, I bought your chocolate chips. They're in the kitchen pantry. Oh, and LuAnn is here too. She just got a late start this morning."

"Thanks. I appreciate it." Tess gestured to Corey and Sandie. "I think Sandie is smitten."

"He's a nice-looking young man." Janice gave the duo another glance. "And they seem to be getting along well."

"Yes. He wants to do an article about her bakery."

"That's nice."

Tess shifted the heavy tea pitcher to her other hand. "Corey told me he's working on a bigger story than the Easter egg hunt and that we might be seeing more of him." As she shot another glance his way and noticed the doe-eyed look on Sandie's face, Tess had to conclude they would probably be seeing more of Sandie Ballard too.

CHAPTER EIGHT

The lunch crowd thinned a little after one forty-five, and Tess made steady work out of tidying up. Sandie and Corey left together, still chatting about her bakery. The vivacious blond seemed more animated than usual as she went on and on about her future plans for expansion.

Tess pondered the situation at hand. She didn't really know much about Corey, except that he knew Griffin from prison. It wasn't really her place to tell Sandie any of that, was it?

"Are Daisy and Miranda back?" Janice asked as she cleared one of the tables.

"No, they're gone for the day on one of their little adventures, as Daisy called it."

"They seem like such a fun, carefree duo."

"Yes." Tess grabbed the linens off the table in front of her. "Wouldn't it be lovely to have that much free time on your hands, to just scat about from here to there?"

Janice shrugged and continued to clear dirty glasses and silverware from her table. "Maybe. I wouldn't trade my life here for that, though. In our world, the adventure comes to us. We don't have to go out and find it. That's an added advantage, I suppose."

"I guess." Janice was right. The Inn Crowd did have their fair share of adventures. Maybe more than their fair share.

After Janice disappeared into the kitchen to help LuAnn and Winnie with the dishes, Tess couldn't stop thinking about Daisy's penchant for adventure. It would be fun to have that much energy and courage at her age, wouldn't it? Tess allowed her imagination to kick in, and she dreamed up a few adventures of her own. Perhaps she would travel. She might go to Italy, to see the countryside. Or maybe Scotland. She'd always heard the landscape there was beautiful.

Tess's thoughts continued to drift from adventure to adventure. How lovely, to have the freedom to travel to such places.

There was that word again: *lovely.*

Tess walked into the kitchen to join the others. The cleanup was taking a little longer than usual, what with the ladies working around Winnie, who was prepping a large slab of beef to marinate overnight in preparation for tomorrow's lunch. They wrapped up around two forty-five, and the ladies each went their own way.

Sometime around three o'clock a box arrived at the front door. Tess smiled as she realized what must be inside. She carried the box to the kitchen and set it on the counter.

Winnie looked up from her work and brushed her hair out of her eyes with the back of her hand. "What have we got here?"

"I do believe it's a surprise for you."

"A surprise?" Winnie's eyes widened. She wiped her hands on her apron and reached to touch the box. "For me? Are you sure?"

"Yes, but let me get Janice and LuAnn in here before you open it. Hold on a minute." She located Janice in the office uploading the photos from her camera to the computer. LuAnn was in the middle of a call with Brad. Tess hated to interrupt her but managed to get the words, "The mixer has arrived!" in.

"Oh, Brad!" LuAnn's voice grew more animated. "I'm going to put you on FaceTime. Hold on." She pushed a button on her phone to get him on video as well as audio. "This way you'll be able to see Winnie's reaction up close and personal!"

Minutes later they all stood in the kitchen, looking on as Winnie opened the box. As soon as images of the mixer came into view, Winnie began to squeal.

"Oh. My. Goodness!" Winnie clamped a hand over her mouth and tears filled her eyes. "Mine just gave up the ghost."

"I know." Tess reached for the instruction manual after Winnie got the box open. "And we wanted to bless you with a new one. I just hope you can figure out how to use it."

"I'll figure it out, if I have to stay up all night reading that thing." Winnie extended her hand, and Tess offered her the manual. "Now I just have to decide what to make with it first. But I still don't know why you did this for me, especially now." Winnie's eyes misted over. "You're too generous."

"Here's how it happened." Tess explained about the money she had been setting aside. She ended the story with the words, "And then Brad said, 'Let me get the stand mixer for Winnie!'"

Winnie clasped her hands to her mouth again. "God bless that man! I'd give him a big kiss if he was here!"

LuAnn held the phone up. "Did you hear that, Brad?"

"I did!"

"Oh, you're there!" Winnie blew a kiss at LuAnn's phone, and they all laughed.

"You're welcome, Winnie. Now, you ladies do me a favor and get my wife out the door. We have a date with Thelma and Irene in about fifteen minutes, and you know how they are if they're kept waiting."

LuAnn laughed as she said goodbye and ended the call. "I'll be back soon," she said on her way out of the kitchen. "Save me some of whatever delicious concoction you make with that new machine, Winnie!"

After she left, Winnie turned back to face the ladies.

"Look, I didn't want to say anything earlier, but I'm pretty sure I know who took that money from the egg the other day."

"You do?" Tess and Janice spoke in unison.

"Yes." Winnie nodded. "It was that yard guy...what's his name again?"

"Griffin?" Tess was surprised by this proclamation from Winnie, who was usually more inclined to give people the benefit of the doubt. "What makes you so sure?"

"I saw with my own eyes that he picked the egg up when he was gathering the clippings from the cedar bushes."

"What? By accident, maybe."

"No accident, at least to my way of thinking. It looked pretty deliberate. I should have told you the minute I saw him with that egg in his hand, but I didn't want to raise any alarm bells unnecessarily."

"If you had mentioned it right away we could have checked it right then and there," Tess said.

"You know what they say about hindsight." Winnie sighed. "Anyway, there's something about that guy that unnerves me a little. I've been keeping a close eye on him ever since he arrived."

"Gracious." Tess sighed. "Maybe I was wrong about him." She paused, overcome by the memory of Griffin praying with Pastor Ben after the Easter service. "I don't really know, to be honest. And I don't want to judge the man too harshly. I saw him in church just yesterday."

"Repenting?" Winnie asked.

Tess suppressed a sigh. "Winnie, really."

"I'm just saying." Winnie went back to work, pulling the mixer's various attachments out of the box.

"Well, he did spend some time with the pastor at the altar, but I'm not going to get into his business."

"You didn't have to. Looks like God already did." Winnie gave her a pointed look.

Tess decided not to argue any further. She would turn this conversation around so that things didn't feel so uncomfortable. "Well, speaking of the Lord, I think this whole story is pretty sweet, in spite of the missing money. I mean, just look at how God works."

"What do you mean?" Winnie fastened the paddle onto the mixer then plugged the machine in.

"Well, you know that verse that says what the enemy meant for evil God used for good?"

"Sure." Winnie nodded.

"Someone with evil intentions stole the money from that egg."

"Obviously." Winnie quirked a brow. "Like I said, I think we all know who that was."

"Winnie."

"I know what I saw."

"Yes, but in spite of that I want to give him the benefit of the doubt, at least for now. Anyway…" Tess dragged out the word in exaggerated tones. "Point is, the money went missing, I made up for it, and then Brad made up for my lack of funds by paying for the mixer. It's been a chain of events that added up to one big blessing for all of us."

"Mostly for me." Winnie grinned. "Now, if you don't mind, I think I'd better see if I can figure this thing out. Looking at it is giving me a hankering for buttermilk pie."

"That's Brad's favorite."

"Exactly." Winnie offered a wink. "I owe that man a favor."

"You love to spoil the fellas, don't you, Winnie?" Janice asked.

"Who, me? I just return favors using food, that's all."

"You're always baking up Thorn's favorites."

"Okay, so I spoil folks a little. Why do you think I made that strawberry lemonade cake? For myself?"

"You knew it was one of my favorites?" Tess guessed.

Winnie nodded. "Well, sure. I pay attention. Last time I made it, you went on and on. So I decided to make another one, just to make you smile."

"It worked. And in case I don't say it often enough, thank you, Winnie. You're a real treasure."

"A diamond in the rough is more like it. Now, let me get to work on something amazing."

Tess walked out into the lobby and caught a glimpse of something shiny under one of the tables in the café. She walked that way and gasped when she realized she was looking at Daisy's diamond and pearl brooch.

"For pity's sake."

Janice looked up from her spot at the front desk. "Everything okay?"

Tess grabbed the fleur-de-lis and took several long strides in Janice's direction, hand extended. "Look what I just found."

"No way." Janice's eyes widened. "Do you think the clasp is broken or something? Why else would it keep falling off?"

"Maybe." Tess checked it out and sure enough, the tiny clasp wasn't working properly. "I need to give her a call, so I guess I'd better look up her number."

"I've got it on her registration. Hang on a sec." Janice scrolled through the index of guests on the computer. "Found it." She scribbled the number onto a sticky note and passed it Tess's way. "You going to call her now?"

"I think I should. She's probably fretting over it."

"If she even remembers it's missing."

Tess made the call, and Daisy answered on the second ring. "Hello?"

"Daisy, this is Tess at Wayfarers."

"Oh, Tess, we're having the most wonderful time! Miranda has brought me to this fabulous place called a—what's it called again, honey?"

Miranda's voice sounded in the background, but Tess couldn't quite make out her words due to static on the line. They must be in a rural area.

"Daisy, I wanted to let you know that I found your brooch on the floor of the lobby this morning."

"What?" The line filled with static again, and she couldn't make out much except a rushed, "Oh my goodness!" from Daisy.

"It looks like the clasp is broken, which is probably why it kept coming off."

"Oh, I'm sure that's it! Tess, please do me a favor and take it up to my room?"

"Sure."

"Bless you. I have a little jewelry box on my dresser. Just drop it inside. I can't thank you enough."

"You're welcome, Daisy. Have a fun trip."

"Oh, we are! What an adventure life is!"

"Yes, it certainly is."

"Have a lovely day, Tess!" Daisy said and then ended the call.

Tess had just picked up the brooch to carry it upstairs when a local police officer named Randy Lewis entered the front door of the inn.

"Tess." Randy took a few steps in her direction. "Can we talk?"

"Sure. Follow me into the office." She led the way, and moments later he was seated across from her. "What's up, Randy?"

He pulled a small tablet from his pocket and flipped it open. "You have a guest named..." He glanced down at his tablet. "Daisy Carmichael?"

"Yes. We sure do." She set the brooch down on the desk and leaned back in the chair.

"And she's got another woman with her? Someone called Miranda?"

"That's right."

He sat up straight in his chair. "Well, you might want to know that Mrs. Carmichael has been reported missing from her home in Syracuse, New York, and her family seems to think Miranda is the one responsible."

CHAPTER NINE

April 4, 1860

Prudence awoke many times in the night to check on her guest. Relief flooded her soul each time she saw the gentle rise and fall of Lolly's chest. When the frail woman awoke late the next morning, Prudence breathed a sigh of relief.

She forced a bright smile as she greeted her guest. "Lolly, good morning. Or should I say good afternoon? It is almost the noon hour."

For a moment, the poor woman looked confused and lost. Then, she seemed to remember where she was, and why.

"My boys..." Lolly struggled to sit up in the bed. "They must be waiting on me."

"Not just yet, Lolly." Prudence gestured for the woman to rest against the pillow once more. "I've prepared a pot of soup. Is thee hungry?"

The elderly woman again attempted to sit up. In doing so, she almost tipped sideways. Prudence ran toward her and grabbed her before she fell over. "Let me help thee."

"Precious girl." As a smile tilted up the lips of the frail woman, her wrinkled face somehow sprang back to life. Those beautiful dark eyes sparkled, as if she had experienced a healing of a miraculous nature. "How kind you are."

"It is no bother. I pray thee slept well?"

"In a bed such as this?" Lolly patted the mattress. "Yes, I slept well." She looked around the cabin, eyes widening in surprise and delight. "Such a fine home you have."

Prudence looked around the humble cottage that she shared with her husband and son. "What we have, we are happy to share, and all the more with those in search of promise."

"Those in search of promise." Lolly's lips curled up, revealing even more wrinkles on her cheeks than before. "You have described me with your words. And God will rain blessings on your head for all you do." Lolly managed to sit aright and looked a bit stronger than before.

"Now, is thee ready for soup? I've made lentil stew."

"As Jacob did make, in Bible days, to tempt his brother Esau."

"That story has not come to mind for some time."

"I know my stories." Lolly lifted a shaky finger and pointed to her head. "The body is weak, but the mind is well. Tack-sharp, my grandson Caleb says."

"Speaking of Caleb, Jason has taken food out for thy grandsons. I do hope thee is able to manage a few spoonfuls."

"For the sake of the cause, I will try." A weak smile followed from Lolly.

"I will bring it to thee."

"To be waited on is such..." Lolly giggled. "A dream, really. Am I still asleep?"

"Thee is awake, and I am happy to see thee in such fine spirits."

"There is much to fill the heart with joy, for I am alive and well, and blessed to have your care. I've spent my days tending to and caring for so many—my master's children, my own boys, and their young'uns. But I'm a queen today, fed in this heavenly bed by an angel in white." She patted the sheets and smiled.

"Angel in white?" Prudence glanced down at her white dress. "Hardly an angel."

Lolly clucked her tongue. "I have no doubt you are, sent straight from the Almighty, precious girl, and do not argue with one my age. You will never win such an argument."

"As thee wish."

A knock sounded at the door just as Prudence hefted a steaming bowl of lentil stew onto a tray for Lolly. She eased the door open an inch or two, using caution, as Jason had instructed. She would not put her guest at risk for any intruder, especially one bent on harm.

Thank goodness, today's guest was quite the opposite.

"Adeline!" Prudence could not help but squeal at the sight of her new friend. "Thee has come for a visit, just as thee promised."

"I never break a promise." The woman's pale skin shimmered with perspiration from the afternoon sun, and her cheeks carried the glow of warmth in them. Heavy glasses covered her eyes that could no longer see, but that never seemed to stop precious Adeline from the tasks at hand. She carried her walking stick in her right hand, as always, for it led the way to worlds unseen.

"But thee has come...alone? However did thee manage it?" Prudence stepped outside and looped her arm through Adeline's.

"Not alone." She gestured to the bushes, where a young man about Adeline's age waved. "Do you know Shepherd Lee?"

"The name is familiar."

"He is one of us," Adeline whispered. "Come to set the captives free."

CHAPTER TEN

Tess could hardly believe her ears. She stared at Officer Randy in stunned silence for a moment and then finally managed, "Wait. Daisy's family has reported her missing? Why?"

He adjusted his position in the chair and glanced at his tablet, then back up at her. "Because it's been more than a week since they've heard from her. She's not responding to calls or texts, and they're worried about her well-being. I was contacted by the police in Syracuse."

Tess still couldn't quite make sense of all of this. "She's perfectly fine, I can assure you. I saw her just this morning and she was as chipper as ever."

"Good to know. Is she here now? I'd like to speak to her."

"No, she's out with her granddaughter."

"Mm-hmm." He scribbled something into his tablet.

"How did the family figure out where she was, anyway? I mean, how did they know to contact you?"

"Her daughter went to a lot of trouble to track her here." He glanced down at the notepad, as if reading some notes he'd written before. "Apparently they share a credit card account with her and were able to track the charge of her room here at the inn. That's how they figured it out."

"Okay, but I'm still confused. Why would they need to track her? That sounds odd. What's the real story here?"

He gave her a pensive look. "Tess, are you absolutely sure Daisy Carmichael is here of her own free will?"

She fought the temptation to laugh out loud. "Here of her own free will? Of course. What are you saying?"

"I'm saying that a Mrs. Victoria Van Cortlandt of Syracuse New York, who claims to be Daisy's oldest daughter, is telling me that her mother has gone missing and she's worried it happened against Daisy's wishes. She's also telling me that Miranda—who is Victoria's niece—cannot be trusted with the elderly woman, that she has ulterior motives for wanting her away from the family, some of which involve the woman's inheritance."

Tess paused to think that possibility through. Was it possible she'd read Miranda wrong? Surely the young woman wasn't dangerous or manipulative, was she? "That seems ludicrous to me," Tess responded after a moment of thinking it through.

"I wouldn't be so sure."

Her thoughts went off in several different directions at once. Miranda hadn't put off any weird vibes. Then again, the family wouldn't have called in the police unless they were worried, right? Tess's heart went into overdrive as she considered the notion that they might have a kidnapper in the inn.

"No, that's just crazy," she said after pondering that notion for a moment. Miranda seemed completely amiable and always treated Daisy with such love and respect. "There's got to be more to the story. You should see them together. Miranda adores Daisy, and vice versa."

Randy shifted in the chair. "Victoria would say that Miranda's so-called affections for her grandmother are a ploy to get on her good side. Apparently, there's a lot of money to inherit when Mrs. Carmichael passes."

Tess's heart felt weighed down by that news. "Well, she's not dead yet, so I'm not sure why we're even talking about that. Is she ill or something?"

"Maybe not physically," Randy said. "But Victoria alluded to a memory loss issue and some other health concerns. They're hoping she will come back home and move into an assisted living center where Victoria can watch over her and keep her safe. They don't think it's wise for her to be out and about."

"I see." Tess chewed on that a while. "She seems pretty clear-headed to me."

"You haven't noticed anything peculiar?"

"No." Tess paused. "Does Victoria have power of attorney over Daisy or something like that? Can they demand she come back?"

"She didn't mention that, but she claimed to be the care-giver. She said that Daisy gets these wild hairs that she's going to run off and do all sorts of crazy things...like the kind of things you'd do in your college years. Jumping out of planes. Driving to Mexico. That sort of stuff."

"Seriously?"

"Yes. Something about a bucket list with crazy things on it."

"She did mention a bucket list," Tess said. "But I certainly didn't assume she meant there were dangerous things on that list. They're off on what she called 'one of our little adventures' today, but it was something sedentary that involved a car ride with Miranda. I don't think they're jumping out of a plane or anything like that."

He shrugged. "From what Victoria said, the old woman is pretty impulsive and has been known to take off on a whim in the past. But this time the family seems to think Miranda somehow coaxed her into leaving. As I said, there's some suspicion that Miranda might actually be trying to get in the grandmother's good graces in order to inherit a vast sum of money when she dies. Have you seen any signs of that? Anything money-related you've taken note of?"

"Daisy paid for the rooms on her credit card, but I assumed that was just their arrangement, since Miranda is her caregiver."

"Hmm." He scribbled something into his tablet. "Anything about Miranda seem...off? Is she money-hungry or anything like that?"

"No. And I don't see her as the inheritance-seeking sort. Besides, like I mentioned earlier, it's a little hard to collect when the deceased isn't actually deceased."

"Right. But Victoria feels this trip will be too hard on Daisy, who, according to her, has a weak heart."

Ack. That made things even worse. Surely Miranda wasn't taking advantage of that weak heart, was she?

"Well, I know they went out for a little road trip today," Tess said. "But I'm not sure where."

"I see."

"Yes, I only happen to know that because Daisy lost her brooch and I found it, so I called her to let her know. She couldn't talk because their cell reception was poor, wherever they were."

"Hmm." Randy flipped his notebook closed. "Thanks for the information. If they get back anytime soon, please give me a call."

"Will do."

He rose and led the way into the lobby, nearly plowing into Griffin Patterson, who came rushing through the front door of the inn.

Griffin took one look at the police officer and paled. He pressed his way past him then turned to watch as Randy left the building.

"Griffin?" Tess took a couple of steps in his direction. "Is everything okay?"

"Yes, ma'am. I was about to ask you the same thing." He glanced back in the direction the officer had gone.

"We're fine here." She offered a smile. That smile faded as soon as she remembered what Winnie had told her less than an hour before, about how she'd seen Griffin pick up the golden egg just before the Easter egg hunt. Should she ask him about that? Maybe the opportunity would present itself.

Griffin looked nervous. He pulled off his baseball cap and rolled it around in his hand, his gaze fixed on it. "I...I was wondering..."

"Wondering what?"

He started to respond but was interrupted by the sound of voices layered over each other. The family Tess had checked in hours earlier bounded down the stairs and entered the lobby, their loud voices ringing out across the room. She greeted them and then watched as the parents went over their plans for the day with the children. Apparently, they were headed out to dinner and then on to the ice cream parlor.

"Would you like to go into the office?" she asked Griffin, once she realized the family planned to stay put in the lobby to discuss their plans.

He nodded and then followed on her heels.

Once inside, she gestured for him to sit. "Nah, I don't need to sit," he said. "This won't take a minute."

"Okay." She went ahead and took a seat in the desk chair. "What's up, Griffin?"

"I'm here on business, actually. I hate to ask, but I'm trying to get into an apartment over on the west side of town. They've got one available, and I'm hoping they'll be willing to rent it to me. I'm not sure, considering my, well…" He paused. "My track record. But my prison chaplain vouched for me and that should help, I hope."

"That's wonderful, Griffin. Is that why you're here, to tell me you can't mow this weekend because you'll be moving?"

"Oh no. I still plan to come. I doubt I'll get the place until the following week, anyway, so I'll be here Saturday, just like normal." His gaze shot back down to the cap in his hands. "I, um…I was just wondering if there was any way you could go ahead and pay me for the whole month in advance so I can come up with what I need to pay the deposit on the place."

"Oh, I see." So that's why he was here.

"Most of the lawn guys I know charge by the month anyway." His words were all business now, as if trying to convince her. "And if we do a set price per month, I'll do all five weeks in the longer months at no additional charge."

"Well, that's nice." She paused to think it through. "So, just pay you through the end of April, then?"

"Yes." He gazed at her intently. "I just need the money for the deposit on the apartment. That's all. I won't skip town on you or anything like that, I promise."

"Well, of course you won't. Just give me a minute, and I'll make out a check." Tess opened the desk drawer and grabbed the checkbook they used for the inn's business account. She hadn't yet settled on a monthly amount with Griffin, but if his monthly rates were as reasonable as his weekly ones, she'd be getting a bargain, especially if he threw in the extra weeks during longer months.

They settled on an amount, and she made out the check. Then, as he folded it and slipped it into his pocket, she saw him sniff the air. "Something smells amazing in here today."

"Oh, Winnie is baking a buttermilk pie as a gift for a friend."

"That sounds good, but I'm smelling something different." He sniffed the air. "Citrusy?"

"Oh, that would be Winnie's strawberry lemonade cake. It's delicious."

"Strawberry lemonade cake?" He patted the pocket where he'd just placed the check.

"Four layers of lemon chiffon, jam-packed with the most amazing filling—lemon curd between some of the layers and strawberry jam between the others. Loaded with fresh strawberries between every layer too. You really just have to experience it to understand."

"You're making my mouth water."

"Mine's been watering all morning. It's one of my favorites. She adds lemon pudding to the whipped cream. It's kind of magical."

"Sounds like it."

"The top is decked out with more strawberries."

"Are you trying to kill me?" His eyes bugged.

Tess laughed. "No, but I'll tell you what…hang around a few minutes and I'll see if I can snag you a piece."

"Isn't the food for your guests?"

"And customers." Tess shrugged. "But, hey, I don't mind being generous now and again, especially to someone who's made our yard look so beautiful."

"Are you sure?"

She nodded. "If I know Winnie, she made more than one, so there will be plenty. You wait right here. I'll put a slice in a to-go container so you can take it with you."

"Wow, thanks." Griffin put his cap back on. "I'm gonna go out and look at the flower beds—I have a couple of ideas to jazz 'em up."

She walked into the kitchen to find Winnie checking on the buttermilk pies she'd just popped into the oven.

"Hey, Winnie. What did you do with the leftover cake?"

"Refrigerator. Whipped cream, remember? It has to be refrigerated."

"Oh, right. Would you mind terribly if I—"

"Ate a slice? Help yourself, honey. You know I don't mind. I was thinking of you when I made it, as you know. I'm hoping these pies will hurry up and bake so I can head home and get off my feet."

"I can keep an eye on them, if you like. Just set the timer."

"No, I'll stick around long enough to get one cooled and wrapped up to carry over to LuAnn's new place. The other I'll pop in the fridge for tomorrow's dessert. You just enjoy that slice of cake."

Tess opened the refrigerator door, and her mouth watered when she saw the luscious cake sitting inside. "Well, it's not for me. I'm giving a slice to Griffin."

"Griffin?" Winnie turned, spoonful of whipped cream in hand. "Is he back?"

"Yes. He came to—" Judging from the look of consternation on Winnie's face, Tess had better not say he'd come for money. "He's offered to fix up our flower beds."

"I like 'em just the way they are, but it's not my place to say." Winnie began to mutter under her breath.

Tess walked back into the office and stopped cold when she saw Griffin holding Daisy's brooch in his hand.

"Griffin?"

He turned to face her and quickly set it down. "Oh, sorry. I just saw this brooch sitting here. I was trying to see the design. It's called a fleur-de-lis."

"Yes, that's right."

"Fleur-de-lis means lily flower in French. That name has a special meaning to my family. We're all from Louisiana."

"I had no idea, Griffin." She slid her hand over the brooch and eased it in her direction, finally dropping it into the top desk drawer. Maybe he hadn't meant to take off with it, but right now she wasn't so sure. Something about the look on his face caused concern.

"Yes, I lived there until I was in my twenties."

"I see." She handed him the container with the cake inside.

He headed off a few minutes later, but she couldn't stop fretting over what she'd seen. The time had come to get that brooch back up to Daisy's room. Tess retrieved it from the drawer and walked up the stairs to the third floor, then used her key to open the door to Sunshine and Daisies. When she stepped inside, the first thing she noticed was the same tea rose perfume scent.

Tess walked to the dresser and saw the little jewelry box Daisy had described. She opened it up and was floored to find multiple pieces inside that looked to be very expensive. Gracious. Should she offer to put these into the safe for Daisy? Probably.

She turned back toward the door and something caught her eye. A note of some sort. Tess's gaze traveled down to the words: *Don't forget cash for Miranda.* Hmm.

Determined to put her concerns out of her mind, Tess headed back downstairs. Just as she reached the lobby, her cell phone rang. She pulled it from her pocket and saw LuAnn's name on the screen.

"Hi LuAnn," she said. "Did you make it in time to the aunts' place?"

"Tess! Oh, I'm so glad you answered."

Tess could tell from the frantic edge to LuAnn's voice that something was wrong. "LuAnn, are you okay?"

LuAnn began to cry. "Oh, Tess…I'm just so shaken up!"

Okay, something was terribly wrong here. "What happened, LuAnn?" Tess asked. "Tell me."

"I was in a car accident, Tess. A bad one."

Chapter Eleven

Tess's heart sailed to her throat. "Oh no! My goodness, are you okay? Please tell me you're not hurt."

"I'm shaken up but fine otherwise. But my poor car." LuAnn paused, and Tess heard the rustle of something like a tissue. "I was driving down the street when an SUV backed out of a driveway going way too fast and plowed right into me. You should see the damage to my car, Tess. It's bad."

"I'm so sorry."

"Me too. I'm just so grateful I was hit on the passenger side and that no one was with me. Brad said the whole—what did you call it again, honey?" She disappeared for a minute and then came back. "The frame. He said the frame might be bent. If that's the case they might total out my vehicle, and then I'd have to get a new one."

"LuAnn, I'm so sorry this happened, but I am glad you're okay."

"Me too. I'm just thanking God it wasn't worse."

Tess couldn't help but shiver as she thought through the possibilities. The idea of losing her good friend was almost more than she could take.

"I'm relieved the accident wasn't my fault," LuAnn said. "The other driver was cited and had to give her insurance information, so that part made me feel better."

"That's good. Is she okay?"

"Yes. Her name is Braelyn. I think she might have whiplash, but otherwise she's fine and so is the baby."

"Baby?"

"Did I forget to mention she had a baby in the car with her? He was in a car seat."

Tess had to sit down at that one. "This story just gets worse and worse."

"He seemed fine too, but they took him to the hospital, just to make sure he's okay. Other than being shaken up, the mom seems fine. Mostly she was upset at herself for causing the accident. She said she turned to see why the baby was fussing and kept backing up. I don't think she realized she was out of the driveway until she hit me."

"Obviously. Poor thing, though. I pray that little baby is fine."

"Yes, me too. And I'm glad she's insured. The officer made sure of that. But you'll never guess who the coverage is with."

"Who?"

"ASAP Insurance. Her agent is that same guy, Rankin, who donated the money for the Easter egg hunt. I'm so glad it's someone local and not one of those big companies."

"Well, that's convenient. At least you won't have to go far to collect."

"True. Gotta look on the bright side, I guess."

"Yes." Tess sniffed the air. The most luscious scent greeted her. She followed it into the kitchen as LuAnn kept on talking about the insurance situation.

"Right. I guess we'll cross that bridge when we come to it. Right now, my car's been towed to the shop and I'm looking into getting a rental."

"Yes, you should. ASAP will probably reimburse you for whatever you spend."

"That's what Brad said. But I'm just so shaken up, I don't know if I even want to drive at all. The idea of getting back behind the wheel terrifies me, if I'm being completely honest."

Tess stopped and stared at the kitchen counter, mesmerized by the delicious smell of Winnie's freshly baked buttermilk pie. Tess gave Winnie a thumbs-up and kept talking. "It's like falling off a horse, LuAnn. You've got to get right back on."

"Everything okay?" Winnie asked.

Tess shook her head. "No, LuAnn was in an accident. Someone hit the side of her car."

Winnie gasped and nearly dropped the second pie, which she'd just taken out of the oven. "Oh no. Is she all right?"

"Tell her I can hear her and yes, I'm all right." LuAnn chuckled through her sniffles.

"She might want to go to the hospital and get checked out," Winnie said as she set the pie down. "I had a cousin who was in a fender bender and she thought everything was okay, but later that night she couldn't move her neck. She ended up getting

$250,000 from the insurance company because of it. Things like that happen."

"I heard that too, and I'll be on the lookout for anything that seems amiss." LuAnn sighed. "Not that I want or need anything other than my car repaired."

"Well, just keep it in mind," Tess said.

"I should probably hang up. Brad wants to leave to pick up the rental car. I'll keep you posted. But please pray this whole thing gets handled smoothly. I'd like to have my own car back as quickly as possible."

"Naturally, and I'm happy to pray. And I'll ask Janice to do the same."

"Thank you. I'm just so grateful that other driver has good insurance. I don't know what I'd do, otherwise."

"Me too. But I'm sure your own insurance company would come to your rescue if it came to that, right?"

"Who knows? Okay, I really need to run."

As she ended the call, Tess felt the sting of tears in her eyes.

"Are you all right?" Winnie asked.

"I'm fine. That just caught me off guard. I'm so glad she's okay."

Janice entered the kitchen, sniffing the air. "Something in here smells divine." She stopped and glanced first at Winnie, then at Tess. "What's happened?"

Tess pulled a chair from the kitchen table and sat down. "LuAnn just called and—"

"She's been in an accident," Winnie blurted out.

"But she's fine," Tess quickly added.

"Oh no! Well, I'm glad she's okay, but tell me everything." Janice sat down across from Tess, who filled her in as best she could, giving the details of the accident.

"This is when I'm glad the law requires every driver to have liability insurance," Janice said when Tess finished telling the tale.

"Me too." Tess realized she'd been bouncing her foot up and down on the floor, so she did her best to calm down. "But I think the bigger issue here is that LuAnn is now scared to drive."

"She'll get over that." Winnie pulled off her apron and set it on the counter. "It might take a few days behind the wheel, but the fear will pass."

"As most fears do," Janice agreed.

"I'm going to wrap up this pie and carry it over to LuAnn and Brad. I'm awfully glad I've got something to offer."

"Please give them our love," Janice said.

"I will. Will you set this other pie in the fridge in a few minutes?"

Tess nodded. "Of course."

"And if that Griffin fellow comes back around, don't offer it to him. It's for the guests." Winnie gave her a knowing look as she headed for the back door.

"Thank you for everything, Winnie," Tess called out as she disappeared from view.

"Griffin was here?" Janice asked.

"Yeah, he stopped to pick up his check. I'll tell you about that in a minute. Before I do, though, someone else came by, and this might be more important news."

"What's that?" Janice asked. "Who?"

"Officer Randy."

"Because…"

"Because apparently Daisy's family in Syracuse, New York, has declared her missing. They are saying that Miranda kidnapped her."

A look of surprise registered on Janice's face. "I might believe you if you said Daisy kidnapped Miranda, but…seriously?"

"I know. I guess there's some family animosity. Daisy's daughter, Miranda's aunt, seems to think that Miranda is deliberately putting her grandmother's life in danger because she's hoping to inherit."

"Well, that's an awful thought."

"I agree. So I guess we need to let Randy know when they get back. He's going to want to talk to Daisy, to make sure she's here of her own free will."

Janice rose and stretched then headed for the pie. "This has been a day of rough news, hasn't it?"

"Yes, but there's more." Tess sighed. "I hate to admit this, Janice, but when Griffin stopped by to pick up his check, I caught him looking at Daisy's brooch."

"What?" Janice carried the pie to the refrigerator and popped it inside.

"Yeah. Actually, I should say I caught him holding her brooch. He said the fleur-de-lis had some special significance to his family."

"And what do you think about that?"

"I don't know." She groaned. "I'd hate to think my instincts about him were wrong. He seems like he's really trying to make a new start, and others have vouched for him."

"Meaning, he's rehabilitated."

"Yes. And he's never done anything to make me suspicious."

Janice gave her a stern look. "Listen, Tess, I'm pretty soft-hearted. We all know that. But maybe it's time to reconsider this guy as an employee. I would hate to put any of our guests at risk."

"It's a little late for that. I just paid him for the full month of April."

"But he hasn't done the work yet," Janice argued.

"It's customary to pay in advance. I think. Anyway, it's done, so he's committed to do the work. And besides, he needed the money for the apartment he's getting over in the west part of town. It should bring some comfort to know that he's working hard to get his life in order again. He said his prison chaplain vouched for him." Tess sighed.

"I'm sorry, Tess. Have we been pushing you too hard about hiring this guy?"

"I don't know, Janice. He's not the only one on my mind right now. I just can't stop thinking about what Randy said about Daisy and Miranda. Do you think there's something fishy in that relationship?"

"You mean, do I think Miranda is somehow out to hurt Daisy so she can end up inheriting a vast sum of money?"

"Yeah, that."

Janice shook her head. "I'd like to think I'm a pretty good judge of character, and if I am, then Miranda's a good person. Maybe there's more to the story. You know? Like, maybe the family in Syracuse is just worried Miranda will inherit, because they want the money themselves."

"Goodness, I hate talking about someone's inheritance when they're still very much alive. If Daisy is half as spry as I think she is, she might outlive us all."

"And have a wonderful time doing it." A smile lit Janice's face. "You've seen how they are. Very adventurous, those two."

"Yes." Tess's stomach rumbled, and she placed her palm on it. "Gracious. I'm getting a little hungry. I didn't have much for lunch."

"Neither did I, actually."

Tess rose and headed to the refrigerator. "I'm hoping there's some of that pasta left over."

Janice joined her at the fridge. "I feel like a sandwich."

Tess glanced her way. "That's funny. You don't *look* like a sandwich." As soon as the words slipped out, they both had a good long laugh.

CHAPTER TWELVE

The rest of Monday evening passed without any word from Daisy or Miranda. Very strange, since Miranda had made a point of telling Tess they would be back by nightfall.

Tess kept checking her phone, but there were no calls. At nine thirty, the Martindale family arrived back from their outing, all smiles, and headed up to their rooms for some TV and game time.

Janice went up to fetch Huck, their canine companion, for one final walk of the day. The gorgeous black-and-white pup came bounding down the stairs, as hyper as always.

The two ladies decided to walk him together but only stayed outside long enough for Huck to do his business and then bark at a neighbor passing by.

By the time they got back inside, it was a little after ten. They usually didn't set the alarm until eleven, but Tess was exhausted and could tell Janice was worn out too. They decided to go ahead and set it, and then they walked up the stairs to their apartment on the fourth floor.

Tom, their tuxedo cat, was happy to see them arrive. He wound his way around Janice's ankles.

Tess double-checked both pets' food and water bowls and leaned down to pat Huck, who seemed glued to her side.

"Looks like Tom has adopted you." Tess pointed at the cat, who couldn't seem to get enough of Janice.

Janice glanced down and smiled. "Yes, he seems a little…"

"Sad? Clingy?"

"I guess that's the word." Janice scooped Tom into her arms and scratched him behind the ears.

"I know it's late, but would you like to watch a show before bed?" Janice asked.

"Sure." Tess figured that would give her an excuse to wait up for Daisy and Miranda. While Janice headed off to her room to change into her pajamas, Tess settled down in her favorite chair in the gathering room and nibbled on a cookie. She would change later. Right now, she just needed time to rest… and to figure out a show they might like to watch.

Tess flipped from channel to channel on the TV, but nothing really looked interesting. Her thoughts kept drifting back to Daisy and Miranda.

"Want a cup of tea?" Janice asked as she walked back into the room. "I think I'm going to have one. Chamomile."

"No, I don't think so. Not tonight."

"You're really preoccupied, aren't you?"

"Yes, unfortunately."

"Missing LuAnn?"

"Actually, I was thinking about Miranda and Daisy. It's a little weird that they didn't come back at all, especially in light of what Randy told me."

"I'm sure everything's fine, Tess. What they do is really none of our business. Now, any preferences on what we watch?"

"No, just nothing with blood and gore right before bed."

"Like that would be my first choice." Janice laughed. She fumbled around with the remote and finally settled on a cooking show.

It didn't take long for both ladies to doze off in their chairs. Tess roused herself sometime around midnight and woke Janice, who couldn't seem to remember what day or time it was.

Tess headed to her room, thoughts still tumbling. She walked over to the dresser to pull off her jewelry. As she placed it on the jewelry plate, Tess's gaze shot to the familiar framed pictures hanging on the wall in front of her. As always, pieces of her heart flittered to her throat as she surveyed the various seasons of her life in photographic form. Snapshots of her memories. That's what Janice would call them.

That remarkable day as a youngster, when her parents took her to the amusement park to ride the roller coaster. The day she married the love of her life, Jeffrey.

Tess paused and let her gaze linger on that photograph. How young they both looked.

"If only we knew then what we know now," she said to the photo.

Then again, if she'd known Jeffrey would pass away before her and leave her alone, she wouldn't have been able to bear it.

She continued to look at the photos, pausing to take in the ones of her children. Jeff Jr. Lizzie. Oh, how happy she was that those moments were forever captured on film so she could enjoy them, even now.

She gave the final picture a close look, flooded with memories of the day it was taken. Standing on the stairway of the inn, she and her two best friends since childhood had celebrated their new venture. They had nicknamed themselves the Inn Crowd, and the moniker stuck, even today.

Even with LuAnn gone.

Gone.

A lump rose to her throat as she thought about Janice's health scare last year. How grateful they were that it turned out to be a false alarm. How blessed, that they all still got to work together every day.

Tess's thoughts shifted back to Daisy, and she whispered a prayer for the woman's safety. Hopefully Randy was wrong and Miranda posed no threat.

Tess did her best to dismiss her fears as she lingered under the hot water in the shower. Afterward, dried and dressed in her coziest pajamas, she settled down to read a book, kept an eye on the clock, and stirred every time she thought she heard a noise downstairs. Surely Daisy and Miranda would turn up before too long. Had she given them the code when they checked in?

She sent a quick text with instructions to Miranda and waited for a response.

Nothing.

At twelve-forty she rose from her bed and paced the room, finally landing at the window, where she peered outside into the nighttime sky. Shimmers of light radiated from a boat on the river. She followed them until they disappeared from view, then crawled back into bed.

Tess began to think more deeply about the story Randy had told her. If the family in Syracuse was right, if this trip posed a real threat, something could really be amiss.

Just as quickly, those thoughts were replaced with visions of the two ladies laughing and talking together. No, Miranda couldn't possibly be a risk to Daisy. The very idea was ludicrous.

Tess finally fell into a fitful sleep. As soon as she awoke the following morning, she walked down to the third floor to check out Sunshine and Daisies. She found it empty, along with Lilac and Sage. Miranda and Daisy had not returned in the night.

"That's it," she said to Janice, who joined her in the third-floor hallway. "I have no choice. I have to call the police."

"You might want to get dressed first, Tess. They're bound to show up at our door, and you don't want to greet them like that."

"True."

Tess dressed for the day then made her way downstairs and into the kitchen, cell phone in hand. She found Winnie making pancakes and bacon for the guests. Tess filled Winnie in, and she seemed genuinely concerned.

"They didn't come back at all? You're sure?"

"Yes, and I'm really getting worried."

She placed a call to Officer Randy, who said he would put the wheels in motion to search for the ladies. Tess could hear the concern in his voice. She felt it too, and all the more as the morning passed and eased its way into the lunch hour.

As she took care of customers, Tess had no time to fret over Daisy and Miranda. But after lunch—as she helped the other ladies tidy up the kitchen—troubling thoughts rose once again.

Just as she dried the last plate, a noise in the lobby alerted her. Tess shot out of the kitchen, her heart in her throat. Only when she saw Daisy and Miranda standing just inside the front door did she breathe a sigh of relief.

"I can't believe I did that!" Daisy stared at the floor in disbelief. At her feet, slivers of shattered glass. "And I just got that on our little adventure!"

"It's okay, Mimi." Miranda knelt and started picking up the pieces of glass. "It was just a trinket. We'll order another one."

"Ladies!" Tess stopped short of running to embrace them. "We were so worried about you. I didn't realize you were going to be gone overnight." She couldn't help but stare at their appearance. Their clothes were a wrinkled mess, and Daisy's usually styled hair was in loose, messy strands around her face. Gone was the usual pancake makeup and lipstick.

"We didn't realize it either," Miranda responded. "Do you have a broom? I want to sweep up this mess. Mimi dropped a little figurine she bought yesterday."

"I'll take care of it." Janice's voice sounded from behind Tess. She disappeared and returned a minute or so later, broom in hand.

Miranda plopped onto the sofa and rested her head against the back of it. "Well, Mimi…you wanted an adventure. We had an adventure."

"So, what happened?" Tess asked. "Are you both all right?"

"We set out to see a library in Cleveland."

"Cleveland?"

"I've wanted to see it my whole life," Daisy said. "We have family ties to the library."

"Really?"

"Yes. It's a long story, but my great-great-grandmother is quite the local hero in Cleveland. Anyway, Mandy is always so good about humoring me when I drag her off on these little adventures. But this time I really got us in a pickle."

"It wasn't your fault, Mimi," Miranda countered. "None of it."

"Tell them the rest, Mandy." Daisy grew more excited as she spoke. "Tell them what happened to us on the way back from the library."

"Right." Mandy sat up straight, her face more animated than before. "So, there we were, in the middle of nowhere, on our way back from Cleveland…"

"Wait, I'm confused. It's interstate all the way from here to Cleveland."

"Not when you travel with Mimi." Miranda rolled her eyes. "Anyway, all of a sudden a raccoon—at least I think it was a raccoon—ran right out in front of my car."

"Did you hit him?" Janice asked.

"No. I swerved to miss him." She paused and blew out a breath. "That's exactly what they tell you *not* to do if a squirrel or rabbit or whatever runs out in front of your car. But I just couldn't bear the idea of running him over, so my instincts kicked in."

"I'm sure I would've done the same thing." Janice reached for the dustpan and filled it with the broken glass.

"Yes, well—"

"We ended up in a ditch!" Daisy clutched her hands to her chest as she interrupted Miranda's story. "Oh, it was so exciting. I wish you could've seen us. The car was good and wedged in the mud."

"It wasn't a shallow ditch," Miranda explained. "Quite the opposite, in fact."

"I'm surprised neither of you was hurt!" Janice stared, wide eyed. "Did the airbags go off?"

"No." Miranda shook her head. "I was surprised too. But I did bruise my wrists against the steering wheel."

"And I banged my knee on the dashboard," Daisy added. "Would've been worse if that seat belt hadn't hugged me so tight."

"We're both okay," Miranda said. "I checked Mimi out to make sure, and she doesn't seem to be hurt anywhere."

"Well that's good," Tess responded. "So, what did you do once you landed in the ditch?"

"I started by calling 911. They came and helped us out of the car. It was easier for me, but Mimi's door was on the side that was wedged."

"I thought they were going to have to use the jaws of life!" Daisy clasped her hands together. "Now that would be a story for my grandchildren, wouldn't it?"

"They helped her climb from the passenger side to the driver's side, and then out of the one door that did work," Miranda explained. "Several wrecker drivers showed up at once."

"They're like vultures, out for the kill." Daisy shivered.

"Well, these guys weren't. They drew straws, and the fellow who got the job checked out my SUV before loading it up. Apparently I'd damaged my—"

"Radiator," Daisy interjected. "She busted the radiator."

"Along with destroying the right front tire and rim." Miranda sighed. "I've got good insurance on the vehicle. No problem there."

"So where did you end up?" Janice still held the dustpan with the broken glass in it.

"The wrecker driver was kind enough to give us a ride to some rinky-dink hotel—"

"*Motel*," Daisy said. "Think *Psycho*."

"I've never seen *Psycho*," Miranda said. "But Mimi went on and on about it while we were at this little motel. It was a rat-trap, for sure, but at least the beds were comfortable. I can't tell you how happy I was to have cash on me. They didn't take credit cards or debit cards. Can you imagine?"

"I never leave for an adventure without giving Mandy emergency cash," Daisy explained. "Just in case. One never knows. We might end up in jail and need bail money."

"Well, I was glad to have it this time." Miranda shivered. "What a day."

"That motel was awful, though," Daisy said. "I didn't get a wink of sleep. Every time I would close my eyes, I'd just see that raccoon's beady eyes staring deep into my soul."

"I slept like a baby. Then, when we woke up this morning, we had to wait it out until the mechanic could replace my radiator and locate the right-sized rim and tire. It was a long day."

"Made worse by the fact that I had no clean clothes and no makeup bag." Daisy sighed. "So, I'm afraid you ladies are getting to see the real me, not the face I usually present. And somehow, you've lived to tell about it."

"You look fine," Janice said. "Don't worry about that." She headed off to dump the trash, broom in one hand, dustpan in the other.

"Oh, but it all started out so well yesterday. We went exploring!" Daisy's eyes lit up. "And when we did, I could almost see myself back in time, traveling the railroad, like my relatives in days of old."

"Your relatives were travelers?"

"They facilitated travel for others."

"On the railroad?"

"Yes. Oh, such an amazing story, one I'm so proud of." Daisy yawned. "We'll just leave it at that for now, though. Maybe I can tell you all about my family after I've slept a few hours."

"Speaking of family..." Tess released a slow breath and braved the next few words. "We've had word from your family in Syracuse, ladies."

Daisy's mouth formed a perfect *O*. "They called here?"

"No, actually." Tess rose and paced the room. "They called the police, and the police came here."

"What?" Miranda looked stunned by this news. "Someone in our family called the police?"

"I guess they're onto us now, Mandy." Daisy pouted. "I thought I'd be able to sneak away for one last trip without anyone knowing, but they've tracked us down. That's a bummer."

"I'm strangely relieved that they know where we are," Miranda said. "It eases my mind."

"Oh, trust me, they know where you are," Tess said. "They tracked your credit card number, Daisy. That's how they knew you were here at Wayfarers."

Daisy's eyes narrowed, and Tess could read the disgust in her expression. "That daughter of mine has a better nose than a bloodhound and twice as much nerve."

Miranda shot a glance Tess's way. "Aunt Victoria worries about Mimi. That's all, really."

Daisy's lips curled down in a pout. "She doesn't want me to have any fun."

"Right now, I think she's more worried that you were taken away from home against your will or that you're in some sort of danger." Tess shrugged. What else could she say, really?

"Against my will?" Daisy snorted.

"That's funny." Miranda rolled her eyes. "And so like Aunt Victoria to come up with something like that...and to involve the police."

"My daughter always did love drama," Daisy said. "But I've told her a thousand times to keep the drama on the stage and let me live my own life. She doesn't listen to me, of course. She thinks I'm... What's the word?"

Miranda shrugged. "I have no idea what she thinks."

"Addlepated. I think that's the word. She thinks I'm old and addlepated and have no business being out and about without her hovering over me like a helicopter."

"Do me a favor and call her anyway?" Tess said. "That way I can report back to the police that you're safe and sound and have made contact with your family."

"If I must, I must." Daisy didn't look happy about it though.

"Yes, do call her," Miranda echoed.

"All right, I shall." Daisy sighed. "I'll do it right away and get it over with. Then I'm going to settle in for a long winter's nap."

They rose, and for the first time Tess noticed that Daisy was hobbling. "Would you like some ice for that knee, Daisy?" Tess asked.

"That would be so kind."

"I'll bring it up to your room."

"Thank you. That would be lovely." Daisy and Miranda walked toward the elevator. As the duo disappeared inside, Tess could still make out Daisy's animated description of the raccoon's beady eyes.

Janice walked back out into the lobby just as the elevator door closed. "That was quite a story."

"Yes. I'm glad they're okay."

"Me too. All's well that ends well. And it sounds like Daisy's family was way off base with their accusations against Miranda."

"Yeah. But I need to put a call in to Randy before he has half the officers in the state out looking for them." Tess made her way into the kitchen, and Janice followed closely behind.

She made a quick call to Randy, who was relieved to hear the lost sheep had returned to the fold. Thankfully, he hadn't yet alerted Daisy's family in Syracuse.

After ending the call, Tess reached for a plastic storage bag to fill with ice for Daisy. "I guess we can safely conclude that Miranda did not kidnap Daisy."

"Still, it's weird that her family thinks that she did."

"Exactly. Daisy is an adventurous spirit, and I'd say that Miranda is just along for the ride. She clearly loves her grandmother."

"She does." Janice's nose wrinkled. "You know, when I see Daisy, I see a woman who's not afraid to grow old. She's very..."

"Carefree?"

"Yes." Janice nodded. "Do you think we'll be like that when we're old? Or do you think we'll be more inclined to lounge around and watch TV?"

"I hope I'll be a little of both—someone who sees there's plenty of life going on outside and wants to join in. And someone who knows when to rest and relax."

"Yes, true." Janice paused, and a faraway look came over her. "But there's something to be said for adventure, don't you think?"

"Agreed."

"And Daisy seems wide open to it, as if she were in her twenties, not her late seventies. She gets this really childlike quality to her voice when she begins to share her stories. She's very animated." Janice shivered. "Especially all that stuff about the raccoon. I can almost see him now."

"Me too." Tess started filling the bag with ice, her thoughts firmly rooted on Daisy and Miranda's story. For someone in her golden years, Daisy sure knew how to weave a colorful tale. "I guess I'd better get this up to her before she dozes off. She sure is hobbling on that knee."

"I noticed that too."

Tess carried the bag up the stairs. When she reached the hallway just outside of Sunshine and Daisies, she noticed the door was slightly ajar.

"It's just me, Daisy," Tess called out. "I've come to bring you—"

"You just try that and see what happens!" Daisy's anger-laced words sounded from inside the room. "If I've told you once, I've told you a thousand times, Victoria, back off and let me live my life! You might be my daughter, but you're not my boss. I'll do as I like, please and thank you!"

Tess froze in place, unsure of what to do next.

As if to answer her question, the door to Miranda's room opened and she stepped out into the hallway.

"Oh, Tess." She smiled when she saw the ice bag in Tess's hand. "Is that for Mimi?"

"Yes, I was just going to take it in to her, but I think she must be on the phone."

"No worries." With her lips still upturned in a smile, Miranda took the bag of ice. "I was just going in to check on her before she takes a nap. Thanks so much for helping out. I'm sure the ice will ease whatever pain she's in."

Based on the level of angst she'd just heard in Daisy's voice, Tess wasn't so sure.

CHAPTER THIRTEEN

April 4, 1860

Prudence stood in the open doorway of her cabin, gazing at her friend. Adeline continued to gesture to the young man standing near the trees along the edge of the property.

"I did not come alone," she repeated. "Shepherd escorted me, but he does not plan to stay. I told him it might be some time. And, might I add, your directions when last we met were concise, down to the step." She offered a wave to Shepherd, and he disappeared into the woods as quietly as they had come.

"I am so glad thee did not attempt the walk alone." The idea of her new friend getting lost in these woods was almost too much for Prudence to bear, particularly in an attempt to come for a visit.

"I had to come. I understand you have a guest in need of care, and I am here to help." Adeline sniffed the air. "Lentil stew."

"Thee is very good."

"What the eyes lack, the nose senses."

"Is thee hungry, Adeline?"

"Perhaps." She tapped her cane against the doorway as if waiting to be invited in.

Prudence ushered her inside and shut the door.

"Now, tell me about our traveler."

"We have three, in fact."

"But one in need of my care." Adeline's brows elevated. "My eyes no longer work, but my nursing skills are still intact."

"Yes, please do come in and meet Lolly." Prudence led Adeline to the chair beside Lolly's bed, and moments later the two ladies were chatting like old friends. Adeline offered spoonfuls of soup to their frail guest, who lapped it up as if she hadn't eaten in days. Perhaps she had not.

"I have heard that you are headed to Syracuse, New York," Adeline said to Lolly.

"Yes, to see my oldest boy, Leon! That's where he lives with his family." Lolly's eyes sparkled. "We will be with him soon, and I will finally see with my own eyes what he has described in his letters."

"What has he told you? I would like to see with my eyes too."

"Your...eyes?" Lolly paused but then picked up where she'd left off. "He tells of a big house and a law practice. My son, a lawyer! Leon writes of buggy rides through the park, of fine clothes, and of greeting neighbors as equals. Oh, my heart is filled with joy at the notion!" She seemed to lose herself to her imagination as she carried on about all the things they would do once she arrived.

Instead of discouraging her from the trip, as Prudence hoped she would do, Adeline encouraged more conversation about Lolly's impending visit with her son and his family.

"Oh, I've actually been to Syracuse when I still had my sight." Adeline's voice grew more animated. "Such a lovely, lovely place. My grand marmee took me when I was only eleven."

"Tell me all about it, honey." Lolly reached for her hand. "I want to hear it all."

"I was there in the summertime, and the weather was lovely. Not too hot, like down south. Just perfect. The houses look a bit different from here. I rode in the most remarkable contraption called an elevator. Have you heard of it?"

"No." Lolly's eyes widened. "But I want to know everything. Tell me."

"It's a small room that moves up and down on a lever, taking you from floor to floor in a building."

"Oh my. For those who cannot walk the stairs?"

"And those who can but choose not to." Adeline giggled. "It was quite the thrill, I do say. Up and down, down and up, we rode it over and over again, just for fun. Grand marmee was quite the adventurer, as I recall."

"Perhaps I shall take an elevator ride as well." Lolly smiled, and a faraway look came over her.

Prudence hated to see the dear woman get her hopes up. How could she plan for tomorrow when today looked so uncertain?

"My boys are with me and will take me there. Together, we shall enter the Promised Land."

"Promised Land." Adeline nodded. "I know of the one with streets of gold and gates of pearl."

"Like the pearls in your brooch, child?" Lolly asked.

Adeline ran her fingers over the brooch that was pinned to her blouse. "There are pearls in the brooch, yes. And other jewels too." Her lips turned up in a smile. "Grand marmee favored me, I must say."

"Such a beautiful shape."

"Fleur-de-lis. She was from France, and her husband-to-be purchased it there as a gift to his young bride before they came to America."

"What a lovely story."

"Yes, she was quite special, and I miss her terribly. She's in heaven waiting for me. One day I will see it, and her, with my own eyes. My vision will be crystal clear, as clear as that lake of glass where we shall worship at our Savior's feet. And I pray, dear Lolly, that you see your promised land—both here and beyond."

"Precious child." Lolly smiled. "I make my plans, but the Lord carries them out. If He is gracious enough to see me through to Syracuse, then I shall have all the milk and honey He will allow. Seeing my boy and his young'uns will be my first glimpse into heaven."

If thee is strong enough for the journey, Prudence wanted to add but didn't. Instead, she reached with a cloth and dabbed the dribbles of lentil stew from Lolly's quivering chin.

"I do not know the day or the year of my birth." Lolly's voice took on a reflective tone. "Best I can figure, I'm ninety-two years of age, but whatever strength I have left, I give to this journey."

Adeline gasped. "My goodness, but God has been good to you, giving you such a life. I am but twenty and six."

"You are just beginning your life, and I am nearly done living mine." Lolly smiled again. "Have you dreams, precious girl? Hidden in your heart?"

"Dreams?" Prudence and Adeline spoke in unison.

"Secret wishes, sweet girls. Tucked into the deepest places in your heart." Lolly rested her hands on her chest and lowered her voice to a whisper. "Things you dare not voice, lest they be argued by well-meaning folk."

"I have dreams." Prudence allowed her imagination to take her to places she had never voiced aloud. "I have always longed to travel to the big city, to see a fancy department store." She laughed. "I must seem so...frivolous...for such a wish."

"Not at all." Lolly waggled a finger in her direction. "You are alive and well and have the joy of many days ahead of you."

"I've always longed to put my feet in the ocean, to feel the salty water against my skin," Adeline said. "Perhaps one day I will."

"Take those dreams and tuck them in the safe places in your heart." Lolly looked back and forth between Prudence and Adeline. "And don't ever give up, no matter how impossible they might seem. Take them out from time to time. Dust them off and remind the Almighty." She extended one hand toward Adeline and the other toward Prudence. "Do you promise?"

Prudence gave her hand a squeeze.

"I...I promise," she said. "But let's not talk about that. I want to see thee strengthened, Lolly. Can thee not stay here for a few days or weeks? Adeline and I could nurse thee back to health, and perhaps then..."

"No, precious." Lolly gave her a stern look. "I shall see my son."

Prudence bit back the words that threatened to follow. Instead, she simply nodded and said, "Then I shall pray to that end."

CHAPTER FOURTEEN

On Friday, the lunch crowd thinned out earlier than usual. By one o'clock they were down to only two customers, a couple of locals who frequented the café. Tess was happy for the reprieve from the chaos of a larger group. LuAnn still hadn't returned to work. In the days since the accident, she'd been battling a sore neck and stiff back, and Tess didn't want to push her.

Janice made a quick trip into the kitchen to grab another pitcher of water, which left Tess and Taylor alone to tend to the customers. Tess was surprised when a moment later Corey walked into the café. Funny, for someone who never frequented the café before the Easter egg hunt, he was almost becoming a regular.

Then again, he had given her a heads-up that he would be returning. Something to do with that article he was writing. About Griffin, perhaps? Or maybe he was hot on the trail of one elderly woman from Syracuse and her granddaughter, who might—or might not—be after her money.

"Good to see you again, Corey." Tess offered him a bright smile.

"Hey, I told you I'd be back."

"You did." She tried not to get in his business but couldn't help asking, "So, how's that new article coming along?"

"Oh, it's coming." For a moment, a cloud seemed to settle over him, and she wondered if he was upset at something.

"Everything okay?"

"Yes." He glanced around the café. "Am I too late for lunch?"

"No. We're just not as busy as usual. Take a seat anywhere you like."

He chose a table near the window and gazed out at the lawn. Tess filled his water glass and handed him a menu. "Here you go."

"Thanks," he said and then gave his order.

Soon Tess brought his soup and sandwich to his table, along with a cup of coffee, which Corey had also ordered.

He grew silent as he glanced down at the food, as if analyzing it closely.

Terrific. Maybe he planned to write an article about Winnie's cooking. Hopefully it would be flattering. "Is there anything else I can get for you, Corey?"

"I see you've got buttermilk pie today. That's one of my favorites."

"You want a slice?"

"Ask me again after I finish this." He took a bite out of his sandwich, gave it a few thoughtful chews, and then looked out the window once again. "I was hoping to have a chat with Griffin. Is he around, by any chance?"

"Not today. He mostly comes on Saturdays."

Corey's brow furrowed. "Well, if you see him, would you tell him I'm looking for him? You wouldn't happen to have his address, would you?"

"I, well, no." She didn't, after all. But even if she did she wouldn't give it to Corey.

"I really need to talk to him, so if you have his number, even—"

Ack. Now what? She did have his number but didn't feel comfortable giving it out. Before she could give it another thought, LuAnn rushed into the café. She slung her purse onto the nearest empty table and dropped into a chair, then planted her head on the tabletop. "Ugh! Can you believe this day?"

Tess took several steps in her friend's direction. "Well, hello to you too. Talk about making an entrance. I didn't think you were coming today."

"Ugh. Sorry." LuAnn looked up and then dropped her head back onto the table. "I hadn't planned to come, but I had to get out anyway to take care of something."

Janice joined them, deep wrinkles creased between her eyes as she saw the condition their friend was in.

"I would ask if everything was all right, but clearly it's not."

"You're right, it's not. You guys are never going to believe what's happening with my insurance claim. I still can't believe it myself."

"What?" Janice and Tess asked in unison.

"That guy, Rankin what's-his-name, won't pay the claim."

"What do you mean, he won't pay the claim?" This made no sense to Tess. "He's an insurance agent. He's got to make good on the claim."

"He said I was to blame for the accident. He had some convoluted reason why, most of it supposedly based on the other woman's word. But at the scene she totally admitted it was her fault. She was really apologetic after she hit me. And the officer agreed."

"Of course she was to blame. A car backs out of a driveway, plows into you, and you're somehow at fault for simply being in the wrong place at the wrong time? He's crazy."

"Exactly!" LuAnn threw her hands up in the air. "Common sense says there's nothing suspect in my behavior that day. I was just driving down the road like any normal person."

"Did he even read the police report?" Janice asked.

"I would think he would be required to. But Brad says that some insurance companies deliberately delay payments on claims so that they can maximize on their profits."

Tess noticed that Corey seemed to be leaning their direction. Eavesdropping, perhaps? He had pulled his phone out and his thumbs were in overdrive. Great. Just what they needed, a snoop in the café. What was he planning to write next, an article about LuAnn's driving skills?

Tess gestured for LuAnn and Janice to follow her to the lobby. When they got there, she glanced back at Corey, then looked into LuAnn's tear-filled eyes. "I think we're safer talking out here."

"Safer?" LuAnn looked perplexed.

"Yeah, kind of a long story, but Corey is back and he seems to be in snooping mode. I have no idea what he's working on, but there's some reason he keeps showing up here. He told me so himself. It's not just for lunch, though he seems to love Winnie's cooking."

"Did he tell you what kind of story?"

"No. But if he does, I'll let you know." She paused and glanced his way, then looked back at LuAnn, who was still clearly distressed. "I'm sorry, LuAnn. Where did we leave off?"

"I was telling you Brad's theory that some insurance companies put off paying claims so they can maximize their profits."

"How does that work?" Janice asked.

"Apparently the longer they hold on to a client's money before they pay out the more interest they earn while the money is banked. Maybe they think some people will just give up and pay for the repairs out of pocket. Some probably do, though I can't imagine it."

"Me neither. If we had that kind of money we wouldn't need insurance," Tess said.

"Exactly. Brad also said that most companies—and I didn't realize this—will turn down claims the first time around, then pay on them after you pressure them."

Tess put her hands on her hips. "So, how does one pressure them, exactly?"

"Yeah, are you going to show up at his office, or what?" Janice echoed.

"I'm going to send a certified letter, to start with, one that carefully documents how the accident took place. I've already tried to write it, but every time I get to the part where my vehicle was hit, I have flashbacks and can actually feel the pain in my neck."

"Maybe I could type it up for you," Janice suggested. "We could go into the office and you could give me a play-by-play of what happened and I'll put it into a letter."

"Oh, good idea, Janice." LuAnn nodded. "I think that would be helpful."

"We should add a diagram to the letter," Tess suggested. "That's what they always do in the movies."

"Brad suggested a diagram too. I think he's already working on it, in fact."

"Perfect." Tess gave her friend a sympathetic hug. "We'll get this taken care of, LuAnn. You won't be alone, I promise."

"Okay." She swiped at her eyes with the back of her hand. "I feel better after talking to you. I'm sorry I'm such a mess lately."

"I don't blame you a bit." Janice rested her hand on LuAnn's arm. "You just take it easy. We'll make sure everything is documented. And when we've got all our ducks in a row, we'll send it to that insurance agent through certified mail."

"And if he doesn't respond after that, Brad says we'll hire an attorney."

"Won't it cost you more for attorney's fees than you'll recoup from the insurance?" Tess asked.

"Nah. Just a letter from the attorney should do it. At least according to—"

"Brad." Tess and Janice finished the sentence for her.

"Yes." She shrugged. "This is just a lot more work than I expected. I shouldn't complain. I have a rental car, so I'm not stranded. But who even knows if Rankin Smith will cover the cost of that? I hope I don't get stuck with that bill too."

"Just hang in there," Janice encouraged her. "Do everything Brad said, and we'll be praying Rankin pays up. He has no choice."

Out of the corner of her eye, Tess caught a glimpse of Corey rising from his table in the café. He left some money next to his cup and then took a final swig of his coffee. On his way to the door he passed them then turned back and cleared his throat.

"Ladies."

"Corey?" Tess glanced his way. "Everything okay?"

"The meal was great, thank you."

"You're welcome. Did you decide to skip the pie?"

"Yes, I don't need it."

She offered a smile. "We hope you'll come back."

"Oh, I will. You can count on it." He paused and appeared to be fighting for words. "I, well, I'm not trying to get in your business, I promise. But I just wanted to let you know that I overheard some of what you were talking about."

Tess pursed her lips. Well, great. "About the insurance, you mean?"

"Yes." He focused his attention on LuAnn. "You ladies might recall that I told you I was following a story, much bigger than an Easter egg hunt."

Tess nodded. "Yes, I remember."

"What I just heard you say confirms what I already knew to be true about this so-called agent, Rankin Smith. Just so you're aware, he's the focus of my story."

"Rankin Smith?" LuAnn's eyes widened. "What about him?"

"Yes. I knew he was fond of Winnie's cooking. I heard him say as much at the brunch after the Easter egg hunt, so I thought he might frequent the place."

"No." Tess shook her head. "I don't recall him hanging out here, other than that one day."

"Bummer. This is turning out to be quite the story."

"What do you mean?" Tess asked. "What kind of story?"

"I mean…" His brow wrinkled, and for a moment she saw anger in his eyes. "Rankin Smith is a crook. And that so-called insurance agency he's running? It's nothing but a scam. You can bet your life on it. And I'm not going to stop until I take the man down, mark my word."

And at that proclamation, Corey turned and walked out the door.

CHAPTER FIFTEEN

On Saturday morning Griffin arrived at nine, right on schedule. He buzzed around the yard, a smile on his face as he worked. Tess watched him from the front window, marveling at his light-spirited gait. She could see his lips moving and wondered if he might be singing. Yes, he was wearing earbuds. No doubt he had music going to drown out the sound of the mower.

Janice approached with a cup of coffee in hand. She turned her attention to the window and sighed. "He's back."

"Yes, like I said, he's paid up through the end of the month, so unless he gives me some reason to fire him, he's staying."

Janice took a swig of her coffee. "He seems to be in good spirits today."

"Yes. When he's done I'm going to take some lemonade out to him."

Tess continued to keep an eye on Griffin as he worked. He started with the lawn, pushing the self-propelled mower all around. Then he edged the borders and used the blower to clean the whole area.

When the time felt right, she filled a glass with lemonade and carried it outside. She reached him just as he grabbed his hedge clippers.

"Well, good morning, Tess." He offered a bright smile.

"You seem in good spirits this morning."

"I have good reason to be."

She offered him the glass of lemonade. "Why is that?"

He took the glass in hand. "I'm going to move in on Monday." Another broad smile lit his face. A swig of lemonade followed. "Mmm. This is good."

"Thank you. It's homemade. Are you saying you got the apartment?"

"I did. My chaplain vouched for me, like I said, and it went through, no problem. All my ducks are lining up in a row, which is great. I just have to build my business a little and then I'll be set."

"I'm so glad things are going well for you."

"Thanks. I'm doing my best, I really am." He took another swig. "This really is good lemonade. Reminds me of what my grandmother used to make."

"You deserve it. It's warm out here."

"It is." He gave her a thoughtful look. "You've been really nice to me, Tess."

"I would hope that everyone would be nice to you, Griffin."

"Hmm. Well, not everyone." He pursed his lips and then finished off the glass of lemonade. He continued to grip the glass, and she could tell he had something more on his mind. "Can I ask a favor?" he asked after a few seconds of silence.

Uh-oh. What did he need now? Hopefully not more money. She nodded. "Sure."

"I know you're the religious sort, like my wife. Would you please pray she takes me back?"

"Griffin, you're married?" Tess couldn't have been any more surprised.

"Yeah. Thirteen years. But I missed out on the last two, for obvious reasons." He shrugged. "Hey, she didn't divorce me. That's gotta count for something, right? It gives a man hope."

"Yes. And you say she's a believer?"

He nodded. "Yeah, she goes to church on the west side of town. That's where she lives now, with our two kids, Charlie and Lily. That's why I chose an apartment complex over there."

"You have children?" The plot thickened.

"Yep. That's why my chaplain thought it was best to go ahead and get a two-bedroom apartment, so there's room for the kids when that time comes. Right now, I can only have supervised visitation."

"How's that going?"

He shrugged again and released a sigh. "I guess that's another prayer request. Charlie was seven when I went in, so he remembers me. But Lily was only three, so I'm a total stranger to her. I missed her first day in kindergarten. I missed…everything."

"I'm so sorry."

"She's our little Fleur-de-lis. Rose and I named her after the flower, in memory of my growing-up years in Louisiana."

So, he really did have a connection to the fleur-de-lis. No wonder he'd reached for that brooch. And how sweet that his wife's name was Rose.

Tess decided she'd better get back to the conversation at hand. "You'll be there to see Lily learn to drive, Griffin, and to leave on her first date."

"Hey now."

She laughed. "And you'll even be there to walk her down the aisle. There are plenty of great years ahead."

"If I'm lucky enough to get to do all that." He smiled. "Which leads me back to what I said earlier. I guess I need a lot of prayer if any of this is going to happen." A sheepish look followed. "And maybe a few recommendations to your friends for more work? I've got solid landscaping skills. I worked for a large company before I, well..."

"Sure, I'll be happy to recommend you. And in case I haven't said it, our yard hasn't looked this nice since we moved in, Griffin. Really. You've got quite the green thumb."

"Every time I see this garden, I want to add some lilies."

"Fleur-de-lis."

"Yes." He smiled. "What do you think? They don't bloom very often, but they're gorgeous when they do."

"I'm sure the other ladies would go along with that, but I'll ask, just to be sure. Would it be costly?"

"Oh no, ma'am. I wouldn't even charge you labor. Just the cost of the plants."

Tess wagged her finger at him. "Now listen here…you've got kiddos to feed. Don't you dare let me catch you taking on freebie jobs, you hear me?"

"Um, yes ma'am." He offered her a bright smile. "Let me know about the flowers."

"I will. And I'll pay you for planting and tending to them, of course."

"Okay." Griffin's gaze shifted downward, as if in shame. "I'm not sure why I told you all that stuff about my wife and kids. I hope you don't mind."

"I don't mind a bit. I'm so excited to see what God does in your journey ahead, and I'm happy to be a listening ear."

"You remind me of my chaplain."

"I do?"

"Yes. You're an encourager, just like he is. And he has a great sense of humor, just like you."

"Yeah, well, my sense of humor gets me in trouble sometimes."

He laughed. "A good sense of humor was one of the things that got me through my time in prison." Griffin grew serious. "A lot has changed for me over the past year or so. I guess you could say prison saved me. I'm definitely not who I used to be."

"Oh?"

"Not that who I used to be was really as bad as all that." This time he looked her squarely in the eye. "Are you wondering how I landed in prison?"

"I, well…I know a little."

"Probably what others have told you. But it comes down to this: I made a mistake. A huge mistake. An opportunity presented itself—to do the wrong thing, I mean—and I took it. I was facing a financial obstacle that felt like a mountain to me, and then, by some…miracle…there was money staring me in the face."

"And you took it."

He released a slow breath. "I can remember it like it was yesterday. I went into Mr. Higley's office to pick up a check for some landscaping I'd done, and he was prepping his night deposit. I took one look at that bag and my heart just went crazy. All I could think about was how much money might be inside."

"Oh my."

"Yeah, my hands started shaking, like they had a mind of their own. Something possessed me. I don't know any other way to explain it. It's almost like I just stepped out of my body and someone else took charge. I've never had anything like that happen before, or since."

"Wow."

"Yeah." He shook his head. "I didn't even think about the fact that most of what was inside that bag would be checks and totally worthless to me. All I know is, Higley turned around to get his checkbook to pay me for the landscaping and I let my hands tell me what to do. I shoved the bag inside my jacket, and when he turned back to face me I just kept talking to him with a big smile on my face, like nothing had happened."

"Guess he figured it out after you left?"

"Yeah." Griffin sighed. "I hadn't been home an hour when the cops showed up. And the really stupid thing is, there was only a couple hundred dollars in cash in the bag. Most of it was checks and money orders…stuff like that. Like I said, they were useless to me."

"One impulsive move changed everything."

"Yeah. It all happened lightning fast. One minute I'm staring at that bag on his desk, my heart thumping. The next they're fingerprinting me at the station. And the next couple years I was secluded from everything and everyone that I cared about. All because of one stupid, impulsive decision that I never planned to make in the first place."

"I've made some impulsive decisions in my life too," Tess acknowledged. "Not to that extent, but I do know what it feels like to be grasping at anything and everything." She paused to think through her next words. "When my husband died—"

"I'm so sorry. I didn't realize you were widowed."

With the wave of a hand she tried to dismiss his concerns. "It's been years now. But in that moment, I was so scared. There were decisions to be made, and I was frozen in place for a while. But that was then and this is now. I'm much more free and easy these days."

"Maybe, but you still don't strike me as the impulsive type, Tess."

"Oh? I don't look like the sort who would jump out of a plane or take a ride in a Nascar?"

"Um, no." He laughed. "Why, are you thinking about either of those things?"

"Not really. I've been thinking a lot about bucket list items, and those two came to mind."

"Bucket list, eh?" He released a breath and raked his hand through his hair. "You want to know what mine is?"

"What's that?"

"For my wife and daughter to forgive me."

"That's a wonderful wish, Griffin."

"Right now, it seems impossible—"

"As most bucket list items do at one point or another. I guess that's why they're 'someday' wishes."

"Someday wishes." He nodded. "Yes. Only, I'd rather have today be my someday, thank you very much." A boyish smile followed.

"Just keep praying."

"I will."

She paused. "Hey, can I ask you a question, Griffin?"

"Sure. Anything."

"That guy, Corey. He was in here the other day, asking about you. Said you had some unfinished business."

Griffin nodded again. "He's right. We do. I don't mind admitting, I've been avoiding him."

"Anything I should be concerned about?"

"No. Not at all."

"One more question, and then I promise to leave you alone."

"Shoot."

"The day of the Easter egg hunt...did you move the golden egg?"

"Yeah, I sure did." He pointed at the spot under the rose-bush. "Someone put it right up against the rosebush. There are like, a thousand thorns on that bush. I was worried one of the kids might get hurt. I did the best I could to trim it back along with the cedar bushes, but it was still a hazard with that golden egg so close. Too much of a risk for the kids. So I moved it a few inches away, just to be safe."

"Ah. Good move."

"Why do you ask?"

She shook her head. "It's not important. I just wondered."

"Hmm." He gave her a look that said, "I don't quite believe that."

Tess just shrugged, unwilling to elaborate.

"I know that people suspect me...of everything. It's the nature of the beast, to be guilty of all because you've been guilty of one thing. But I'm clean as a whistle these days, so rest easy."

"Oh, I'm resting easy, all right. No worries at all, at least not on my end."

"Good, because I'd hate to think I'd somehow disappointed you. You're one of the few people who's shown me true kind-ness and mercy since I got out, and I'm beyond grateful. You have no idea." He grinned. "Pastor Ben said you were good people."

"I do my best."

"You do that."

Tess turned to go back inside. When she reached the side-walk, she was approached by two strangers—a woman in an expensive outfit wearing top-of-the-line heels, and a sour-faced man who looked to be doing his best to keep up with her.

"Are you here to check in?" Tess asked.

"Certainly not." The woman's lips curled downward. "I'm Victoria Carmichael Van Cortlandt, and I'm here to find my mother and talk some sense into her."

CHAPTER SIXTEEN

Tess led the way inside and gestured to the sofa in the lobby. "If you'll just have a seat, Mrs. Van Cortlandt, I'll go up and tell your mother you're here."

The woman did not look happy with this arrangement. Her eyes narrowed to overly made-up slits as she said, "No thank you. I'll go up myself. Just give me her room number."

Tess gave the woman a closer look. She was beautiful but in an oddly pretentious way. Perhaps it was the upturned nose. Or maybe it could be blamed on the platinum blond updo, which had been pulled a bit too taut, giving her face a severe look.

"Oh, we never do that." Tess shook her head. "Sorry, but it's protocol. I can't possibly give out a guest's room number."

The man quirked a brow. "Even if my wife happens to be her daughter?"

"I, well…" She shook her head. "I'm happy to call her room, if you like, and let her know you're here."

"I could do as much myself."

"But she probably wouldn't come down, either way," Mr. Van Cortlandt said.

"True." Mrs. Van Cortlandt sighed and reached into her expensive handbag for a compact, which she opened. "Stubborn woman." She stared at her reflection, smacked her lips, and closed the compact.

LuAnn descended the stairs into the lobby. She must have picked up on a weird vibe, because she headed Tess's way with a concerned look on her face. "Everything okay?"

"Yes, I wonder if you would mind running up to the third floor to get Daisy. You might also ask Miranda to come down."

"We don't need Mandy." The woman shoved the compact back into her handbag and fussed with her tightly coiffed hair. "That will only complicate things. We're better off with just my mother, thank you."

Complicated or not, Miranda exited the elevator with Daisy a few minutes later. LuAnn wasn't with them but came back into the lobby via the stairs a few seconds later.

Tess could tell from the look on Daisy's face that this was going to be a tough conversation. She wanted to slip out, but they had her way blocked, so she pretended to busy herself at the front desk.

"So, you've come for me, have you?" Daisy put her hands on her hips. "Thinking you'll fetch me back and put me in that old folks' home you've got picked out for me?"

Victoria rolled her eyes. "Mother, you know better than that." She opened her arms. "Aren't you even going to greet me? Dougie and I have come a long way."

Daisy released a sigh and gave her daughter a hug that seemed, at least from Tess's point of view, a bit strained. Instead of hugging her son-in-law, Daisy offered him a curt nod. It seemed a bit odd that Victoria never even acknowledged Miranda's presence. This was her niece, after all, right?

LuAnn stood at the foot of the stairs for a moment, then pointed herself in the direction of the kitchen, stopping just short of the door. Likely to listen in on the conversation.

"Is there someplace a little more private we can talk?" Victoria gave her mother a pensive look. "Your room, maybe?"

Daisy shook her head. "We'll stay down here."

Tess decided this might be a good time to interject an idea. "There's no one in the café at this time of day. Would you like to visit in there? I could even bring you some refreshments."

"*Visit* might be a stretch," Victoria's husband responded.

"That would be lovely, Tess." Daisy flashed her a warm smile.

Tess led the way into the café and gestured to a table near the window. "This should be comfortable. Now, how about I fix you all some coffee and cake. How would that be?"

"Yes, please." Daisy clasped her hands together in obvious delight at the idea of an afternoon snack. No doubt she would need the fortitude it would offer, faced with a Goliath like Victoria.

"Same," Miranda echoed.

"None for me." Victoria put up her hand, as if warding off any such notion. "I'm counting carbs."

"I'd like a slice of cake and a cup of coffee," Mr. Van Cortlandt said. "Two sugars, heavy cream."

"He'll have a cup of black coffee and no cake." Victoria gave him a side-eye. "Are we or are we not watching our sugars, Dougie?"

"I, well…" He paused and then gazed at Tess. "I'll have a coffee with artificial sweetener, please. Skip the cake, I guess."

"Sure." Tess headed into the kitchen where she found Janice reorganizing the contents of the refrigerator. LuAnn joined them a few seconds later.

"Wow," she said.

"Yeah, I agree." Tess rolled her eyes.

"I'm trying to picture what Thanksgiving would look like at their house." LuAnn leaned against the counter and appeared to be thinking that idea through. She shivered.

"A lot like what we just saw, I would imagine."

"What did I miss?" Janice poked her head out of the refrigerator and gave them an inquisitive look. "Something big going on?"

"Daisy's family has arrived. Her highness Victoria Carmichael Van Cortlandt and husband, Dougie, who shall not consume cake, at risk of peril."

"Gracious."

Tess quickly prepared the refreshments then entered the café with four cups of steaming coffee and two pieces of cake on a serving tray. The family appeared to be hot and heavy into an argument, with Daisy taking the lead.

"What's all this nonsense you've been spouting to the police about my heart?" she asked her daughter.

Victoria took the cup of coffee that Tess offered and set it on the table. "Mother, you have a weak heart and you know it."

"My heart is as solid as steel. I don't know where you come up with these things."

"But your cardiologist said—"

"He said I have A-fib, a common condition for people of all ages. I don't show any signs of blockage or other valve issues to cause concern. So don't blame your concerns about my well-being on my heart. If anyone here has a hard heart, it's you, not me."

"Mother!"

Talk about wishing she could disappear. Still, Tess had three more cups of coffee to serve, along with Daisy's and Miranda's slices of cake. She practically tossed them on the table and then headed to the swinging doors with the tray. Out of the corner of her eye she caught a glimpse of LuAnn peeking through them and blocking the route to the kitchen.

"No, I mean it, Victoria," Daisy responded. "You've never tried to see anything my way. You want to push me around and make all my decisions for me. And when I try to push back, you put up walls. So don't go talking to me about heart conditions. The only one in the room who has one is you."

Victoria flinched, and her gaze shifted down to the tablecloth. She fingered it and remained silent for a while before speaking. "I…I don't know what to say in response to that, Mother. I've done my best to care for you."

"But that's just it." Daisy put both hands on the table and stood. "I don't need caring for, at least not yet."

"Then why do you always insist upon taking Mandy with you when you go off on these little jaunts of yours?"

"So that I'm not alone." Daisy's expression softened as she gave her granddaughter a tender glance. "I still long for companionship, just like anyone else. No one can blame me for that."

"If you would just come back home, Mother—"

"I will. In my time."

Tess chose this moment to nudge LuAnn and return to the kitchen. She kept the swinging doors cracked so that she could keep an eye on the goings-on in the café.

"You think because I'm old that I've lost my faculties." Daisy's cheeks flamed pink. "Well, I want you to know, every marble in my head is intact."

"Mother, I never said you'd lost your faculties. But you're seventy-eight years old. I think it makes sense for you to—"

"Settle into the nursing home and wait to die? No, thank you."

"I never said that." Victoria wiped her eyes.

Daisy seemed to soften at this reaction from her daughter. "Look, I agree that the house is too big for me. Even with Miranda filling up some of that space. And I certainly don't want her to give up her life just to care for me, if things reach that point."

"I'm fine, Mimi," Miranda said with the wave of a hand. "You know me. I'm easy."

"Yes, sweet girl, you are."

"I'm happy to hang with you."

Daisy faced Victoria, a look of determination coming over her. "Tori, I don't expect you to understand this, because you're young."

"I'm fifty-five, Mother."

"You're young. And you don't see it yet, but you will. You'll reach an age where people begin to expect you to just stop living. And I'm not done with my life yet."

"If you move into assisted living, you'll have friends. You'll play cards. You'll watch shows together. You'll have community meals."

"Which will all be fine when I'm ready for it. But I won't get to do the things on my bucket list."

"Bucket list?" Victoria and her husband spoke in unison.

"Yes." Daisy reached into the pocket of her colorful slacks, pulled out a slip of paper, and unfolded it. "Now, many of the things on this list Miranda and I have already done, but there are still a few things left."

Victoria crossed her arms and leaned back in her chair. "Like...?"

"Well, for one, this trip to Ohio. I came because my great-great-grandmother lived here at one time. I wanted to see the place where Adeline lived and worked. I've always known of her, but I don't feel that I've truly known her, if that makes sense. I'm getting a chance to experience some of her story, now that I'm finally here. And then it was critical to visit the library in Cleveland, of course. That was an important stop. It was number seven on my list."

Victoria's brows arched. "What library in Cleveland?"

Daisy pinched her eyes shut and shook her head. "That's just it, Tori. If you paid attention, you would know. Oh, I do wish you'd been with us, so you could learn more about where this family comes from."

"It's where we are now that matters to me."

"Where we are now is solely because of where we've been. Don't you see that? If you had come with us to Cleveland, you would have seen that we were treated like celebrities. The historian was so tickled to meet one of Adeline Lee's relatives in the flesh. She was quite the local hero back in the day, you know."

This certainly got Tess's attention. She didn't want to interrupt but couldn't help herself. With the coffeepot in hand, she walked back into the café to refill their cups.

"Did I overhear you say Adeline?" she asked as she topped off Mr. Van Cortlandt's coffee.

"Yes." Daisy looked her way. "My great-great-grandmother. She lived in this area."

"I've read of an Adeline in the diary I told you about, the one dating back to the mid 1800s. I wonder if it's the same woman."

"Oh, I'd love to see it, to compare notes." Daisy's eyes lit up. She turned to face her daughter. "See, Victoria? Another connection to the past."

"I'm happy you're finding ties to our ancestors, but I really don't see what other fascinations this part of the country holds."

"Getting to know Adeline's hometown was number six on my list. But let's not forget about numbers eight and nine."

"The mind reels," Mr. Van Cortlandt said as he spooned sweetener into his coffee.

Daisy nodded. "Yes, Victoria. There's more to her story, and I want to follow the trail west."

Tess stepped away from the table, more than a little curious about where Daisy and Miranda were headed next. She set the coffeepot down and eased her way toward the opening on the parlor side.

"I hope you will follow it all the way back home." Victoria took a sip of coffee and made a face. She pushed the cup back a few inches, as if having it too close caused pain.

"I will, when the time is right," Daisy said. "I'll confess, it's a little late to see the seven wonders of the world, so I've already crossed that one off, which narrowed my bucket list down from ten items to nine."

"Thank you." Victoria smoothed a wrinkle in the tablecloth.

"And I checked off the trip to Paris ages ago. I took that three years back with you, Victoria. That was number two, by the way." She offered her daughter a warm smile.

"Yes, and we had a lovely time but it wore you out, Mother."

"It wore *you* out, as I recall. I was fine."

"What else is on the list?"

"The Caribbean cruise we took last year, Mimi," Miranda interjected. "That was number three."

"Yes, and singing a solo in front of the church," Daisy added with a crooked grin. "That was number five." She giggled. "Oh, what a day that was!"

"Hey, you've still got it, Mimi." Miranda's eye lit up. "And boy, did you ever prove it with that version of 'Victory in Jesus.'

"They're still talking about it at Old Oaks Presbyterian," Daisy responded with a proud smile.

"Yes." Victoria quirked a brow. "They are. Indeed. So, let's cut to the chase. Just tell me what you haven't yet crossed off of your list. Other than the seven wonders of the world."

Daisy's brow wrinkled, and she quickly folded the paper. "That's for me to know, at least for now. If I tell you, you will just say I can't do them."

"Please, Mother, just tell me there's nothing crazy on that list."

From the way Miranda chewed at her bottom lip, Tess could tell there must be.

"Life is an adventure, Victoria." Daisy's expression hardened once again, and her voice tightened as she spoke. "I want to live it. Fully live it."

Victoria fingered the coffee cup, concern registering in her eyes. "And if something happens to you while you're living, then what?"

"Then I'll die living." Daisy shrugged. "There are worse ways to go, right?"

Tess almost chimed in with a hearty, "Right!" but decided to stay out of it. None of this was her business, after all, though she was a little curious about numbers eight and nine.

Apparently, Victoria was still curious too. She wouldn't let up until Daisy finally confessed that number eight had something to do with the town of Cincinnati, where Adeline also traveled in her adventures to visit good friends.

"See, Aunt Victoria?" Miranda planted her hands on her hips. "Now, that doesn't sound too dangerous, does it?"

"You could get in a car accident on the way there," Victoria countered. "Things like that happen."

"Yes, and I could get hit by a bus crossing any street back home in Syracuse. But I can't live in fear, sweetheart. As long as

there's breath in my lungs and I'm of a mind to be adventurous, I shall. And no one will stop me." Daisy paused when her
daughter's lips curled downward. "But I will promise to come
home and behave when I've crossed that final item off my list.
Agreed?"

Victoria sighed. "I'd still feel better if I knew for sure what
you're doing in Cincinnati." She shifted her gaze to Miranda.
"I don't suppose you'll fill me in on the details?"

"I'm sworn to secrecy." Miranda put her fingers up, as if
taking the Girl Scout pledge. "My lips are sealed. But I can tell
you that at least one of the items is perfectly tame."

"Just one?"

"Yes." Miranda nodded. Daisy elbowed her, and Miranda
pretended to zip her lips. "But that's all you're getting from
me."

"So you won't come back home with us today, Mother
Carmichael?" her son-in-law asked.

Daisy shook her head. "No. I would say my little adventures
will take about another week or so, and then I'll be happy to
come back. When I do, you can kill the fatted calf and invite
the whole neighborhood. Tell them the prodigal has returned
home."

Victoria released an exaggerated sigh. "So, we've wasted a
trip."

"Not wasted at all. We got to see each other and eat some
of Winnie's delicious strawberry lemonade cake." Daisy paused.
"Well, I got to eat some. You'll never know what you missed by
opting out."

"I have a feeling that's true in many ways, not just as it relates to cake." Victoria rose. She glanced at her husband. "I suppose we'll have to make reservations at a hotel, then."

He nodded and reached for his phone.

Daisy shook her head. "Oh, don't do that, dear. I'm sure Tess has a lovely room here you can stay in. The inn isn't full. Right, Tess?"

Tess stepped back into the room. "That's right. I can always put you on the same floor, in Woodbine and Roses. It's very spacious and—"

"Here?" Crinkles formed between Victoria's brows. "No offense, but we're accustomed to staying in a completely different sort of place."

"And good riddance to you," Tess wanted to say but didn't.

Mr. Van Cortlandt reached for his cell phone and scrolled until he located the number for a hotel that suited his wife. Once he made their reservations, he and Victoria rose, ready to be on their way. Daisy and Miranda said their goodbyes to their family.

Tess walked Victoria to the lobby and thanked them for coming. "If you need anything else while you're in town, don't hesitate to ask."

"All right." Victoria gave her a curt nod. "Thank you for the coffee."

"You're welcome." She offered a bright smile.

They pointed themselves toward the front door, and Tess turned back toward the café. She stopped cold when she heard Mr. Van Cortlandt say, "We'll never get her to sign that power of attorney now, Victoria."

Really? So, that was why they were here?

Tess walked back into the café and found Miranda and Daisy deep in conversation. They looked up as she retrieved the coffeepot.

"Don't mind me," she said, and then headed toward the kitchen.

"No, wait a moment, Tess." Daisy rested her palm on the table. "Come sit with us. There's so much I want to tell you."

"About…?"

"My great-great-grandmother, Adeline! I need to know if she's the same one you were talking about, in that diary."

"I promise to check it out, as soon as I can."

"My Adeline helped people move along the Underground Railroad."

"She did? Oh, my goodness, it must be the same woman. I'll find the diary, and we'll do some exploring."

"Perfect."

"Our Adeline was completely blind," Miranda explained. "She played a key role in the library we visited in Cleveland. It's the Ohio Library for the Blind and Physically Disabled."

"Goodness, that's fascinating."

"Yes, that's what makes her story so remarkable," Daisy said. "Adeline accomplished great things, in spite of her disability. One day she had her vision, the next she did not. Something precious to her was stolen." Daisy's voice broke.

Tess wasn't sure what to do. Something had triggered this emotional response from Daisy, but what?

After a moment, Daisy snapped back to attention. "I'm sorry. Mandy's mother, my youngest, passed away from cancer a few years back," she explained. "Her life was cut short, but what time she did have, she spent to the full."

"Oh, Daisy, I'm so sorry." Tess rested her hand on the woman's arm. "That's heartbreaking." She turned her attention to Miranda and said, "I'm truly sorry for the loss of your mother. How difficult."

Miranda nodded. "Some days it feels like a million light years since I saw her last. But other days, it's as fresh as if it happened yesterday." Her eyes flooded with tears. "Anyway, she would have loved this trip with Mimi. Sometimes I like to picture events like this with her in them."

Tess looked back and forth between the two women, suddenly understanding their unique bond. "I'm sure it's very hard."

Daisy nodded. "It is. My heart was so broken at first that I could barely function. But this precious girl has been a lifesaver." She reached out and grabbed Miranda's hand. "We were always close, but after Lydia passed we truly—"

"Bonded." Miranda smiled. "But she's right that we were always close. From the time I was young, I loved to go to Mimi's house. It was hard for my mother to pry me away." She gave her grandmother a wink. "And it wasn't just because you gave me treats and took me on fun adventures. I've always loved hanging out with you."

"I feel the same. Especially since your grandpa passed and I've been in that big old house all alone." Daisy turned to face

Tess. "There's nothing worse than the sound of silence in a house that used to be filled with laughter."

"Yes, I understand." And she did, much as she wished she didn't. After Jeffrey's death, she'd felt the same way. That was why purchasing the inn gave her an opportunity to reinvent herself, to have a little...adventure.

"Mandy resembles her mother in so many ways—that blond hair, the freckles." Daisy's eyes clouded once again. Just as quickly she seemed to snap out of it. "Happier thoughts! That's what we'll think. And we'll go on living and make the best of every day." Her gaze shifted to Miranda. "Right, sweet girl?"

"Absolutely, Mimi. Our days are meant to be lived to the fullest."

"With as much joy as we can squeeze in. And that's just what I plan to do. I won't take one step toward Syracuse until I've crossed number eight and nine off my bucket list." Daisy pushed her chair back and stood. "But right now, this old gal needs a nap. I won't have the energy for any adventures if I don't get my beauty sleep." She took a couple of steps toward Tess and rested her hand on her arm. "You are a fine hostess, sweet girl. Thank you for treating my daughter and son-in-law with such kindness, in spite of their behavior."

"Of course. They were our guests."

"Yes, well, I'm still more grateful than you know. Now, don't forget to check into that story in the diary so we can compare notes. Promise?"

"I promise," Tess said. "In fact, I'll get right on it."

Chapter Seventeen

April 4, 1860

Prudence tidied up the kitchen as Adeline and Lolly continued their visit, then she rocked little Moses to sleep. Just as she got him settled onto his cot, a rap sounded at the door. She cracked it open and peeked outside to discover Lolly's two grandsons, Caleb and George.

"We've a mind to leave in the morning, missus," Caleb said. "We's already lost one day."

"In the morning? But, Caleb, I don't think thy grandmother is well enough to travel."

He released a sigh. "Missus, we ain't gonna argue that. Grand-Lolly ain't in no shape for any of this. But we cain't say no to her. It's been nigh on three years since she made us promise we would take her to the Promised Land." He chuckled. "I might be grown, but if my Grand-Lolly gives me the side-eye, I say 'Yes'm' in a hurry."

"I do understand that."

"She's bound and determined, ma'am," George added. "This has been her dream, from the day her son Leon sent for her to come, fifteen years ago."

"That's a long time to wait to see a dream come true."

"Yes." Caleb smiled. "And iff'n the Almighty is willin' to see us through to New York, she will rest easy."

"She will." Prudence bit back a sigh. "So the morning, then? I shall see thee off with a hearty meal and plenty of food for the days to come."

"And we thank you, ma'am," George said. "In case we haven't said it proper-like, we's grateful for all you done. And that lentil stew filled a hole in my belly that ain't been filled for days."

"Thee is welcome. There are times when I wish I could do so much more. While compliments are being passed, I must say, thee are both very good men."

Caleb shook his head. "We just do what any grandsons would do."

"Far above what others might do," Prudence responded. "I do not know if she will make the trip. As I'm sure thee know, she is not long for this life."

"Just keep her talkin'," Caleb said. "As long as she's fillin' your head with those fancy stories of hers, she's of the mind to go on livin'."

Prudence couldn't help but chuckle. "She's in good company with my friend Adeline. They are both of a fanciful nature."

George did not seem to find pleasure in this conversation. He kicked his toes against the dirt, creases forming between his furrowed brows. "All that talk of fancy places and such ain't gonna do her no good. War's comin', and soon. We needs to get to Syracuse before it starts, and then I need to figger a way to get back home to fetch my wife and children."

"I pray thee favor in all thy comings and goings," Prudence said.

The hardness in his face seemed to soften a bit, which gave her courage to keep speaking.

"There's coming a day when these troubles will be past." Prudence felt courage rise up in her soul. "Abraham Lincoln could be our president, and when that happens—"

"It'll change nuthin', 'cept'n to rile folks up all the more." George yanked off his hat and swiped his hand against his tight curls. "Forgive me, ma'am. I ain't lookin' fer a fight with ya. I just knows how it is back where I come from. Ain't no man—Lincoln or other—gonna change those people's hearts. So, you can keep him, far as I'm concerned."

"Only God can change the heart of a man."

"Yes." George's jaw flinched. "And if you can think of a way to hurry Him up, that'd be right nice."

"I do know how to pray, but whether or not I can stir the hand of God is another matter." She offered the young men a faint smile and then excused herself to go back inside the house.

She approached Lolly's bedside just in time to hear the ladies dreaming up more ideas for places they would one day love to travel. Lolly explained that she had been taught to read by her master's daughter as a child.

"That sweet gal would share her storybooks with me when no one was lookin'." Lolly giggled. "My, the places we did travel in those books! I always did wish I could see those places for real, but it never did happen."

"Where would you go, if you could?" Adeline asked.

"Paris." Lolly's deep brown eyes glistened with excitement. "I would stroll alongside the Seine with my arms stretched wide, and I would not care who was lookin'. And I would do it as a free woman."

"Grand marmee lived in Paris before moving to America. She shared so many lovely stories about her time there." Adeline sighed. "In my mind's eye, I can see it all so clearly."

"What does thee see?" Prudence asked, as she leaned forward.

Adeline's face brightened. "Oh, I see beautiful rivers and tall buildings. I see the Arc de Triomphe and the Notre Dame Cathedral. I've seen them so beautifully described in her stories and in the books in her library. She loved to tell me about her home country."

"Does thee still read, Adeline?" Prudence asked.

"There are many books available in braille," she responded. "Though not as many as I'd like. But I have a very clear memory of the tales I read before I lost my sight. Through the eyes of my favorite authors I traveled the world, just like Lolly here."

"Yes, thee must tell us all about them, so we can travel there with thee," Prudence said. "In our imaginations, I mean."

"I read the most magnificent tales of world travelers. Through their eyes I've seen the Roman Colosseum. It was so real I could hear the sound of the gladiators inside. And I've traversed the barren deserts of Africa." She placed her palm against her face. "Just reading about them made me perspire."

"It's hard to imagine all of those places," Prudence said. "I cannot fathom a trip so far from home."

"Which is why I'm grateful for books." Adeline's lips curled down. "Not that all books are available in braille, but if I have my way, more will be."

"What do you mean?" Lolly asked.

"I want to work as a translator to turn more books into braille for the blind. Then, maybe, one day all blind children can travel the world through the books they read—hundreds and thousands of glorious books!"

"You are a remarkable woman, Adeline." These words came from Lolly, who looked as if she might drift off to sleep.

Adeline patted her hand. "No, *you* are a remarkable woman, Lolly. I aspire to be more like you."

"Old?" Lolly's lips tipped up in a playful smile.

"Well, I do hope I live a long, long time, for there is much to be done. But I meant I wish I had your courage to take off and leave my home, to go to the place where my heart was drawing me."

Lolly reached to grab Adeline's hand. "Make me a promise, girl."

"What sort of promise?" Adeline asked. "I must know before I consent."

"Go in my place."

"Where?"

"To Paris!"

Adeline laughed. "However could I do that, what with my..."

"God will give you eyes to see how it will happen."

Adeline grew quiet, and Prudence wondered what she might be thinking.

Lolly broke the silence. "Can I ask a question, Adeline?"

"Of course. Anything."

"How did you lose your sight? You said earlier that you were not blind when you went to Syracuse. So how did it happen?"

Adeline paused, as if reliving the story was too painful. "I went to the doctor with an eye infection three years ago," she said after a few moments of silence. "The treatment he used caused the blindness. One day, without warning, I lost all of my ability to see the world through these natural eyes."

She took a breath, and her face brightened. "But what a gift God gave me! He opened my spiritual eyes in ways I never dreamed, and He heightened my senses so that I might see the world through its scents, its flavors, its cheerful voices, and even through its cries. I have eyes to see worlds beyond this place where the Lord has placed me now. And Lolly, I will pray about what you have asked. If the Lord wills me to see

Paris—through its sounds, its smells, and its flavors, I shall see it."

"Thank you, precious girl. You must live until you die." Lolly's eyes fluttered closed, and after a moment she drifted off to sleep. Judging from the smile on her face, Prudence couldn't help but think that she must be dreaming about Paris.

CHAPTER EIGHTEEN

On Sunday after church Tess invited LuAnn and Brad over for lunch. She had put a delicious pot roast on to cook before leaving for church, and the vegetables were perfect by the time they arrived home.

After a hearty meal, everyone settled down in the lobby to visit. Before long, Brad dozed off on the sofa. Tess excused herself to go upstairs to fetch her copy of Prudence Willard's diary. Once she had it in hand, she searched through it for the name Adeline.

"Aha. April 1860."

It didn't take long to discover that the woman in Prudence's story was, indeed, blind. That would mean she was Daisy Carmichael's great-great-grandmother after all. What an amazing discovery. Tess could hardly wait to tell her. She headed back downstairs and found Brad still snoring on the sofa and LuAnn and Janice in the kitchen, baking oatmeal cookies.

"Any word from Daisy and Miranda?" Tess asked as she stuck her finger in the bowl of cookie dough.

Janice pretended to slap her hand away. "No, not a peep. They're both snoozing, I guess."

"Like Brad. I didn't realize he snores."

"Mm-hmm." LuAnn groaned. "Oh, the things I've learned. He also throws his socks on the floor. You know how I am about keeping things tidy. The man doesn't seem to know we have a dirty clothes hamper."

The ladies continued to swap stories about married life until their laughter finally woke Brad up. He ventured into the kitchen just as the first tray of cookies was cooling, the hair on the top of his head standing straight up. Tess did her best not to laugh.

"What's so funny in here?"

"Oh, nothing," LuAnn said. "Just girl talk."

"Kind of glad I missed it, then."

"We are too," LuAnn said and then laughed all over again.

They took their cookies and coffee to the table, but Tess thought she heard the elevator, so she grabbed the diary and headed to the lobby.

"Mmm, I smell cookies!" Daisy grinned as she stepped out of the elevator. "Just what the doctor ordered!"

Tess held up the diary, and Daisy squealed.

"Do you have news for me?"

"I do." She gestured for Daisy to join her on the sofa.

Daisy wriggled into the spot on Tess's right and clasped her hands together. "This is so exciting."

"It is," Tess agreed. She could hardly wait to share what she had learned.

Janice entered the lobby with a plate of cookies, still warm from the oven, if the aroma was any indication. "Daisy, I've got oatmeal-raisin cookies, if you're interested."

"Am I ever! But Janice and LuAnn, you must join us. Tess was just about to tell me what she's learned about my great-great-grandmother.

"Sure." Janice set the plate of cookies on the coffee table and settled onto the sofa to Tess's left. LuAnn walked behind the sofa and peered over their shoulders.

Daisy beamed as she glanced Tess's way. "Now, what have you found?"

"Check out Prudence's diary entry from March 3, 1860." Tess began to read aloud. 'Today I met the most wonderful woman. Her name is Adeline, and she has come to help us with our travelers. I could not imagine how someone without vision could be of help, but she has proven me wrong already. There is little she cannot do.'"

"Oh, Tess, that's her. That's my great-great-grandmother. But tell me again who Prudence was? That name doesn't sound familiar."

Tess filled Daisy in, telling her all about Prudence Willard, the woman who once worked at the inn long before it was called Wayfarers.

"It was the Riverfront House back in those days," Tess explained.

"Oh, yes. I think I knew that."

"Prudence was a key player in the Underground Railroad. I'm not sure we'll ever know exactly how many people she and her husband, Jason, helped move along the road, but the number is very high."

"And your Prudence knew my great-great-grandmother. This is truly a find, Tess." Daisy's eyes grew misty. "I want to share this story with Victoria so she will understand why I care so much about Adeline and about our rich history here in Ohio. I'm so proud that my relative was supportive of those in need and worked hard to see them free."

Tess flipped the pages in the diary until she landed on something else she wanted to share. "Listen to this, Daisy. Here's another entry, just a few weeks later. 'Adeline amazes us all. She brings friends of every race and creed to the cause of freedom. Yesterday we were introduced to her friend, Shepherd Lee, a handsome young man from Cincinnati. He is the brother of her dearest friend, who will visit when next in town. Shepherd is a skilled craftsman and will be helpful to the cause. He has come all this way from Cincinnati to stay with her family, that he might join our ranks in saving the oppressed from peril.'"

Daisy clasped her hands together at her chest and grinned. "Cincinnati, just as I said! And Shepherd Lee!"

"Is *that* why you're going to Cincinnati next?" Tess asked. "Because Adeline's friend hailed from there?"

"That's part of it, yes." Daisy gave Tess a coy look. "There might be a bit more to it, but one would have to refer to my bucket list to know the full details."

"Ah, I see."

"I guess now would be as good a time as any to reveal number eight on my list. I wasn't willing to tell Victoria, but you might be able to coax it out of me."

"Well I'd be lying if I said the question hadn't piqued my interest," Tess responded. "Are you wanting to share?"

"I might be persuaded. But promise you won't judge me or give me a lecture about how I'm too old?"

"Hmm." Tess wasn't altogether sure she could make that promise. After all, seventy-eight was a little old for anything too risky.

Daisy bounced up and down in her seat. "First, try to guess."

"Um, zip-lining across the Amazon jungle?"

"Hardly. I hate bugs."

"Okay." Tess paused and chewed her lip. "Waterskiing in the Caribbean?"

"No, but another Caribbean cruise does sound good. I might have to add a number eleven to my list."

"I give up." Tess shrugged. "What's number seven?"

"We're headed to Cincinnati so I can go parasailing over the Ohio River and see the area from up above."

"Parasailing?" Janice squeaked out.

Daisy's eyes glistened, and her voice grew more animated. "Yes, doesn't it sound glorious?"

Tess wasn't sure if it sounded glorious or terrifying.

"We did so much research to find a company along the Ohio that's open this time of year," Daisy explained. "The house that Shepherd Lee and his sister lived in is now on the historic homes tour, so we hope to see the inside of it."

"Yes, but let's go back to the parasailing part." Janice shook her head. "Are you absolutely sure?"

Daisy nodded. "We've been building up to this for some time. Everything else has been crossed off my list now except that and one other thing, which is more personal in nature."

"So, this is the trip to Cincinnati you mentioned to your daughter." Janice grinned. "And she was worried about a car accident. Goodness. Little does she know her mother will be taking to flight."

Daisy giggled. "Picture me, soaring through the air, ready to see life from a different point of view."

"That sounds dreamy!" Tess clasped her hands together. "Truly. I would love to soar across the river and look down below."

Daisy nodded. "I got the idea from the most wonderful novel I read a few years back about an enslaved man in Barbados who escaped his masters by hopping onboard a hot air balloon."

"Is that true?" Janice asked. "Did it really happen?"

"No, it was just fiction, but I got to thinking about how marvelous it might be, to escape your problems by flying across the sky like that. At first I thought to take a hot air balloon ride, but I wanted something more adventurous. Mandy stumbled across the parasailing idea, and I was hooked. And what better place to do it than right here in Ohio, where my great-great-grandparents actually helped people escape slavery."

"I'm just floored by the idea," Tess said. "It's perfect, Daisy."

"So you're not going to try to talk me out of it?"

"Talk you out of it?" Tess laughed. "More likely, you're going to have to talk me out of taking a ride myself."

"Well, come on, then! We'll be companions in flight."

Tess gave it thought…for a moment. When she saw Janice's wide-eyed stare, she thought the better of it. "I'll save it for another time. Maybe I'll add it to my own bucket list. Who knows."

"I'm hoping Mandy will video the whole thing on that phone of hers. She knows all about technology."

"What do I know, Mimi?" Miranda descended the stairs into the lobby with a yawn. "Sorry, I didn't mean to sleep for so long."

Daisy gave her an empathetic look. "You needed it, honey. I've kept you hopping lately."

"True. But what were you saying about a video?"

"These ladies want to see a video of the two of us parasailing on Wednesday."

Miranda's eyes widened. "Mimi! You swore me to secrecy! We weren't going to tell anyone we're going parasailing, remember?"

Daisy shrugged. "That was then. This is now. Besides, Tori is really the only one I was concerned about knowing. But hey, maybe we'll send her the video too. That'll really make her day, don't you think?"

Miranda plopped down on the sofa and groaned. "She'll kill me. Or worse, she'll say I'm irresponsible."

"There are worse things one could be called, sweet girl." Daisy reached over and took her hand. "But if you insist upon keeping it a secret, I shall. We never breathed a word about parachuting out of an airplane while we were in the Caribbean. So I can say without hesitation that you are truly a young woman who knows how to keep her word!"

CHAPTER NINETEEN

W ait...You jumped out of a plane?" Janice asked.

"Shh." Daisy put her finger over her lips. "Just pretend you didn't hear that part. But that was number four on my bucket list."

LuAnn and Brad entered the lobby from the kitchen.

"What's going on out here?" LuAnn asked. "It got loud all of a sudden."

"We're absorbing the news that Daisy jumped out of an airplane in the Caribbean and is about to go parasailing in Cincinnati," Janice said. "Other than that, not much is going on."

"Wait...what?" Brad looked back and forth between them. "Did I hear that right?"

"You heard right," Tess said.

"Did you jump out of a plane too?" LuAnn directed the question at Miranda.

"Well, it wasn't my first choice, but to keep up with Mimi I have to do some crazy things."

"Yes, but you're young," Janice argued. "You have your whole life ahead of you. What if something had happened to you to prevent that?"

Miranda reached for an oatmeal cookie. "I get your point, but I'm not that young."

"Hold up." Brad put his hand up in the air. "Just so I'm understanding this correctly, you two ladies are planning to parasail in Cincinnati?"

"It's true," Daisy said. "Over a section of the Ohio where my great-great-grandmother once visited. And we're trying to talk Tess into joining us."

LuAnn turned Tess's way with a look of disbelief on her face. "Tess, you're not really interested in parasailing, are you?"

She paused to think it through, then shrugged. "I think it sounds wonderful. Why?"

"Don't you remember that big story about the people who were killed parasailing a while back? It was all over the news."

"Actually, that was a hot air balloon incident, not parasailing. And I'm not saying I'm really going to do it. But it's fun to think outside the box like that, don't you think?"

Janice reached for a cookie. "I'm pretty comfortable inside my box."

"But don't you think sometimes we're all a little...predictable?" Tess asked.

Brad shrugged. "I guess, but is that a bad thing?"

"Predictable is highly overrated, at least in my opinion." Daisy offered Brad a playful wink.

Tess nodded. "I agree. I mean, think about our ancestors. They had to do brave things all the time. Really brave things.

Have you read *Little House on the Prairie*? Laura and her family faced bears and fires and even wild natives."

"We're not living in the old days," LuAnn said.

"Hence my comment about how easy we've got it."

Janice placed her hands on her hips. "I don't know where you're coming up with all this, Tess. I'd say we all put in a hard day's work every single day. I know a lot of people our age who don't work as much as we do."

"Well, that's true. But compared to people in the days of old, we're pretty spoiled. We're not riding around in wagons or forging rivers or anything like that. We've lost our sense of adventure."

"Completely untrue," LuAnn countered. "If that were the case, we wouldn't own this inn right now."

"Yeah, I guess you're right."

It was a different kind of adventure Tess was referring to, but she didn't want to get into an argument with Janice or LuAnn. It might be fun to do something daring once in a while, just to see what she was capable of.

"I would just like to go on record as saying parasailing isn't for me," Janice said decidedly. "It's not on my bucket list."

Daisy flashed a sweet smile. "You'll have to think of other things that do sound exciting to you."

"Oh, I've already come up with one thing."

"What's that, Janice?" Daisy asked.

"I would love to save up for a good camera. Like, a really nice one that can capture breathtaking images."

"That's a bucket list item, a camera?" Tess asked. "I thought bucket list items were supposed to be activities you participated in."

"But that's just it. If I had the kind of camera I'm talking about, I could have adventures all over the place. There's just something so special about capturing a moment in the frame of a camera. It's like time stands still."

"What kind of camera are we talking here?" Daisy asked.

Janice seemed to lose herself to her thoughts. When she did speak, her words took on a faraway, dreamy tone. "One with excellent processing speed. That's what you need to capture quality images. Probably one of the mirrorless cameras, if I'm dreaming big. Advanced optics. Impressive ISO sensitivity range." She carried on, talking about the kind of lens she'd like to have and all the various zoom ranges, but almost lost Tess altogether.

"She's done her research," Brad said. "I've never even heard of a Ninja 5 touchscreen video recording monitor, have you?"

"Um, no," Tess admitted. "I can barely get the camera on my phone to work."

"Same." He shrugged and swallowed a cookie in two bites.

Janice shifted gears and started talking about her new-found passion for capturing flowers on film, but she lost Tess once again. How could someone be this ecstatic about flowers?

"It's the perfect time of year to capture photos," Miranda said. "And your yard guy is sure making the gardens come to life. You'll have plenty to take pictures of."

Daisy offered Janice a bright smile. "I love your idea of capturing images of all your adventures, Janice. I can almost see them now."

"Well, first I need the camera." Janice laughed. "The one I have now is twenty years old. It's good enough, but not what I'd really like to have. A girl can dream though, can't she?"

"Of course she can," Daisy responded. "They don't charge you anything to dream. People say I'm a dreamer, but I've never minded being called that. We don't know how many days we have left, but I refuse to be one of those people who curls up in a ball and pretends the story has already ended when it hasn't."

"I think a lot of people do that, regardless of age," Janice said. "I've been through seasons where I just gave up."

"Pain will do that to a person. But I'm not ready to stop just yet." Daisy glanced Janice's way once more. "Are you?"

"When you put it like that, no." Janice shook her head. "I'm not. Just please don't ask me to jump off anything higher than a curb."

"I won't," Daisy said. "But don't fret if I want to do things that sound scary to you. None of us knows how much time he has. I want to teach my grandchildren and my friends to embrace life with a fullness that goes beyond what they've experienced so far."

"The Bible would call that fullness of joy," Tess said.

Daisy's eyes sparkled. "Then that's what I want, fullness of joy."

"What about all of you?" Miranda asked. "What's on your bucket list?"

"I like a little adventure as well as the next person," Brad said. "But I won't be jumping out of any planes or anything like that."

"Right, but there are lots of other things we could do with the later years of our life," LuAnn countered.

"Like?"

She paused and appeared to be thinking. "I've always wanted to sit in the audience for my favorite TV game show."

"That might be fun," Tess agreed. "What else?"

All at once LuAnn's face lit up in a way Tess hadn't seen in a while. "Oh, I know! I would absolutely love to go island hopping in Greece."

"Greece?" Brad looked startled. "Why Greece?"

"Harkens back to my days as an English teacher, I suppose. I want to see the birthplace of literary epics like the *Iliad* and the *Odyssey*. I've seen pictures, of course, and I've seen it in movies. Those bright blue waters are just breathtaking. Can you even imagine swimming in them?"

Brad shrugged. "We've got the Atlantic."

"It hardly compares to the Mediterranean." LuAnn went off about a scene she'd watched in a movie where a young couple got married in a boat on the Mediterranean Sea. She grew more animated with each word.

This led to a lengthy discussion of LuAnn's love of travel, which somehow led to talking about gelato, which made Daisy decide she must have ice cream.

"There's a wonderful little ice cream shop not far from here," Tess explained.

"I'll drive, Mimi. Just let me run upstairs and grab my purse and keys."

"Okay, sweet girl."

Daisy struggled to stand but finally made it up from the sofa with Brad's help. "I would never turn down a hot fudge sundae."

"They are delicious," Tess agreed.

"Then come with us. We'll all have ice cream."

"Oh, no thank you." Tess smiled. "I've got plenty of sweets here, if I'm so inclined. But I really feel like putting my feet up, to be honest."

"Then you do that. And if you stumble across any more diary entries about my grandmother, please let me know."

"Will do."

Miranda reappeared moments later with her purse strapped to her shoulder. She led the way out the front door with Daisy chattering all the way behind her.

Once the door closed, a lengthy discussion ensued about whether or not Daisy had lost her mind, wanting to do something as dangerous as parasailing. Tess listened but did not chime in, as the others all came to the conclusion that life was dangerous enough without all the risky activities. She wasn't so sure.

Tess headed up to her room later that evening to prepare for bed, her thoughts still focused on Daisy and Miranda. It might be nice, to soar over your circumstances, to look down on all the people scurrying around below. To breathe in the fresh air and feel the breeze on your face.

These images flitted across her imagination as she dozed off. Only when she awoke with a start a short while later did Tess realize her dream had turned into a nightmare, in which she was falling, falling, falling.

She sat up on the edge of the bed and caught her breath. Maybe flying was for the birds, after all.

CHAPTER TWENTY

While Tess and LuAnn prepped the café for guests on Monday, Tess asked her, "Is Rankin Smith still saying he won't pay your claim?"

"It's infuriating." LuAnn's expression hardened. "It's not even about the money at this point." She placed silverware sets on the tables. "To me, it's a matter of principle. He has the police reports showing I wasn't at fault. The woman who caused the accident has perfectly good coverage. He's got to do the right thing."

"I agree." Tess continued to work alongside LuAnn setting up. "And if he doesn't, there are other courses of action you can take. I've been looking into it."

"We have too." LuAnn sighed. "I sure hope he makes this easy on us and just pays the claim, though. Those other options can be time consuming and are sure to raise my blood pressure. The last thing I want right now is a fight. I'm praying for a peaceful resolution."

"Then I'll pray for that too." Tess led the way into the kitchen where she found Winnie and Janice working on several items for the lunch menu. LuAnn joined them, helping Winnie with the chicken and wild rice soup.

"Did you ever get a chance to talk to Corey about the article he's writing about Rankin Smith?" Tess asked her.

"No." LuAnn shook her head.

"Well, speaking of articles Corey is writing…according to Sandie he's meeting her here for lunch today, so maybe you'll get your chance to talk to him about ASAP yourself." Tess took her apron off and hung it on a peg in the pantry.

"He's meeting Sandie for lunch?" LuAnn's eyes widened. "That's interesting."

"Yes, he's writing an article about her bakery." Tess walked back out into the lobby just as Corey entered the front door of the inn. She offered him a welcoming smile. "Good to see you again."

"Thanks." He gave her a nod. "Told you I'd be a regular."

"Because of the story you're chasing?"

"That's part of it." He smiled. "I do love Winnie's cooking too. That's a big plus."

"Well, speaking of that story you're researching, I know LuAnn would love to talk to you more about her situation with Rankin. He still hasn't acknowledged her claim."

"I'm not surprised." He glanced at his watch. "I've got a couple of minutes until Sandie gets here."

"LuAnn's in the kitchen. I'll go get her." Tess walked into the kitchen and told LuAnn that Corey had arrived and was willing to talk about the situation with ASAP.

"Will you stick around and listen to what he has to say too?" LuAnn asked. "I'm so distracted today I might not remember all the details to share with Brad later."

"Sure."

LuAnn led the way into the lobby and greeted Corey. "Thanks for talking to me. I was hoping for some sort of update from you. How are things going with Rankin on your end? He still won't pay my claim."

"Mine either." Corey sighed. "I've had a claim with him for over a year, and he absolutely refuses to pay. He's claiming some sort of loophole, but I've looked over the contract, and he's wrong. Completely wrong."

LuAnn sighed. "What sort of claim, if you don't mind my asking?"

"My wife died fourteen months ago."

"Oh, Corey, I'm so sorry!" Tess couldn't help but interrupt. "Are you saying it was a life insurance claim he didn't pay?"

"Yes." He nodded. "And it's ridiculous. You wouldn't believe the efforts I've gone to, to track the guy down. He's got to pay." Corey fished around in his pocket, finally coming out with his wallet. He pulled out a card and pressed it into Tess's hand. "That's my business card. If the guy shows up, let me know, okay? Just give me a call—on my cell or at my office."

Tess took the card and slipped it into the pocket of her slacks. She would have to remember to put it in her purse later, so it would be handy, just in case Rankin ever did show up.

"And I thought my case was awful." LuAnn shook her head. "That's despicable."

Corey's jaw flinched. "I've been by his office six times over the past couple of months and he's been conveniently absent, even on the days when I called and told him that I was on my way."

"So strange." Tess sighed. Both Corey and LuAnn had been badly treated by this guy. "That's no way to run a business."

"No, it's not. And he has no idea what I'm up against."

"What you're up against?" Tess wasn't sure what he meant by that.

Corey began to pace the room, his words taking on a frantic tone. "I need that money. And I need it soon, or there are going to be dire consequences."

"Dire consequences?" Tess echoed.

He didn't respond. Instead, his words grew more frantic. "Yes, and that's why I've got to get Rankin to pay her claim. It was her dying wish that I would…" He paused, and his gaze shifted to the floor. "Anyway, it's important that Rankin pay that life insurance claim. I've got places to go, people to see. If he knew what I was up against, he would have paid long ago."

"Maybe not." Tess couldn't help but wonder what Corey's wife's dying wish had been. For him to travel, maybe? That whole "places to go, people to see" line made her think so.

Before she could ask, Sandie Ballard barreled through the lobby toward the café, all smiles. The young woman looked considerably different from last time—today she wore a lovely outfit without a bit of batter on it. And her hair was nicely styled. Even her makeup looked picture perfect.

Tess greeted her with a smile. "Sandie, I'm so glad to see you again. You look lovely."

"Oh?" Her cheeks flushed pink. "Thank you."

"We get you twice in one week. That's marvelous."

Corey turned to her, a smile on his face.

"I'm here for my closeup, Mr. Demille!" She flushed. "I mean, I'm here for my interview. Are you ready?"

"Yes." He glanced LuAnn's way. "You leave Rankin to me. I've got a plan for him."

Tess noticed that worry lines creased LuAnn's forehead at that news. Hopefully Corey wasn't planning anything bad.

Tess seated Sandie and Corey at a nearby table and took their drink orders. Before long, the room filled with more patrons, many of them friends of the Inn Crowd.

Tess went from table to table, visiting and filling glasses with water, tea, and sodas. Before long, the clanking of silverware against dishes blended in harmonious melody with the sound of voices raised in laughter and conversation.

Daisy and Miranda arrived in the café for their final meal at the inn before heading off to Cincinnati. Instead of their usual table for two, Daisy asked for a table for four, explaining that Victoria and her husband would be joining them for one last meal together before they parted ways. *Wow, this should be interesting.*

Sure enough, the duo arrived a short while later and joined Daisy and Miranda at the table next to Sandie and Corey. Tess could tell that Victoria was in a rough mood, so other than taking her drink order, she steered clear of the woman.

Tess happened to walk by Sandie and Corey's table just in time to see Sandie bat her eyelashes at him and invite him to visit her bakery.

"I think you'll love it!" She dabbed at her lips with her cloth napkin. "It's so colorful and bright. And I make some delicious treats, if that sort of thing tempts you in any way."

"Excuse me for a minute. I want to make this call while it's on my mind." He rose, phone in hand, and stepped to the edge of the room, where he appeared to punch in a number. Seconds later he began to speak in a voice loud enough to be overheard by everyone in the small café.

Victoria glanced up from her table, disgust on her face as he carried on. "I hate it when people do that. He needs to go outside."

Tess had to agree, and all the more as Corey's voice grew louder. He appeared to be leaving a message. She eased her way to the opposite side of the room, the whole thing feeling very awkward.

Janice sidled up next to her with a concerned look on her face. "Heavens, it really bugs me when people do that. Doesn't he realize we're all a captive audience?"

"I don't think he cares."

LuAnn approached from the kitchen, loaded down with water glasses. She drew near the other ladies, glanced Corey's way, then looked back at them. "What's all the hollering about? Building on fire?"

"No, but people are going to flee like the building's in flames if he doesn't calm down," Janice responded. "He's going to drive away the customers."

"We need to ask him to take that outside." Tess took a couple of steps in Corey's direction just in time to hear him say, "You're going to pay for this, Rankin, if it's the last thing you do."

LuAnn shook her head. "Sounds like our conversation with him earlier must've gotten him riled up."

"Guess so," Tess acknowledged. "But I refuse to feel guilty about it. He agreed to talk to you about Rankin."

"True. But I hate that he's disrupting our guests."

"Yeah. Agreed."

Tess looked on as Corey shoved his phone back into his pocket and returned to his table. She decided this was as good a time as any to confront him about his behavior.

"I'm sorry about my phone call just now." Corey leaned back in his chair, a look of chagrin on his face. "Sometimes I just get worked up."

"Yes, I see that."

He released a slow breath and glanced Sandie's way. "I do apologize. I picked the wrong time to make that call. I hope you can all forgive me. If you knew the backstory, I feel sure you would—" Corey's gaze shifted to the window, and he shot from his seat to peer through the glass. "Do you see what I see?"

"What's that?" Tess joined him and stared out, not noticing anything peculiar.

Corey pointed through the glass. "That car with the ASAP Insurance decal on the side. And it looks like he's pulling into your parking lot."

"What?" LuAnn looked over at them, deep creases forming on her brow.

"I'm going to go out there and talk to him." Corey turned toward the lobby. "I'll be right back."

He tore out of the café, ran through the lobby, and bounded out the front door.

Tess stared out the window as Corey headed straight for Rankin's car. However, as soon as Rankin saw him, he backed out, tires squealing, and took off at record speed down the street.

By now, everyone in the café was at the window, staring out at the scene unfolding in front of them.

"This is better than a movie," Daisy said as she leaned against the glass. "And without the price of a ticket!"

Corey waved his arms in the air, visibly upset. Tess didn't blame him. But she did blame him for heading to his car without paying for his lunch. She watched as he climbed into his SUV, threw it into reverse, and took off down the road after Rankin.

CHAPTER TWENTY-ONE

On the following morning Tess awoke, somewhat depressed. A dense fog hung over the river and seemed to bring with it a heaviness that transported itself to the Inn Crowd. They went about their morning routine in the same way as always, but with gray skies looming, their hearts just didn't seem to be in it.

"I do hope this lifts," Tess said as they gazed out the window just after feeding their guests breakfast. "And I pray it's not raining in Cincinnati."

Less than ten minutes later, Daisy and Miranda exited the elevator.

"This is the day." Janice's lips curled down in a pout as she walked toward Daisy and wrapped her arms around the older woman. "I'm going to miss you both so much." She stepped back and sighed, then gave Miranda a hug.

"And we're going to miss you too." Daisy slipped her purse strap over her shoulder. "But you know me, ladies. I've got places to go, people to see. There's a life to be lived and para-sailing to do!

Janice cringed. "I still can't believe you're actually going through with that."

"When we get to Cincinnati this afternoon, we'll spend the rest of the day resting up and eating some yummy food. Our reservation to fly is tomorrow afternoon."

Daisy's purse strap slipped off her shoulder, and she adjusted it. "I do hope the weather is pretty tomorrow. April showers and all that."

"I've checked the app on my phone, Mimi, and it's going to be lovely."

"Lovely." Daisy's winsome smile showed her appreciation of that notion. "Have I ever mentioned that I just love the word *lovely*? I don't know who came up with it, but I'd like to thank them. I think it's just…"

"Lovely," they all said together.

"You have mentioned it," Tess said. "But I'm inclined to agree." She gave Daisy a warm hug and said, "Now, promise you'll hold on tight while you're up there, sailing above your circumstances?"

"Well, of course!"

"And Miranda, get lots of pictures," Janice said. "That way we'll feel like we're up there with you."

"Yes, of course. Just don't post it on that social media thing," Daisy admonished Miranda. "Your aunt Tori will come and haul me off to a home, for sure."

Miranda took her Girl Scout's honor pose again. "I won't."

"So Victoria still doesn't know?" Tess asked.

"No, and it's going to stay that way until I get back to Syracuse." A wistful look came over Daisy. "I must admit, it will be nice to be back home again." Just as quickly, her expression shifted. "Oh, but it will be blissful to fly over parts of Ohio and see the countryside as Adeline saw it when she flew in a hot air balloon over the Ohio River all those years ago."

"Adeline?" Miranda's brow wrinkled. "In a hot air balloon?"

"Yes, she helped enslaved people escape in a hot air balloon. Don't you remember, sweet girl? I've told you."

"I remember the fictional story about the enslaved man in Barbados flying in a hot air balloon, but that's all."

"Oh." For a moment, Daisy's eyes clouded over and she looked lost. Just as quickly, she snapped to attention. "That's right, honey. Silly me. Adeline never flew in a hot air balloon. But she did help free people from their shackles."

"Yes, she did." Miranda offered her grandmother a compassionate smile.

Daisy walked into the café to grab a muffin, and Tess approached Miranda. "Do you think she's…"

"Losing her memory?" Miranda released a sigh. "She's always telling Aunt Victoria that she's not, but I've seen more and more signs of it on this trip. I've been keeping a watchful eye on things, for sure, and have even been documenting things she says and does to share with her doctor next week."

"I see."

"When this little adventure is over, we're going back home to New York. She'll have crossed everything off her list at that point and I, for one, will be very relieved."

"I do hope she doesn't give up being active after that," Janice said. "Some older people do, especially when they have to move out of their homes."

"Right." Miranda's brow wrinkled, and she appeared to be thinking their words through. "I've given that some thought, myself. She's been living for the things on this list. But maybe, after she's moved into assisted living, I can help her put together a completely different kind of list."

"Like…" Tess gave Miranda a curious look.

"Like…work on her genealogy chart. Or talk to her cousin in France, the one she's always talking about but never talking to. There are all sorts of adventures she can have that won't require taking flight. And I promise, ladies…" Miranda's eyes filled with tears. "Even though I won't be living with her anymore, I'll still be very close. The apartment complex I've chosen is just three miles from where she'll be. I'll check in on her all the time and make her days as enjoyable as I can. But, as social as she is, I have no doubt she'll fit right in. She might even meet Mr. Right."

"I'm living proof that it happens, even for those of us who are up there in age," LuAnn interjected.

"You're hardly up there in age, LuAnn." Miranda laughed. "But that would be something, if Mimi found a mister."

"*Mimi and the Mister.* Sounds like a good title for a book." Tess laughed. "You'll have to tell her I said so, but wait until you're on the road. She'll get a laugh out of it."

Daisy approached with a muffin in one hand and a to-go cup in the other. She lifted both hands and said, "Fortification!"

then laughed. Her purse strap slipped off her shoulder once more, nearly causing her to drop the cup.

"Let me hold that for you, Mimi. I don't want you to get burned." Miranda reached out and took the cup, then helped her grandmother adjust the purse once again.

Tess happened to notice the fleur-de-lis pinned to Daisy's sweater. "Are you sure that's safe?" She pointed to it.

"Yes, Mandy fixed the clasp on it last night. I'm so excited to be wearing it again. It's going to be the last time."

"The last time?" Janice asked. "Why is that?"

"Refer to number nine on my list and you'll know." Daisy winked. "When we reach the Cincinnati home of Adeline's good friend, I'll pin it on our girl here, and it will be hers, until she's ready to pass it on."

"What a wonderful idea," Tess said. "Please take pictures."

"We shall." Daisy paused and sniffed the air, her eyes fluttering closed. "Ah, Wayfarers, how I shall miss thee! Most of all, I'll miss those amazing smells that greet me each and every morning." Her eyes popped back open. "You know, I often think of my great-great-grandmother, how she lost her vision. She was reliant on her other senses to see the world. I want to capture it all the same way, especially the scents. And you've certainly tantalized me here with Winnie's coffee in the morning, and those luscious pastries of hers."

"And the bread," Miranda threw in. "Let's not forget the bread."

"And the cakes, and the pies, and all of those yummy casseroles you ladies serve up in the café." Daisy glanced down at her midsection. "Oh, it's been years since I've eaten like this, and it's all my nose's fault!"

Tess couldn't help but laugh.

"Mama used to say I would cut it off to spite my face, but I can tell you that's not the case here. If I lost my sense of smell, Wayfarers would lose its nasal sparkle."

"Nasal sparkle." Janice chuckled. "I'll add that to our brochures as one of our offerings here at Wayfarers."

"Do." Daisy nodded. "You'll draw them in by the hundreds. Wayfarers will be full to the brim, which will be absolutely..."

"Lovely." They all spoke the word in unison and laughed.

Daisy walked to the front window and gestured for the other ladies to join her.

"Tess, Janice...look outside. What do you see?"

"I see..." Tess looked around at the same view she witnessed firsthand every day—the cobblestone streets, the nearby buildings, the people moving to and fro.

"I see the front lawn of Wayfarers with a very heavy sky overhead," Janice said.

"I see a familiar, comfortable home that we love," Tess added.

"Would you like to know what I see?" Daisy flashed a bright smile. After the ladies nodded, she said, "I see a holy patch of land, planted in this very spot for a set-apart purpose. And all who lived, or continue to live, here have a calling on their lives to serve and bless others. Capture that image in your mind, precious friends. Set it to memory like a photograph and don't ever forget it. You were made for Wayfarers, and Wayfarers was made for you."

Tess felt the sting of tears in her eyes at the images the elderly woman's words presented. "That's...that's beautiful, Daisy."

"For over one hundred and fifty years God has led people through this patch of land, often leaving one place and heading to another. And their lives were transformed here."

"Yes, that's true," Tess agreed.

"My great-great-grandmother's life was forever changed because of someone she met here. And those changes went on to affect thousands, maybe even millions of lives. Don't discount the fact that lives are still being changed as people come through here, Tess. They are, you know."

Tess pushed back the lump in her throat. "Thank you for that reminder, Daisy. I promise to capture it like a photograph."

LuAnn walked in just as they said their final goodbyes.

"I'm so glad I made it in time," she said as she gave them each a quick hug. "Brad said to tell you he's going to miss you."

Daisy's lips curled down. "We'll miss him too. We'll miss all of you, in fact."

Tess looked on as the two ladies pulled away from the inn, moments later. "The inn just won't be the same without the two of them, will it?"

"Not at all," Janice said.

They didn't have to worry about missing Daisy for long. Less than five minutes later, Tess's phone rang. She recognized Daisy's number at once.

Daisy sounded a bit breathless as she spoke. "Put me on speakerphone, Tess. I have something to tell Janice."

"Okay." She did as instructed.

"I almost forgot something, Janice," Daisy said. "It's a little surprise, just for you. I left it in my room on the dresser."

"You did?" Janice looked flabbergasted by this news.

"Yes, wrapped in pretty gold paper. I can't wait to hear what you think."

"We'll let you know, I promise." Janice flew up the stairs, a woman on a mission.

"Let it serve as a reminder of me," Daisy said. "In case you're ever tempted to forget."

"Oh, trust me," Miranda's voice sounded. "They'll never forget you, Mimi! You're the loveliest guest they've ever had."

They both had a good laugh, then said their goodbyes.

Tess smiled. "That woman is a wonder, isn't she?"

"She is," LuAnn agreed. "But I'm dying to know what she left for Janice."

Tess barely had time to agree before Janice barreled back down the stairs and took a seat on the sofa, gold-wrapped package in hand. "There's a card." She pulled the card out from under the ribbon and opened it. She read it to herself, but Tess couldn't hold it in.

"Come on, Janice. What did she say?"

"That life is for the living and we need to capture every moment while we can. That's sweet, isn't it?"

"Sure is, and sounds just like something she would say." Tess stared at the package in Janice's hands. "Now, are you going to open that, or am I going to have to come over there and pry it out of your hands?"

Janice grinned and then ripped the paper. When she saw the box inside, she gasped aloud. "Goodness gracious goat!"

Tess could hardly believe her eyes. "Is that what I think it is?"

"If you mean, is this a top-of-the-line camera, complete with high-powered lens, then yes." Janice tore into the box, her hands now trembling. "What was she thinking?"

"That she wants you to capture the special moments in life and that you need a great camera to do it."

"You said so yourself," LuAnn reminded her.

"We teased you about it, as I recall." Tess felt bad about that now.

"She was paying attention." Janice hugged the box to her chest. "But what a gift to give someone you barely know. Should I keep it or insist she take it back?"

"Are you kidding?" LuAnn laughed. "You're keeping it!"

"Okay, okay." Janice went to work, unfastening the box and emptying its contents onto the coffee table. Moments later, she loaded the camera with the accompanying battery.

"You two pose," she instructed.

Tess and LuAnn attempted a goofy pose on the sofa but nearly lost their balance and fell off. Unfortunately, Janice caught a shot of that.

"Put that on social media, and it'll be the last thing you ever post!" Tess warned, then doubled over in laughter. "Can you even imagine my kids seeing their mother looking like such a goober?"

"Hey, better than your kids seeing you parasailing over the Ohio River," Janice countered.

"Who knows? I might do that someday. Or maybe even something more exciting."

"Like what?" Janice caught a shot of Huck sneaking down the stairs.

"Oh, I don't know." She paused to think about it. "Like white-water rafting down the Colorado River at the bottom of the Grand Canyon."

"I saw that at a 3D theater once," Janice said. "That was good enough for me.

"Or maybe seeing the Great Barrier Reef," Tess added.

"Or the northern lights!" Janice pointed the camera up and caught a picture of the pressed tin ceiling.

"I'm still settled on going to Greece," LuAnn said. "No one is going to knock that one off my list."

"What about an African safari?" Tess suggested. "You could get some amazing pictures there, Janice."

"I could." Janice sighed. "Now that I have the perfect camera, I must visit the seven wonders of the world. Or at least touch as many continents as I can while I'm still alive." She snapped a picture of the banister with its mushroom-shaped newel cap.

"I wouldn't mind a Mediterranean cruise," LuAnn threw in. That way I could see all of the Greek islands and go other places too. Like…"

"Italy!" Tess squealed. "Yes, please."

"Or Paris. Ooh-la-la!" Janice snapped another photo of the antique gold cash register at the front desk. "I would dress the two of you up to look like Audrey Hepburn, then take your photographs standing in front of the Eiffel Tower."

"As long as you don't dress me up like Marilyn Monroe and stand me on top of a subway grate, I'm good with that." Tess laughed.

"Taking pictures of everything we just described sounds absolutely heavenly." Janice leaned back against the sofa and continued to peer through the lens of the camera.

Tess nudged her with her elbow. "Hey, do you remember what you once said about why you like photography?"

Janice gave her an inquisitive look. "I don't remember the details, just that I love it."

"You told us that you love it because when you capture a moment in the frame it's like time stands still."

"Oh, right." A delicious smile curled up the edges of Janice's lips. "I remember."

"I think that's where Daisy got the idea. It's her way of honoring your request to capture those special moments, like you did at the Easter egg hunt."

"I wish I'd captured more photos of my kids when they were little." Janice sighed.

"Me too," Tess said. "Sometimes life marches by so fast that I can't even remember the details of what I've left behind."

"What's that old song about capturing time in a bottle?" LuAnn asked. "Oh, if only…"

"We can't really stop time," Tess observed. "It just keeps marching on, whether we want it to or not."

"There's a part of me that's really glad time doesn't stand still," Janice responded. "If the clock had stopped when I was in my twenties, when my babies were young, I would never have met my grandchildren. And I would never have seen my babies as grown, responsible, and godly people. Time can be a real blessing, in that way."

Tess nodded in agreement. "True, but we can take photographs along the way. That's what Daisy is doing with that bucket list of hers. Those things on her list are photographs. She's capturing them and committing them to her personal history and leaving behind an image for her kids and grandkids to see."

Janice glanced up from the camera with a soft smile. "That's a lovely thought, Tess."

"Every now and again I have a lovely thought." Tess laughed at her use of the word. "But, really…I think that's why you love photography so much, Janice, because it's the only way we can really make time stop, while we're clicking that button to capture the image."

"I'm grateful for all of the magical moments in my life, the ones caught on film and the ones that weren't," LuAnn said.

"Me too." Tess paused and gazed out the front window, trying to see the view as Daisy had seen it. "And from now on, I'm going to celebrate every photographic moment God gives me. Each one is a blessing and I want to capture it and put it to memory, then pass it on to my kids and grandkids."

"Amen." As if to punctuate the point, Janice caught one more photo—this time of Tess peering out the window.

Chapter Twenty-Two

April 4, 1860

When Adeline heard that Lolly and her grandsons would be leaving in the morning, she insisted upon staying the night.

"You sleep, Pru," she said tenderly. "I will watch over Lolly and make sure she has all she needs through the nighttime hours."

Prudence wanted to argue but knew better. Lolly would be in the best possible hands with Adeline there, so Prudence prepared foods for the travelers to carry on their journey, then settled down for the night with prayers for Lolly and her grandsons in her heart.

Jason roused Prudence long before daybreak with the words, "It is time, Pru."

Moses stirred and whimpered, but she soothed him with her hand on his back, then tiptoed to the cupboard to get the food she had prepared the night before. She checked in on Lolly to find her sleeping peacefully with Adeline still seated in the chair next to the bed. The precious young woman had dozed off.

Though she hated to do so, Prudence knew she must wake them both. She made sure the travelers had a hearty breakfast and then gave the boys the extra food for the road. Prudence could hardly believe her eyes when she saw the contraption Jason had made. He called it a carrying bed.

"It's just two sticks of wood with muslin between," he said. "But it should ease the burden a bit."

"Thee is a Godsend, Jason." Prudence gave him an admiring look. "And clever, as well."

Just as the morning sun eased its way up the eastern edge of the property, Jason helped George and Caleb load Lolly onto the makeshift bed. Once they had her situated, Adeline leaned down to give the elderly woman a kiss on the cheek.

"You are headed off on a journey far superior to any I've read about in any of those books I told you about," she said.

Lolly's eyes widened. "What does it look like? Can you see it?"

"Oh, yes." A lone tear trickled down Adeline's cheek. "I see the two of us, meeting again—in a place so lovely nothing can compare. I see your children and your children's children gathered around you, singing praises to the One who brought you through it all. And Lolly, I see you, healed and whole, a woman of strength. Can *you* see it?"

"I can. In here." Lolly rested a hand on her heart, though Adeline wouldn't see the gesture.

Adeline must have understood for she said, "Then let that knowledge give you the courage you need as you travel to see your son. The Lord be with you as you go."

"Bless you." Lolly extended her hand in Prudence's direction. "How can I thank you, child?"

Prudence took her hand and gave it a gentle squeeze. "I am the one who has been blessed, Lolly. Godspeed. We will be praying as thee goes."

"Thank you, sweet girl."

Prudence did all she could to press any fears or concerns aside as George and Caleb disappeared into the shadows of the trees on the edge of the property.

"Let us pray for their journey, Prudence. Shall we?"

Before she could respond, Adeline reached over until she caught Prudence's hand.

"Heavenly Father, You are Lord of all. You created us, body, soul, and spirit. You see your daughter, Lolly. You know the desires of her heart, Father, and You see the weakness of her body. We do boldly implore You, as we read in Your Word, to carry her all the way to the Promised Land in safety. Guard over her, we pray. Be with her boys, that they might garner strength for the journey, Lord. Amen."

Prudence ushered up a quiet, "Amen."

"You are fearful of what cannot be seen, Prudence." Adeline smiled. "But rest easy. The Lord giveth and the Lord taketh away. Should He see Lolly through to Syracuse, we shall rejoice. And should He call her home, we shall also rejoice."

Prudence whispered a quiet, "Amen," then turned back toward the cabin to tend to her son.

CHAPTER TWENTY-THREE

After Daisy and Miranda left, the ladies went through their usual routine at the inn. LuAnn slipped out around two o'clock, explaining that she had some work to do at home. A few hours later, Tess received a call from LuAnn, asking if she and Janice could swing by "the mansion," as they were fond of calling LuAnn's new home.

"Must be important," Janice said. "Otherwise, I think she would've waited until the morning to tell us."

"True. Maybe Brad finally caught up with Rankin Smith and got him to agree to pay the claim."

"Maybe." Janice shrugged. "Or maybe she and Brad have some sort of personal news."

Tess offered to drive, and moments later they pulled up to the Bickerton mansion. Tess led the way to the front door of the massive Victorian house, and, as always, was overwhelmed by the sheer beauty of it all.

For a moment, she stood in silence on the wraparound porch, transported back to that day when she, Janice, and LuAnn first visited this stately old home, which had its roots in the anti-slavery movement. How ironic that one of them was now mistress of the manor. What would it be like, she wondered, to live in such a towering home on two full acres of land?

Tess squinted and used her hand to cover her eyes from the beams of sunlight flooding down onto them. "Look at how far the old place has come." She gestured to the beautiful home. "And now one of our dearest friends is mistress of it all."

"You sound like Elizabeth in *Pride and Prejudice*." Janice laughed. "'Mistress of it all.' Where do you come up with these things?"

Before Tess could answer, Janice let out a squeal. "Oh, Tess! Look!" She pointed to the flower beds to their right. "The pansies are in bloom. So are the impatiens. I wish I'd brought my camera."

"They're gorgeous. Quite the kaleidoscope of color, I'd say."

"Just begging for a photo op." Janice's mood seemed to brighten. "That's what I'll do, Tess. I'll ask LuAnn if she minds if I photograph Bickerton Mansion. It will be a great way to learn the features of my new camera. With all of the gorgeous fountains and statues on the property, I'll never be at a loss for things to photograph."

"That's for sure." The beautifully landscaped lawn provided a colorful entrance to the grand home with its turrets, leaded glass windows, and deep redbrick exterior...perfect for photographing.

"It's funny," Janice said. "I didn't realize how beautiful life looked through the lens until I stopped moving so fast."

"That'll preach," Tess said and then rang the bell.

Moments later the door swung wide and LuAnn ushered them inside the immaculate foyer. "Come on in. We can visit in the parlor."

"Visit in the parlor." Tess fought the giggle that threatened to escape. "That sounds so...Southern."

"Doesn't it, though?" LuAnn kept walking. "I feel a bit like a Southerner living here. Strange, how a place can do that to you." She led the way to the expansive front parlor with its stunning fireplace.

Tess looked around the room, seeing it with fresh eyes. "In case I haven't said it before, LuAnn, I just love the way this room turned out."

"Quite the contrast from the old brocade window treatments and Oriental rugs that Thelma and Irene used to keep in here." LuAnn gestured for them to sit.

Tess nodded as she took a seat in the wingback chair. She remembered the room as it had been three years ago. In those days, Brad's aunts kept the place like a museum.

"Hey, at least you can see those gorgeous oak floors, now that the rugs are up," Janice observed.

"They took a lot of time and effort to whip back into shape," Tess responded. "But it was worth every bit of it."

LuAnn offered them mugs of hot coffee. After settling down with cup in hand, Tess was finally able to ask the obvious question: "LuAnn, what's going on?"

"I did a bit of snooping on the computer."

"Snooping?" Janice took a sip of her coffee and then set the cup on the end table.

"Yes, I googled ASAP Insurance Company to see if I could locate someone else who was struggling to get a claim paid."

"And did you?" Tess asked.

"Yes, I found some complaints. All in Ohio."

This certainly piqued Tess's curiosity. "Did you reach out to any of them?"

"Not yet. That's why you're here. It's going to take a little more research to track these people down. But once we do, I was hoping we could make some calls together."

"Sure," Tess agreed. "I'd like to get to the bottom of this."

"I'll help," Janice added.

"Thanks, but before we do, I did make one call, and it was eye opening. You're not going to believe this. It's about the woman who caused my accident."

"Braelyn, right?" Tess asked.

LuAnn nodded. "Yes. Well, it turns out she *did* have whiplash. And the baby ended up having to be kept overnight in the hospital for observation, just to be safe. The medical bills are going to be huge. Knowing that, she reached out to Rankin to let him know what to expect, but he's already told her that her policy doesn't cover overnight stays in the hospital."

"That's ridiculous," Janice said. "If she has full coverage it should cover hospitalization due to injury caused in the vehicle."

"Exactly, and that's what I told her. She's really upset because he's led her to believe he won't pay her claim. He's still insisting that I was to blame for the accident and that she'll have to deal with my insurance company if she wants to see any money. Isn't that awful?"

"Your company won't pay unless the accident was your fault, though." Tess sighed. "What a mess."

"Exactly. And I'm certainly not liable for anyone else's medical bills."

"How can he get away with that?" Janice leaned forward and rested her elbows on her knees.

"It's just a ploy, I'm sure. Anyway, I told Braelyn my predicament and she told me hers. It looks like we're in this together, so at least I don't feel alone."

"Right, and remember, Corey has a similar story," Tess reminded her.

"I would like to talk to him again, but let's start with a couple of these other people that I found online, shall we? I wrote down the names."

"But how is a name going to help unless we have a phone number or email address?" Janice asked.

"Social media," Tess said. "I'll look them up."

LuAnn reached for a notebook and flipped the pages until she found what she was looking for. "First up is a lady named Seraphina Homayoun." She paused. "I'll have to check, but I think I stumbled across her story on Twitter, which means I already have access to one of her social media accounts. We can always reach out to her there, but who knows if she'll see it."

"I'll look up her account," Tess said. "How do you spell the name, again?"

"I'm probably butchering that last name but it's spelled h-o-m-a-y-o-u-n."

Tess pulled out her phone and opened the Twitter app. "Or, similar, anyway. "I found a Seraphina Basara Homayoun."

"That has to be it. Does it say where she lives?"

Tess scrolled on her phone until she saw the woman's location. "She lives in the Canton area, looks like." Tess located the post in question and decided to comment on it with the words, "Please inbox me. Dealing with same issue." Then she shot off a private message to the woman, giving LuAnn's contact information.

"Wow, you're quick." LuAnn gave her an admiring look.

"I'd like to see if I can find her on any other social media sites." Tess did a bit of research and finally found Seraphina on another social media outlet. "She's definitely in Canton. Married. Has two kids."

"So, that means Rankin used to do business in Canton?" Janice asked. "Or maybe he insures people from all over the state?"

"Who knows? I'll private message her here too and see if she writes back." Tess started to compose the note, then decided to add LuAnn's phone number to the message, in case the woman wanted to talk.

It took a little longer to find the second name on LuAnn's list—a man named Jeremiah Weston. From what Tess could gather, he didn't spend much time on social media. His one and only account looked as if it hadn't been used in some time. She left him a private message anyway.

"What's the next name, LuAnn?" Tess asked. "Maybe we'll have more luck with this one."

"It's..." LuAnn's eyes widened as she read the name aloud. "For pity's sake, it's Sally Jamison."

"As in, Sally and Sal's Bathe and Groom?" Janice's eyes widened in disbelief. "*That* Sally Jamison?"

"Sure looks like it. I'll pull up the phone number."

Moments later, they had Sally Jamison on speakerphone. She told a harrowing tale about a traffic accident on the interstate that had injured her husband, Sal, and caused him to be life-flighted to the hospital in Columbus.

"Sally, I had no idea," Tess responded. "I'm so sorry to hear this."

The woman went on to say that her dealings with Rankin Smith had been anything but good and that she was in the process of filing a complaint with the Better Business Bureau. She suggested LuAnn do the same.

When they ended the call, Tess set her phone aside and leaned back against the sofa. By now her coffee was cold, so LuAnn offered to top off her cup.

"So, this guy Rankin is really up to no good," LuAnn said as she poured. "I don't know if it makes me feel better or worse that he's done this to multiple people."

"You're not the first person he's tried to cheat, that's for sure," Tess said. "But that was a good idea Sally had, to file a complaint with the Better Business Bureau. I'm going to look him up on the BBB site to see if anyone else has filed any complaints about him. Could I use your laptop, LuAnn?"

"Sure, or I'll just do it myself." LuAnn went to fetch her laptop and then joined the ladies on the sofa. A couple of minutes later, she scrolled the internet until she landed on the BBB site. She typed the company's name into the search box.

"Oh, I do see that a complaint was filed." She scanned it and took in the details before realizing how familiar they sounded. "Ah. This must be Corey. It mentions a life insurance claim that wasn't paid."

"Nothing else, though?" Janice peered over LuAnn's shoulder. "That's kind of shocking."

"Some people don't think to file with the Better Business Bureau," Tess said. "But I've thought of another place to check."

"Where's that?" Janice asked.

"The state insurance board." Tess took the laptop and navigated to the website for the state insurance board. Once there, she looked over the process of filing a complaint.

"Looks like you have to go through the attorney general's office." She glanced at LuAnn. "You ready to do this?"

LuAnn shrugged. "I mean, I don't know. It's only been a little more than a week since the accident. What do you think?"

"I would do it, and also pass this information on to Corey. He's got a claim with Rankin too."

"Yes, as we all heard loud and clear."

After a little more discussion, the ladies decided the time had come to take some action. No more pussyfooting around with this Rankin Smith guy. They would go to his office tomorrow morning and give him a piece of their collective minds.

"Let me just make sure Brad is okay with it," LuAnn said. "He's already sent all the documentation by certified mail, so I know that Rankin has everything he needs. If I show up in person, it might just make him angry."

"Or it might spur him to action," Tess debated. "I think that's the more likely scenario."

"But you heard what Corey said yesterday," LuAnn reminded her. "He's been by Rankin's office six times over the past two months and hasn't found him yet."

"Yes. But we've got to try, LuAnn. Otherwise, the guy might skip town or something."

"Do you really think that's possible?"

"Possible?" Tess echoed. "I not only think it's possible, I'd be willing to bet the farm on it."

CHAPTER TWENTY-FOUR

The next afternoon Tess offered to drive to Rankin's office. They left the inn around two thirty, headed toward town, ready to slay this dragon, once and for all.

"I'm going to give him a piece of my mind when I see him," LuAnn said. "I've held back too long."

"Did you tell Brad we were going?" Tess asked.

"I was going to run it by him, but he had a big meeting this morning and was so preoccupied, I didn't bother. I'll cook him a nice supper tonight and tell him what I've done."

"After the fact?" Janice asked.

"Hey, it's easier to ask for forgiveness, don't you think?" LuAnn laughed. "But seriously, he trusts me. We just need to be careful."

Off in the distance thunder rumbled. Dark skies hovered like an eerie blanket and Tess wondered if, perhaps, they'd chosen the wrong day to be so brave.

"Is that lightning?" LuAnn pointed out the window to the right. Unfortunately, a loud peal of thunder kept Tess from responding. She gripped the steering wheel and held on for dear life as rain came pelting down.

"Whoa, Nellie." She turned on the windshield wipers.

"Man. Looks like a bad one." Janice's voice sounded from the back seat. "I haven't been paying attention to the weather. Didn't even realize we were expecting rain."

"April can't make up its mind," LuAnn said. "Half the time the skies overhead are blue and cloudless. The other half, we're having a monsoon."

Thank goodness the torrent slowed a bit as they got closer to the part of town where Rankin's office was located.

"I just have one request, if you don't mind," Janice said as they drew near. She pointed to the Better Batter, Sandie Ballard's bakery, which was to their right. "Can we stop in there after confronting Rankin? I'm going to need some extra sustenance."

"You betcha," Tess agreed. "I'm all for that."

She located a parking spot along the edge of the street. Minutes later, the ladies were inside the Town Center building, looking for ASAP Insurance's suite. It wasn't listed on the board up front. They went up and down the various hallways, looking for a sign that read ASAP.

"This place smells old." Tess wrinkled her nose. "Musty."

"Yeah, I couldn't work here," Janice agreed.

"This is it." LuAnn pointed at a door to their right. "Weird that the business name isn't on the door, but I know this is the right suite number. I remember it from the letter I mailed." She tried the door, but it wouldn't open.

"Strange." LuAnn's nose wrinkled, as if the smell of the place bothered her. "It's locked."

"Maybe he's out with a customer," Janice suggested.

"Maybe." LuAnn shrugged.

Tess peered through the glass to see the interior of the office. She couldn't make out much. She knocked on the door, and they waited. And waited. And waited some more.

"Maybe his office is in back?" Janice suggested. "Try again, Tess."

Tess knocked once more, this time much louder. Still, no one answered.

"What kind of insurance agent is closed to customers?" Janice asked.

"This kind." Tess pointed at the door again. She fought the temptation to say more.

"Well, doesn't that just figure?" LuAnn groaned. "I finally get brave enough to come down here, and he's not even around."

"I think it's strange." Tess turned to leave.

"Well, I vote for going to the bakery. At least something good will come out of this venture. But first..." LuAnn pointed to a door on the opposite side of the hallway that read LADIES. "I've got to make a pit stop. Anyone else?"

"Not me." Janice shook her head.

"Me neither. We'll wait for you out here." Tess leaned against the wall, deep in thought. Why would an insurance company not have its name on the door? What kind of business was Rankin Smith running, anyway?

A man approached from the end of the hallway. He walked straight to Rankin's door and tried to turn the handle.

"He's not here," Tess said.

"Again. Convenient." The man rolled his eyes then glanced at Tess. "You work for ASAP?"

"No, I don't."

"I'm trying to reach Rankin Smith." The man pulled off his baseball cap and ran his fingers through unruly hair.

"You're in the right place," Janice said. "This is his office."

"Yeah, I know." The guy shoved his cap back on his head. "I rented it to him six months ago."

"Oh, I see." Tess frowned. *Interesting.*

The man's gaze narrowed as he looked them over. "You ladies customers? Looking for him like everyone else?"

"Well, we're not," Janice said. "But our friend..." Her words trailed off as she pointed in the direction of the restroom where LuAnn had disappeared.

The man glanced at his watch. "Listen, I've gotta go. But if you do catch up with Smith, remind him that he owes me rent money."

"Rent money?" Tess echoed.

"Yeah. He came in here that first month talking a big game about how successful his business was, but I haven't seen my share of it. If he doesn't get the rent money to me by next Saturday, I'm kicking him out. Tell him that, why don't you."

"I don't really think it's my place to—"

Before Tess could finish the sentence, the man turned and walked away.

"Wow," Janice said. "So, Rankin's business is failing?"

"Either that or he's very forgetful." Tess shrugged. "LuAnn will be interested in what he had to say."

"What who had to say?"

Tess pivoted and discovered her friend standing right in front of her, a small bottle of sanitizer in her hand. "Don't use that bathroom, by the way." LuAnn shivered as she squirted the sanitizer into her palm. "Disgusting."

"Ugh." Tess grimaced. "I'll take your word for it."

"Now, what were you saying?" LuAnn tossed the bottle back into her purse and rubbed her hands together.

Tess filled her in on what the man had told them and LuAnn groaned. "Are you telling me his business is failing?"

"I don't know, LuAnn." Tess released a sigh. "He's behind on his rent, though."

LuAnn's jaw flinched. "This story just keeps getting worse and worse. I'm so over it."

"It's definitely time to take this case to a higher court," Tess said.

LuAnn finished rubbing her hands together. "I read online that I can appeal to the state board of insurance, but I sure hate to go that route. Can you imagine how complicated things might get, especially if Rankin is some sort of scam artist."

"Is that what you're thinking?" Janice asked.

LuAnn shrugged. "Who knows at this point? Let's just get out of here. I'm craving one of Sandie's cinnamon rolls. Maybe I'll feel better after I eat one."

Tess had to admit, that did sound good.

When they reached the lobby of the building, Tess caught a glimpse of Corey parking his car out front. "Ladies, look." She pointed at his vehicle.

They watched through the front window as Rankin's landlord approached Corey and spoke to him. Tess could tell the landlord was really losing his temper, and Corey didn't look much happier.

The landlord took off toward his vehicle, and Corey got back into his car and left.

"Guess he heard Rankin wasn't here," Tess said.

"Let's get out of here." LuAnn barreled toward the front door, and moments later the ladies walked out into the bright morning sun.

Janice glanced up at the sky. "Well, that storm cleared up quickly."

"Yeah, it unnerved me a little," Tess admitted. "I'm glad it's behind us."

"Me too." LuAnn pointed herself in the direction of the bakery. "I've had enough fun for one day."

They'd only taken a couple of steps when Tess's phone dinged. She pulled it from her purse and gasped when she saw a text from Miranda with an attachment to be downloaded.

"Oh, my goodness. Hold on, ladies." She stopped walking and fussed with her phone. "A video just came through."

"From who?"

"Miranda. You've got to see this."

They watched the video together, completely mesmerized by what they saw.

"Goodness gracious goat!" Janice clamped a hand over her mouth then pulled it away. "She did it. She actually did it."

CHAPTER TWENTY-FIVE

Tess stared at the video in awe. "She did it, all right, and it sounds like she had a delightful time too!" She texted a response to Miranda that read, Wow! CONGRATULATIONS! WE'RE LIKE PROUD MOTHER HENS OVER HERE, WATCHING THIS VIDEO!

Seconds later, Tess's phone rang. She realized it was a video call from Miranda's phone.

"I did it!" Daisy's voice was half-squeal, half-childish giggle. "Oh, it was the most glorious experience of my life, ladies. I highly recommend it. The Ohio looked marvelous from up above. I could almost see Adeline walking along the banks of the river, headed for Marietta. The scenery was breathtaking, and flying through the air like that..." She disappeared for a moment, then returned. "It was like I was an angel up there, just looking over everything below. Truly glorious."

"The video was wonderful," Janice called out. "We're so proud of you!"

"Thank you." Daisy giggled. "We'll send you the video of Miranda parasailing. I'm not quite the picture-taker she is, so it moves around a bit, but you'll get the idea."

"We can't wait to see it," LuAnn responded.

"I heard about your book title, Tess!" Daisy said, after they finished talking about Miranda's flight.

"My book title?" Whatever was she talking about?

"*Mimi and the Mister!*" Daisy giggled. "So funny!"

"Oh, *that* book title." Tess couldn't help but laugh. "I'm thinking you're going to write that one, not me. When you get to your new digs, I mean. You can add book-writing to your new bucket list."

"I think I will. Thanks for giving me the idea. I've always wanted to write a book."

"Really?"

"Yes, I don't know why I didn't think to put it on my bucket list in the first place. But there's still plenty of time. I'll need something to do in that old folks' home."

"Mimi, it's not an old folks' home." Miranda's voice sounded in the background.

"Anyway, I'd better let you ladies go and pay attention. Our pilot is a handsome fellow. Maybe he's my mister." She turned the camera and showed a close-up of a fellow who looked to be in his early forties, standing along the river's edge next to them.

"I'm married!" The pilot pointed to his wedding ring, then went right back to work loading up another customer ready for flight.

"Well, pooh. He's spoken for." Daisy laughed. "Guess my mister will just have to be the fictional sort. But I'll send you a copy of my book as soon as it hits the bestseller list, ladies. I promise! I'll even dedicate it to you."

"No, dedicate it to Miranda," Janice suggested. "She's the wind beneath your wings."

Daisy kissed Miranda's cheek. "Yes, she is. Gotta go, ladies! It's been fun."

The call ended almost as quickly as it had begun.

"That's one invincible lady," Tess said as she pressed her phone back into her pocket. "And I'd also say that Miranda was right."

"About…" Janice gave her a curious look.

"She said there were other bucket lists, yet to be written."

"Oh, right." Janice nodded. "Things she can do once she's moved into the assisted living facility, you mean?"

"Yes." Tess nodded. "Sounds like Daisy's already getting creative, thinking of a few things she can add to her new list. I'm proud of her."

"And I wouldn't be a bit surprised to hear there's a real mister in her story a year or two from now," LuAnn added. "She's absolutely charming. There's likely a hero yet to be added to her story."

Tess thought that through. "Oh, I don't know. I'd say she's hero enough, all by herself."

"Now, can we please go to the bakery?" Janice asked. "I'm dying for something sweet."

They walked to the Better Batter, just three doors down from their current location. When they opened the door, the most amazing scents greeted them.

Janice stopped just inside, pinched her eyes shut, and threw her hands up in the air, as if in a trance.

"What in the world?" Tess nudged her with her elbow. "Are you all right?"

"I...I..." She sniffed the air. "I think I've just realized what heaven is going to smell like."

"She's usually not like this," LuAnn explained to a customer who was trying to get by.

"That's right. She's usually the quietest one of the bunch," Tess added. "And the least dramatic."

Janice's eyes popped open. "Cinnamon."

Tess nodded. "Yes, and sugar. Key ingredients to cinnamon rolls."

"Must. Have. This place smells like heaven," Janice repeated.

Tess couldn't help but agree.

"Looks like it too." Janice pointed to the colorful walls. "I always love coming in here."

The bakery's colorful decor always made Tess happy too, and today's visit did not disappoint. The varying shades of pink and lime green were just the ticket. Oh, but those glass cases, filled with delectable baked goods! Who could resist them?

She walked up to one of them for a closer look and practically drooled over the cookies with sprinkles, the brightly colored cupcakes, those adorably decorated cake balls, the tiered cakes, and breads. Lots and lots of breads.

Sandie approached from the register with a broad smile on her face. "Well, good morning, ladies. What brings you around?"

"I'm here on official business." Janice pointed to the cinnamon rolls. "I need a dozen of those to take back to the inn."

"Done. Anything else?"

"I want a bear claw, Sandie," LuAnn said.

"And I'll take a pecan twist. I just love those." Tess adjusted her purse on her shoulder.

Sandie filled their order and they paid, then took a seat at one of the little wrought iron café tables near the front of the room. After taking care of another customer, Sandie walked their way.

"What do you think?"

"I think it's delicious." LuAnn licked her fingers.

They made small talk for a while, and then Tess asked if she could have a couple of minutes alone with Sandie.

"Sure, follow me back to my storeroom. I have to grab something anyway. Follow me." Sandie hollered out instructions to her coworker, a teenage girl sporting a blond ponytail and cheerful expression. Then Sandie led the way to the storage room, which was loaded with Rising Star baking products. "All of this is thanks to Winnie," Sandie said as she gestured to the many bags of flour, baking powder, and baking soda.

Tess looked around the room, mesmerized. "Everything in here is so...white." Massive bags of Rising Star flour filled the metal baking shelf to her right, jammed so tight you couldn't squeeze a penny between them. And to her left, the oversized shelf unit was jam-packed with sugar, baking soda, baking powder, and cornstarch.

Sandie closed her eyes and moved her hands in a circular motion toward her face. "Can you smell that?"

"Smell what?"

"Sugar. Isn't it divine?" She giggled. "I still can't believe how generous Winnie was when she won that baking competition. I'm set with flour and baking powder."

"Oh, she's very generous. She's also..." Tess wrinkled her nose. "Very, very cautious."

"About flour?"

"No." Tess laughed. "Something else entirely. That's kind of why I'm here. I wanted to chat with you about Corey."

"Oh, right." Sandie's bright smile faded. "You mean because of what happened at the café? The way he acted on the phone and then his big disappearing act after the fact?"

"Well, partly, but there's more to the story than that and I feel like you deserve to know."

"Goodness. Sounds serious."

Tess shook her head. "I just wanted to let you know that Corey mentioned in passing that he knew our lawn guy from prison."

"From prison?"

"Yes. That's really all I know, but I thought it was worth mentioning."

Sandie's nose wrinkled as she reached for a bag of flour and hefted it to her shoulder. "Are you telling me I should stay away from him?"

Tess cringed. "Well, no. I just want you to be careful."

They walked back out into the bakery just as the bell above the front door jangled. Tess was surprised to see Griffin walk in with a woman about his age and two adorable children. Only when one of them hollered out the words, "Daddy, look!" did she realize he had brought his family.

Chapter Twenty-Six

Tess waved at Griffin from across the room and then took several steps in his direction.

"Tess, what a great surprise. I've been telling my wife all about you and the other ladies. Rose, this is Tess. Tess, meet my wife and children."

"This is a pleasant surprise. I'm so glad you're all here." She reached out and shook the young woman's hand.

Then Griffin introduced the children. Tess turned her attention to the little boy. "Charlie, it's good to meet you." She directed her next words at the girl. "Lily, I love your name."

"Thank you." The girl smiled.

"Fleur-de-lis." Tess gave her a wink.

"He told you that?" She gave her father an inquisitive look.

He smiled at Tess. "That was my fascination with the brooch."

"I thought so." Tess turned her attention to his wife. "Griffin's been a fixture around our place over the last few weeks. We're so happy to have him. He's really given the lawn a face-lift. And it's the perfect season for that too, now that spring has sprung."

"His business is doing well, thanks to people like you." Rose smiled. "Thank you for hiring him."

Sandie took their order, all smiles. "I don't think I've seen you guys in here before."

"This is our first time," Charlie said. His eyes grew wide as he pointed to the colorful cookies inside the glass case. "Yum!"

"So, what brings you in?" Sandie asked after taking their order.

"Oh, my chaplain, Corey, recommended it. He said that he's doing a piece for the paper on you."

Tess wasn't quite sure she'd heard right.

"Corey?" Sandie almost dropped the change. "Corey from the paper?"

"Yes, that's right." Griffin nodded and took the change she offered him.

Tess couldn't quite believe what she was hearing. Oh, goodness. Well, that certainly explained how the two men knew each other.

"He's a chaplain?" Sandie scrambled to get the change into Griffin's palm.

"Well, yeah. When he's not working at the paper, which he does on the side. But I met him when he was working, well..." Griffin's words faded off. "Not at the paper."

"At the prison," Charlie said. "My dad was in prison."

Griffin flinched but didn't say anything.

"So, you're saying that Corey *works* at the prison as a chaplain?" Sandie's words were directed at Griffin, but she turned to face Tess with an expression that asked, "Really?!"

Tess simply shrugged. What else could she do, short of apologizing to Sandie for raising any suspicions about him in the first place.

"Yeah, well, he's one of several chaplains. He's been there for years." Griffin took a bite of his chocolate chunk cookie. "But when he moved to Marietta after his wife died he took the job at the paper, so he's been pretty busy with that too."

"This is all so…surprising." Tess wasn't sure what else she could say, but it certainly put everything in a new light. She could hardly wait to tell the other ladies, who were engaged in a lively conversation about parasailing.

She introduced Griffin's wife and children to Janice and LuAnn, and the family took the table next to theirs. They visited for some time until the bell jangled above the door once again. Tess could hardly believe her eyes when she saw the little girl, Brianna, who had won the prize egg, standing there with her mother and with a man who must be her father. She was even more astounded when Griffin rose and walked their way. He threw his arms around the man and embraced him like one would an old friend.

Griffin's wife must've noticed the look of confusion on Tess's face. "That's Harrison. He works in the prison ministry too. He's also a chaplain. That's why Griffin brought us down here today, to meet Harrison and his wife and daughter. He thought we would all hit it off."

"Goodness." It was the only word she could think of.

Brianna's mother approached the table and smiled when she saw Tess and the other ladies. "Hey! I recognize you all from that day at the Easter egg hunt. I'm Joy."

"Yes, nice to see you again, Joy. I'm Tess." She extended her hand.

Introductions were made all around, and before long the incoming family took the one remaining table near Griffin and his wife and kids.

"So, let me get this straight." Janice spoke in a low voice to Tess and LuAnn while the other families chatted amongst themselves. "Corey—the one who was yelling on the phone—is in some sort of prison ministry. And this guy—the one whose daughter pitched a fit at the Easter egg hunt—is also a chaplain? And the person they were ministering to was Griffin. Do I have it right?"

"I think you have it right."

"This is a fascinating twist." LuAnn laughed. "I'd have to say we jumped to a few conclusions."

"Did we ever. I think Griffin arranged their meeting today, so that his wife could see the people who have led him to the Lord."

Brianna and Charlie sprinted back over to the cookie case, and the adults continued their discussion.

Joy turned to Tess, Janice, and LuAnn, an apologetic expression on her face. "I'm glad Brianna stepped away for a bit. I just had to tell you all something."

"Oh, what's that?" Tess asked.

"I was horribly embarrassed that Brianna reacted the way she did at the Easter egg hunt. I know you ladies were as shocked as the rest of us to find that money gone."

"Yes, we were," Janice said.

Joy shook her head. "And I know you somehow made up the difference, but I'm sure that had to sting."

"Well, God has used that for good," Tess explained. "It's quite the story, actually."

Harrison walked up with a box of sweets, which he handed to Joy. "Are we talking about Bri's outlandish behavior the day of the Easter egg hunt? I heard all about it."

"Yes, I apologized, honey." Joy opened the box, and her eyes widened as she looked inside. "Oh, wow, this looks delicious." She turned back to visit with Griffin's wife.

Harrison remained standing in front of Tess and the other ladies. She could tell he had something on his mind. "I just wanted to say that I was embarrassed to hear about Brianna's behavior that day, even though I didn't witness it firsthand. She's in a weird stage where she throws fits, kind of like she did when she was little. We're working with her on it, but it's still awkward when it happens, especially in public."

"Lots of girls go through it, especially at this age."

"I guess, but that doesn't make it any less embarrassing or any more right. So here's what I decided to do, so that Brianna could learn a little lesson from the whole thing. I asked her to consider giving a percentage of her winnings away to the children's hospital in Memphis."

"St. Jude's?"

"Yes." Harrison beamed. "She wrote a little note explaining where the money came from—how she'd won it in a golden egg and all that—and they wrote back just today, with an invitation for our family to come to the hospital to share the story at a big fundraising event they're holding in a few weeks."

"Wow!" Tess's heart nearly burst at this news.

"And none of this would have happened if things hadn't gone wrong with the egg. I never would have thought to ask her to consider donating, except to shift her thinking from herself to someone else, if that makes sense."

"Perfect sense."

"I'm just saying, it started out being bad—the money being missing and all—but in the end it worked out for good."

"The same thing happened on our end," Tess said. "It's like that verse, 'What the enemy meant for evil—'"

"'God used for good.'" Harrison smiled. "I have a whole story about how God honored our actions to make good on the golden egg monies, but that's a story for another day. Just trust me when I say that everything worked out for the good." His brow wrinkled. "Did you ever find out who took the money from the egg in the first place?"

"No." She shook her head. "But we're closer to seeing who didn't take it, so that's progress, I suppose."

"I see. Well, I wanted to let you know. I told Brianna to take the golden egg with her when we go to St. Jude's. She can tell them the whole story."

"Be sure to get pictures."

"Oh, I will."

Tess was struck with an idea. "Maybe Corey will write up a story and put it in the paper."

"Could be. He'd probably love that."

Tess paused, thinking through her next words. "Hey, speaking of Corey, can I ask you a couple of questions, apart from the others?"

"Sure."

She rose and took a couple of steps away from the group. He followed her.

"You're close friends with him?" Tess asked.

"Corey is more than a close friend. I was his pastor for years."

"Oh, wow." This story just kept getting better and better.

"I quit about five years back to focus on the prison ministry," Harrison explained. "And I knew he would be the perfect addition to our team. At first, he wasn't interested in going, but after a while I think I wore him down. We go in once a month and do a Bible study with the guys. That's why I missed the Easter egg hunt, because I was at the prison."

"I see."

He chuckled. "I use the term 'Bible study' loosely. Mostly we just tell them our stories."

"Your testimonies. And that's how you and Corey met Griffin."

Harrison laughed and then shot a glance at Griffin, who continued to visit with the two wives. "Yes. Trust me when I say that Griffin wasn't interested in what they were selling. We were pretty persistent, though. We finally made inroads." He paused, and Tess could read the emotion in his face. "I'm pretty passionate about reaching all those guys, and so is Corey. We both wanted to keep up with Griffin after his release but lost touch pretty quickly."

"Until that day at the Easter egg hunt," Tess said. "Corey recognized Griffin."

"Yes, he was so excited. But he forgot to get his new address, so it took some maneuvering to find him. Corey kept going back to your place, hoping to see him. We had this idea..."

"Did I hear my name over here?"

Tess turned to discover Griffin had joined them.

"I was just about to tell Tess all about the idea Corey and I came up with."

"Oh. That." Griffin's gaze shifted to the ground and then back up again. "Corey's really been pushing me."

"We all have." Harrison gave him a knowing look.

"To do what?" Tess couldn't quite understand what they were getting at.

"It's that ministry of his." Griffin took a bite of his cookie and then spoke around it. "These guys seem to think I should join them. Personally, I think they're both nuts, but that's just me."

Tess could hardly believe her ears. "Griffin, are you telling me that all this time Corey was trying to track you down to talk you into spreading the gospel?"

"Yeah. And trust me, I'm not ready for that, at least not yet." He gave Tess an inquisitive look. "Why?"

"Oh, I don't know. When he told me that he knew you from prison, I actually thought he was—"

"Oh!" Griffin laughed. "You thought he was an ex-con like me."

This got a belly laugh from Harrison, who apparently found the whole thing hysterical.

"What's going on over here?" Both wives approached and before long Janice and LuAnn joined them.

"Oh, nothing much," Harrison said. "Only, these ladies thought that Corey was an inmate at the prison, not a chaplain."

"What a mess!" Tess put her hands up and then laughed. "I'm relieved everyone thinks it's funny. That makes me feel less guilty for having suspicions. It's just that he kept asking me for your contact information. He told me you two had unfinished business. I thought maybe he meant…"

Griffin and Harrison both doubled over again.

"Oh, that's priceless," Harrison slapped Griffin on the back. "You and Corey…unfinished business." Just as quickly, he stopped laughing. "But that reminds me, you never did give us an answer. Are you going to join the ministry, or not?"

Griffin gave him a pensive look. "I'm not ready for that. But as soon as I am, I'll let you know. Right now, my focus is on my family." He gave his wife a shy glance, and she diverted her attention to the kids.

Before long they were all seated again.

"When we get it wrong, we get it wrong." Janice laughed. "But at least we can admit it."

"I have one more question about Corey," LuAnn said. "If it's none of my business, I will understand. But he told us he's working on a story for the paper—"

Harrison's face clouded over. "About his wife's death, you mean?"

"Yes. About the insurance company."

"Yes." Harrison took a swig of his water. "We know all about that. We've been praying about if for almost a year now. I guess you've already heard that his wife Kelly died in a terrible car accident. She was six months pregnant with their son. He didn't make it either."

"Oh no!" Janice cried out.

"That's horrible." Tess shook her head.

LuAnn rested her palms on the table. "That poor man."

"It happened about a year and a half ago," Harrison explained. "It was the other driver's fault. He fell asleep at the wheel and went head-first into Kelly's lane. The coroner said Kelly died instantly, taking the baby with her."

Tess felt the sting of tears in her eyes. "This breaks my heart. And now the insurance company won't pay the claim."

"Right. Kelly was such a good friend. And my wife and I were there with Corey when he buried her, so I feel like we have a vested interest in helping him get the money from the accident." Harrison paused. "You know why he wants that money, right?"

"I...well, it's really none of our business," Tess said.

"I'm sure he wouldn't mind you knowing, especially since your family is in the same boat with that Rankin fellow. Kelly did missions work in Nicaragua."

"Oh, wow," Tess said. Now this was interesting.

"Yes, we all went on a mission trip together a few years back. She fell in love with the kids at an orphanage in Managua and wanted to help renovate their building. It was in deplorable condition."

"That's so sad," Janice said.

"Yes. Really bad. Kids sleeping on mats on the floor. Hardly any food to eat. She and Corey supported them monthly—I'm sure he still does—but she always had this dream of helping the orphanage rebuild. That's why Corey is so anxious to get the life insurance money, so that he can carry out her dream."

"Oh my goodness," Tess said. "It was on her bucket list. And he's going to see that it happens."

"If he gets the money."

Tess reached to squeeze Harrison's hand. "Then we'll pray he gets it, one way or another."

She would have said more, but at that very moment something outside the window caught her attention—Rankin Smith, headed toward his office.

"Ugh! Not again." Sandie groaned. "I'm done with that guy."

"Done with *that* guy?" Tess asked as she pointed to the window.

"Yes!" Sandie's expression tightened. "He can leave the state for all I care and never come back again!"

CHAPTER TWENTY-SEVEN

S andie, what do you mean?" Tess stared at her friend in disbelief. "Tell us everything you know about that man."

"I know he's in here every single day, wearing me out, asking for freebies."

"Freebies?"

"Yeah, I've got samples most of the time, but to say he takes advantage of it would be the understatement of the century."

"Have you seen him more, or less lately? Say, over the past three or four days?"

"About the same. He was here just this morning. Looking pretty rough, I might add. If I didn't know any better, I'd say he's sleeping in those clothes." She pointed at the window, though Rankin had now disappeared from view. "They were a wrinkled mess. Nothing new there. But why are you asking, Tess?"

"I'll tell you later, but you've been very helpful." Tess reached for her purse and signaled the other ladies to join her. They took a few steps toward the bakery door, but Sandie bolted their way, her brow wrinkled.

"One more thing, Tess—when I saw him this morning he said something about wanting snacks for the road, like he had a big trip coming up."

"Ugh. Thanks again, Sandie. That helps a lot."

With Tess taking the lead, the ladies barreled out of the bakery just in time to see Rankin disappear into Town Center.

"He's in there," LuAnn said. "And I'm going after him." She shot into the Town Center building and buzzed down the hall with the other ladies directly behind her.

"S-slow d-down, LuAnn." Janice's pants could be heard from behind Tess, who was also having trouble keeping up with LuAnn.

They reached the door of the ASAP office and LuAnn tried the knob, only to discover the door locked. She banged on the door, but no one answered.

"I know you're in there!" LuAnn called out as the light in the office flipped off.

Tess could hear someone banging around inside, but their knocking and hollering did no good. Rankin wasn't coming out.

"Ugh." LuAnn leaned against the wall and groaned. "I guess we can no longer wonder if he's avoiding me." She turned back toward the door and called out, "Talk to me now, Rankin, or I'm going to the state insurance board."

More noise sounded from inside the now-darkened room, as if things were being thrown around, but he did not respond.

"I'm done." LuAnn threw her hands up in the air. "Come on, ladies. Let's go back to my place. You can help me craft that letter to the state insurance board while all of this is fresh on my mind."

Tess drove them back to the Bickerton mansion, her thoughts in a whirl. They pulled up to discover Brad getting out of his car. LuAnn filled him in on their adventures.

"Wait, you went to Rankin's office...without me?"

"Yes, you were so busy, and I hated to bother you."

"LuAnn." He shook his head. "But he wasn't there?"

"Not at first, but he came back," LuAnn explained. "We saw him. But he's not coming out and he's not responding—to me or anyone else, from what I can gather."

"So, are you ready to file a complaint?" Brad asked her.

She nodded. "The ladies are going to help me fill out whatever paperwork needs to be filled out. I'm turning this guy in to the state board."

"Atta girl." He gave her a kiss on the forehead. "I'll be in in a minute. Just need to unload a few things from the car into the garage."

She nodded, then led the way into the house. The ladies settled into the parlor, and LuAnn filled glasses with iced tea.

"I want to dive right in," she said. "But I feel like I need to include Corey, now that we know he's a victim and not some sort of perpetrator."

"Good idea," Tess agreed.

"Why don't you call him, Tess? Ask him to meet up with us."

"Today?"

LuAnn shook her head. "No. What about tomorrow afternoon at the inn? After lunch. That will give us time to figure out what paperwork we need to fill out. But do call him so he's aware we're going this route. Maybe he needs to do the same. It might be helpful if we both filed simultaneously. You know?"

"Right. I've got his card in my purse. Let me find it." Tess reached into her purse for Corey's business card. When she located it, she picked up the phone and punched in his number.

He answered on the third ring. "Hello?"

"Corey, this is Tess Wallace from Wayfarers." She put the call on speaker so the other ladies could hear.

"Tess, good to hear from you. Is everything okay?"

"Well, not exactly. There's a lot to catch you up on. We've had a bit of a run-in with Rankin. Well, not really a run-in, but we…" She paused. "Let me back up."

"Okay."

"It started when we went by his office this afternoon. We noticed the sign was missing from his door."

"Wait. You were there this afternoon?" Corey sounded perplexed. "I was too."

"Yes, we saw you."

"And you didn't say anything?"

She sighed. "I'll explain that part later. But we ran into Rankin's landlord."

"Chris McDougal. That's why I was there, to meet up with him. I put my reporting skills to work and did some research to track him down a while back. I located him in the Town Center directory and reached out to see what he knows about Rankin."

"Wow, I'm impressed," Janice chimed in. "You've done your legwork."

Tess did her best to pay attention to Corey, who kept on talking.

"I've been at this almost a year." He sighed. "Anyway, I've been scoping out Rankin's office for a while now and something about that whole situation is off. I clued Chris in to the fact that he might be packing up to skip town."

"Yes, I think you're right," LuAnn said. "I banged on the door, and he wouldn't answer. I know he was in there."

"She's getting ahead of herself," Tess explained. "We actually went twice, once before the bakery and once after."

"The bakery." His smile came through in his voice. "I had a call from Griffin. He said they ran into you today. Sounds like it was quite the party."

"You've got some great friends, Corey," Tess said. "We were very impressed with all of them."

"So I heard." He laughed. "They told me you thought I was an ex-con."

Tess did her best not to groan aloud. "Yeah, sorry about that."

"My fault. I should have clarified that first day when I told you I knew Griffin from the prison. I can see how you followed that train of thought all the way to the station. But I've never been in prison, except to share the gospel."

"That's so great, Corey," Janice said. "I'm proud of you for that."

"Yes, we're grateful for your work with Griffin and the other inmates," Tess added. "His wife was there today, by the way."

"That's what he said. He's been hoping she could meet Harrison's wife, Joy. I think they'll make a good team. And it will be nice for Griffin's wife to see him hanging out with solid Christian families."

"Corey, they told us all about your wife's plan to build the orphanage," Janice said. "She sounds like an absolutely wonderful woman."

"Yes, that's why I need the money from the claim, to follow through with her dream. Didn't I tell you about that? I'm sorry. Sometimes the grief is still overwhelming."

"It's okay. And knowing it now makes the situation even more pressing, to our way of thinking," LuAnn said. "It's one thing to steal from you, it's another to steal from children in an orphanage."

"Right." He sighed. "This has been a long battle on their behalf, but I'm not giving up, no matter what."

"It's an admirable thing you're doing, Corey," Janice said. "We love the idea of the orphanage."

Tess had one more question. Something had been troubling her. "Corey, you told me once that there were going to be dire consequences if you didn't get the money soon. You were referring to the children at the orphanage, not something else?"

"Yes." He paused. "I should have been more specific, sorry. Every day that passes is another day those children go without. I've done what I could out of my own pocket, but think of what a difference a hundred thousand dollars would make to those kids."

"I can't even imagine." Tess shook her head.

"It was my wife's deepest wish to help those children. She desperately wanted to impact their lives in a major way."

"Then we will pray that God brings a resolution to this story that works to their favor," Janice said.

"Thank you. To be honest, I've been so distracted with my animosity toward Rankin Smith that I haven't been the easiest to be around of late." He sighed again. "Harrison has witnessed a few outbursts on my part. And I'm afraid you ladies also saw that firsthand when I had my little episode in the café. Oh, and by the way, I still owe you for lunch. I plan to come back and make good on that."

"No worries, Corey." These words came from LuAnn.

"You've been more than gracious. I just get so worked up when I see how Smith has treated his clients."

LuAnn rose and paced the room. "Corey, we did some research online and learned that multiple people have filed complaints."

"Yes," he said. "I tracked down a couple, but they weren't open to talking to me. As soon as they heard I was writing an article, they tucked their tails between their legs and ran away."

"I guess that's understandable," Tess said. "Not everyone wants to go public with their story."

"Right." He paused. "But we've got to stop this guy before he moves on and does this elsewhere. He's already hit up people in Canton and a couple of other small towns in Ohio. I can't believe he's gotten away with this for so long, but he just seems to slip in and out of places like a phantom."

"LuAnn is giving thought to filing a complaint with the state insurance board," Tess said. "Have you considered that?"

"I've thought about it, but the process is long and agonizing, at least for some."

"Might be worth it, though," LuAnn called from across the room. "From what we understand, if they rule in your favor, it can result in the agent losing his license."

"Good. He needs to lose his license."

"I was thinking we could do it together," LuAnn explained. "And maybe I can reach out to some of the others who have been hurt by Rankin and they can file too. If we all come in with a bang, the state board will take the issue more seriously, don't you think?"

"Yes, I agree. And sure, I'll file if you do."

"Perfect. Would you like to come for lunch tomorrow?"

"Sure. Sounds good. I've got a couple of things to do at the office, but then I'll come over. I'm always up for Winnie's cooking."

Tess ended the call moments later and was just about to dive into a conversation with the other ladies when LuAnn's phone rang.

LuAnn pulled it from her pocket and glanced at the screen. "Oh, wow. That's a Canton area code." She answered it and put it on speaker right away.

The voice on the other end of the phone was filled with emotion. But there was no mistaking her words: "LuAnn, my name is Seraphina Houmana, and I'm calling to talk to you about ASAP Insurance. I hope you've got a few minutes, because boy, do I have a story to tell."

CHAPTER TWENTY-EIGHT

Seraphina's story ripped out Tess's heart and brought tears to her friends' eyes. She told an emotional tale of a car accident two years prior that seriously injured both of her children and physically impaired one of them for life. The man who caused the accident, a neighbor of hers in Canton, was insured by Rankin Smith.

"The company wasn't called ASAP," she explained. "It was AAA Affordable. And the agent didn't go by Rankin Smith, either. The card I was given said Grayson Anderson. So all of my searches, at least my initial ones, were for a man with that name."

"Only, he's not Grayson Anderson?" Tess asked. "He's Rankin Smith?"

"I don't think he's Rankin Smith, either," Seraphina explained. "But I have yet to find a real name. I started tracking stories of insurance scams across the state. There were quite a few here in Canton around the same time as mine, but then I noticed a shift...to other towns. First, to Youngstown and then Marietta."

"So this is his MO." Tess felt her anger growing as she realized the gravity of what Rankin had done, not just to Corey, not just to LuAnn, but to this woman and dozens of others like her.

"He bounces from town to town, setting up shop and then pocketing money from customers. He stays long enough to pitch the product but not long enough to pay out any claims."

"Yes," Seraphina responded. "Then he's off to a new place with a new office, a new business name, and new name for himself. So far, he's gone by Liam, Mitchell, Grayson, and Rankin."

"Interesting," LuAnn said. "Those are all names of characters from a detective show I watch."

"Seriously?" Seraphina asked. "Well, go figure."

"Yes." LuAnn paused and then snapped her fingers. "There's another prominent male character in that show, a guy named Vincent. He's the main character, actually."

"That might come in handy as I search for people who've been scammed in other towns," Seraphina said. "Who knows? He probably started in Akron as Vincent. Nothing would surprise me at this point. He's been at this a while, for sure. I've spoken to several others—probably half a dozen or so—and they're ready to file complaints too. So, we should have quite a case against the man."

"If only we can catch him before he slips away," Tess said.

"Right."

They ended the call with Seraphina, and Tess rose from her chair. "Well, there you have it, folks. Thanks to Seraphina we know that Rankin Smith isn't Rankin Smith. Whoever he is hasn't paid his rent and is likely on his way out of town."

The ladies discussed the subject a bit longer and then LuAnn placed a call to Officer Randy to give him a heads-up about what they had learned about Rankin Smith. She put the call on speaker.

"Unless we catch him in an actual crime, we can't go in and arrest him on your hearsay, LuAnn," he explained. "These kinds of matters are best dealt with by going through the—"

"State insurance board," the ladies said together.

"Yes." He paused. "Now, if you caught him in a local crime of some sort, that I could prosecute. But something of this nature is beyond us, sorry. I do promise to keep an eye on him, though."

"I doubt he'll be around long enough to keep an eye on," Brad said. "But thanks, Randy."

Tess was tempted to say, "Thanks for nothing," but decided against it.

She and Janice headed home long after the sun had set. She fed the animals, took Huck for a quick walk, and then tumbled into bed. Her dreams that night were scattered and erratic. They included all the children she'd met at the bakery, as well as Seraphina's children, who faded from the story as the dream went along.

Tess awoke feeling miserable. She couldn't tell if she was coming down with something or if the terrible night's sleep had left its mark on her joints and tendons. Regardless, she rose and went through her morning routine, including checking in new guests.

By early afternoon she was feeling better. Corey arrived after the lunch crowd left, just in time for a slice of peach pie

Winnie had baked. LuAnn and Tess ushered him into the café, and they all sat down together.

"Where is Janice?" LuAnn asked.

"In the office working on something." Tess shrugged. "We can fill her in later."

"Would you like coffee with that pie, Corey?" Winnie asked as she set the plate with his slice of pie down in front of him.

"Yes, please." He flashed a bright smile.

She disappeared into the kitchen and returned moments later with a steaming cup of coffee.

He jabbed a fork into the pie, took a bite, and then leaned back in his chair with a look of delirium on his face. "Winnie, this pie is remarkable."

"Thank you." She offered him a warm smile. "That's a recipe passed down from generations ago."

"It reminds me so much of the peach pie my wife used to make. I've never found one so much like it until now." He took another bite.

Tess squirmed in her chair. "Corey, before we dive into the insurance stuff, can I get one question out of the way?"

"Sure, I'm an open book." He took a swig of his coffee and set the mug back down.

"That morning of the Easter egg hunt, you knelt down and whispered something in Brianna's ear. I'm ashamed to admit it now, but I thought maybe you were telling her where the golden egg was. I suspected you'd seen it when you went over to talk to Griffin."

"What?" He looked mortified by this. "No way. I never even noticed the golden egg at all, to be honest. As for what I told Brianna..." He sighed. "I guess you might call it a bribe. I told her that I wanted to take her out for ice cream after the hunt was over, as long as she behaved for her mommy." A louder sigh escaped. "I guess we saw how that worked out."

"Oh well. She was having a rough morning."

"She has a lot of those. My wife was so good with her. I always knew Kelly would have made a wonderful mother. If you could have seen the way she loved not just Brianna, but those kids at that orphanage..." His words drifted off. "Trust me, there will never be another one like her. She had such amazing plans for her future. You wouldn't believe all the things Kelly wanted to do but never got the chance."

Tess pressed her palms against the table and stood abruptly, overcome with emotion. "Here's what we're going to do, Corey."

"What's that?" He looked up, fork midair with a piece of pie dangling from the end.

"We're going to help you raise the money to donate to that orphanage in Nicaragua."

"Wait...what?" He set the fork down.

"Yes." Tess's voice grew more animated as she spoke. "Just because Rankin—or whatever his name is today—didn't come through for you, that doesn't mean you can't see your wife's fondest wish come true. This was something huge on her bucket list, and I think we can all work together as a community to see it come to pass."

"Oh, Tess, this is a marvelous idea." LuAnn clasped her hands together and grinned. "I want to help. Brad can promote around town, and I can set up one of those online fundraiser sites. I'll also reach out to all of my friends on social media."

"I will too." Tess nodded.

"I think this is a marvelous idea, Tess, but I don't know what to say." Corey leaned back in his chair. "Kelly would be blown away that you're even thinking of doing this in her honor." He rose and flung his arms around Tess. "I'm so grateful."

"Happy to be of service." Tess paused, so many lovely thoughts tumbling through her head. "That's one of the things on my bucket list, actually," she said after a moment. "To be able to do more for others, I mean."

"I'd say this is a good start, for sure."

"What's a good start?" Janice entered the café, open laptop in hand. "What did I miss?"

"We're going to help Corey raise the funds to build the orphanage in Managua in his wife's honor."

"Oh, perfect idea!" She took a seat and set the laptop down in front of her. "Sign me up! Sorry I'm late, by the way."

"It's okay." Tess glanced down at the screen. "What are you doing?"

"Hmm?" She looked up from her laptop. "I transferred the pictures from the Easter egg hunt onto the laptop so I can finish editing them. I want to update the inn's website with a few when I'm finished."

Corey groaned as he saw a photo of himself. "Promise you won't post that picture of me."

"Okay, if you say so. But I think you made it into one of the videos I took that day too. Hang on and I'll pull it up."

She found the video in question and hit the PLAY button. Tess couldn't help but smile as she watched the events that took place on the lawn before the children arrived.

"I was just playing around with the camera's video feature," Janice explained. "But I caught you coming up the walkway, Corey."

The video carried on until Tess saw something that stopped her cold.

"Wait. Pause the video a minute, Janice." She pointed at the laptop screen. "Go back."

"What for, Tess?"

"Just go back about a minute or so."

Janice backed the video up and played it again. When it reached the point where Tess saw Rankin on the screen with the golden egg in his hand, she squealed, "Stop!"

Janice stopped the video right away. "Okay…"

"Don't you see? You had the answer all along, Janice."

"I did?"

"Yes. Rankin is in the corner by the daffodils. Take a look at that clip. You caught the whole thing."

"I can't believe I didn't notice it before." Janice replayed the clip.

"Yes!" LuAnn pointed at the screen. "He's definitely got the egg in his hand, and he put it back just seconds before Brad blew the whistle."

"I'd say we have a phone call to make." Tess reached for her cell phone.

"Who are we calling?" LuAnn asked.

"Officer Randy. Did he, or did he not say that we needed a local crime we could pin on Rankin, one that Randy could prosecute?"

"Why, yes, he did." LuAnn smiled. "Now let's pray we can catch the guy before he skips town."

CHAPTER TWENTY-NINE

Tess placed the call to Officer Randy, and he agreed to arrest Rankin...if he could find him.

"You say you've got proof that he stole the money?" Randy asked.

"Yes."

"Shoot me a copy of that video to my email address, would you? After I look it over, I'll put out a call and we'll bring him in for questioning."

"Go get him!" LuAnn called out.

"You ladies stay put," Officer Randy instructed Tess. "I've got officers on the way."

"Stay put?" Tess echoed. LuAnn shook her head.

"I'm not staying put," she said as soon as Tess ended the call. "This is one arrest I want to see firsthand."

"If he's even still there," Janice said.

Corey offered to drive, and minutes later they pulled into a parking spot at Town Center. Three police cars swarmed the building moments later, and a crowd gathered outside of the bakery and several other businesses as well.

"I think we'd better stay in the car," Corey advised.

Tess agreed. She watched in shock as two of the officers emerged from the building moments later with Rankin in custody.

LuAnn let out a whoop, and Corey voiced a loud, "Hallelujah!"

When the officers got Rankin to their car, they pressed him inside the back seat. Tess bolted from Corey's vehicle and headed over to Sandie, who watched the goings-on with her jaw dropped.

"I don't believe it." She glanced Tess's way. "Did you have something to do with this?"

"Maybe a little."

"I can't believe they got him." She swiped some flour off her cheek. "I thought he'd left town."

"We were hoping...and praying." Tess glanced in the direction of the patrol cars and gasped when she saw LuAnn headed straight for them. "Oh no!"

Tess barreled down the sidewalk until she caught up with her. From the back seat of the patrol car, Rankin carried on about how the cops had the wrong guy.

"You can't prove anything," he seethed. His gaze shot to LuAnn, and his eyes narrowed to slits.

"By the way, slick move on stealing three hundred dollars from the children of Marietta at the Easter egg hunt," Tess said to him. "But God already made good on that, so no worries."

"God?" He snorted.

"Yes." Tess brushed a loose hair out of her face. "He blessed us for giving the money to the child who won. And then we blessed someone else with a new stand mixer. She blessed our guests with great food. And one of those guests"—she gestured to Corey, who stood several feet away—"a man you know quite well, since you scammed him too…blessed us by linking arms to track you down. Oh, and the little girl who won? She blessed children with cancer in Memphis. *That's* the chain of blessing you created by stealing that money the children of Marietta that day. So I suppose we should be thanking you for all the blessings."

He rolled his eyes and leaned back against the seat, pain etched on his face as his handcuffed arms contorted behind him. "You people are very confusing."

"Aren't we, though?" Tess laughed. "But don't worry, Rankin. You'll get a better taste of us in the weeks to come, as we track down more of the people you scammed. You really got around, by the way…Vincent."

His eyes grew wider than ever.

The officer slammed the back door of the patrol car as Corey approached.

"I guess it's safe to say the police got their man."

"Police, nothing." Tess laughed again. "We got our man. And boy oh boy, was he ever a hard egg to crack."

Chapter Thirty

May 30, 1860

Prudence was slumbering with her son in her arms when a rap at the cabin door roused her. She laid her little one down. Cracking the door open, she saw Adeline and Shepherd Lee standing there. Adeline held a piece of stationery in her hand, which she raised as soon as the door opened.

"Oh, Prudence!" She continued to wave the paper in the air.

"What is it, Adeline?"

"I've heard from Lolly's family in Syracuse."

Prudence's heart began to thump. She stepped outside, so as not to wake the baby. "Yes? What has thee heard? Did she make it?"

"She arrived, but less than a week later she passed in her sleep. They've buried her in the family cemetery."

"Oh my." Prudence's heart swelled with the realization that Lolly had lived to see her promised land, both the natural and now the spiritual. "Free at last."

"Yes, free at last," Shepherd said. "In the best possible way one obtains freedom."

"She inspired me in so many ways." Adeline's eyes filled with tears, and she swiped the moisture away with the back of her hand. "I've been thinking about what she said, about living until you die."

"Yes, as have I."

"I've dared to dream again, to hope again..." A smile tipped up the edges of her lips, and her cheeks turned pink. "I do hope to fulfill my promise to Lolly, when the time is right, Pru. I'm not sure how I will manage it, but one day I will go to Paris and will fulfill her wish, to see it all through her eyes."

"I have no doubt thee will, Adeline." Prudence reached to squeeze her friend's hand. "And when thee does, just know that I will be there with thee, in spirit."

CHAPTER THIRTY-ONE

On the Saturday after the police arrested Rankin Smith, Tess decided to give Prudence's diary a closer look. She couldn't stop the nagging feeling that she'd overlooked something. She scrolled past the now-familiar sections about Adeline to the entries from the following year. When she reached two additional entries, Tess wanted to jump for joy. She could hardly wait to share what she'd found with Daisy. But first, to tell Janice and LuAnn.

She raced downstairs and found Janice in the kitchen with Winnie, who was baking another strawberry lemonade cake.

"Who's that for?"

Winnie wiped her hands on her apron. "It's for that nice yard man. I heard all about his family—his wife and those two kids. And I remembered that strawberry lemonade cake was a favorite of his, so I decided, since it's Saturday and all, that I would bake him a cake as a thank-you for all he's done. I know not everyone will see it my way, but I believe the man is rehabilitated."

"Do you, now?" Tess did her best not to chuckle aloud.

"I do. And I figured, if he had a whole cake to take home, he could share it with the family. People bond around cake, you know."

"Yes, they do." Tess couldn't help but smile. "I think it's a fantastic idea, Winnie, and I'm sure the whole family will love it."

Winnie turned back to her work, and Janice took a few steps in Tess's direction.

"Is that Prudence's diary, Tess?" she asked.

"Yes, I have something to show you. You're not going to believe it, Janice."

Before she could say another word, LuAnn rushed into the kitchen from the back door.

"Ladies! Stop everything you're doing! I have news."

Tess didn't interrupt her to say that she had news as well. She simply let her friend forge ahead.

LuAnn stopped to catch her breath. "You're not going to believe what Brad has done." She broke into a happy dance. "He's booked a tour of the Greek islands for the two of us."

"No way." Janice's mouth fell open.

"Yes. Not until next spring, but I can't wait!"

"LuAnn, that's one of the sweetest things I've ever heard. Brad just earned extra points for that one."

"I'm so jealous!" Janice released a lingering sigh. "Tell us all about it."

"Well, we fly into Venice."

"Italy?" Janice's eyes bugged.

"Yes. The first ten days will be on a Mediterranean cruise that will take us up and down most of the Italian coast and then the Greek isles. We'll have two nights in Santorini. Can you imagine?"

"Heavens." Tess could imagine, all right.

"After that we'll end the cruise in Athens, where we'll be staying at a wonderful hotel for another four days of sightseeing and fun. He said we can book some guided tours when we get there if we like. Or maybe we'll just lounge around on the beach."

"I hope you'll get to see the Parthenon."

"Oh, for sure. And the Acropolis. We're already planning both of those. But there are so many other options."

On and on she went, talking about her upcoming trip and how amazing her husband was. Tess couldn't dispute that fact, but she had a little news of her own.

Thank goodness for Winnie. She turned back from decorating the cake and said, "Now, what was it you were saying about that diary, Tess?"

"Oh, right." Tess held it up. "I've learned something rather shocking. I can't believe I overlooked it before."

"About…?" LuAnn asked.

"Adeline. According to an entry I just found, she actually went to Paris."

"What?" Janice squealed. "Goodness gracious goat! That's so cool. I wonder if Daisy knows."

"I'm going to call her when things slow down."

"What does it say?" Janice asked.

"Wait till you hear." Tess opened the diary and flipped to the entry. She read, "'I could not believe my ears when I heard the good news. Adeline sold her most precious possession, the brooch her grandmother passed down to her, so that she might travel to Paris. She sent a postcard postmarked Paris, France, with just two words scribbled on it: For Lolly.'"

The room grew silent when Tess stopped reading.

"Whoa." Janice shook her head. "Not what I was expecting."

"Right, but that's the long and short of it."

"I just can't believe it." LuAnn turned thoughtful a moment. "She was willing to give up something that meant the world to her so that she could experience Paris…for Lolly. That's remarkable."

"Very," Tess agreed. "But that should tell you how deeply she cared about keeping her word. She was willing to give what she had, a very valuable gift, indeed."

Janice looked puzzled. "And yet somehow it survived and is in Daisy's possession today."

Tess smiled. "That's the best part. This is an entry three months later. 'Oh, how my heart wanted to sing when I heard the news from Adeline. Her precious friend Shepherd purchased the brooch and presented it to her when he asked her to marry him. I've never seen my friend more delighted than when he pinned the brooch onto her shawl once and for all.'"

"Shepherd Lee?" LuAnn asked. "The abolitionist who walked Adeline to Prudence's home?"

"One and the same," Tess said. "But the best part of the story is yet to come."

"I can't believe there's more than that," Janice said. "I'm overwhelmed already."

"Just wait." Tess could hardly wait to share the rest. "Adeline went on to become a publisher."

"What?" LuAnn gasped. "Are you serious?"

"Yes. Her company published books in braille. Hundreds of them."

"Oh that's wonderful." Janice's eyes glistened.

Tess nodded. "I'll call her when things settle down and share all of these entries I've found. But doesn't it touch your heart to know that God used Lolly's trip to change Adeline's life?"

"It does. And He's still in the business of doing that."

Tess's thoughts drifted for a moment. "You know, I've been thinking about something."

"What's that?" LuAnn asked.

"How the world is filled with givers and takers."

"True, that," Winnie said from her spot at the counter, where she continued to work on the cake.

"I want to be a giver." Tess paused to think through her next words. "When people look back on my life, I want them to see a woman who was more interested in the needs of others than her own life. I want to be an Adeline or a Prudence or a Shepherd. I never want to be a Rankin, only thinking of myself."

Janice rested her hand on Tess's arm. "No one could ever see you as a taker, Tess. You're one of the most giving people I know."

"I hope so," Tess said. "We're all going to leave a legacy of one kind or another. Even someone like Griffin, who's got a past. He's hurt others, but he's a new man. It's not too late for him to leave those beautiful children of his a legacy they can be proud of."

"Amen," Winnie chimed in.

LuAnn nodded. "You're right. And you're good and kind, Tess, seeing the best in him from the get-go."

Winnie cleared her throat but said nothing. Instead, she started humming "Amazing Grace."

"I just felt for him, is all. But I've been thinking a lot about this whole legacy thing, and I've had a revelation, of sorts. If you take a good look at Daisy's bucket list you'll see that most everything on it was for Mandy, not for herself. She wanted to bring the legacy of her family alive to her granddaughter while there was still time. It's actually a gift she was giving, not something she was taking for herself."

"You're so right, Tess," Janice said. "I hadn't thought about it, but that's so true."

Their conversation was interrupted by a familiar voice ringing out from the lobby. "Yoo-hoo. Anyone here?"

Tess set the diary down on the counter and walked out into the lobby to discover Sandie Ballard.

"Hey there. Good to see you."

"Good to see you too. I stopped by to ask Winnie some questions about her buttermilk pie recipe." Sandie's gaze shifted to the front window and her mouth fell into a perfect *O* when she saw Corey and Griffin entering the front lawn, headed for the daffodils. "Oh no! I didn't know Corey was coming here today. If I had, I would have worn something nice. Fixed my hair."

Tess chuckled. "You look smashing, as always, Sandie."

"Well, come on! What are we waiting for?" Sandie took Tess by the arm and practically pulled her out into the front yard and over to the two men.

"Hey." Corey offered Sandie a welcoming smile as she bounded his direction. "I didn't know you were going to be here today."

"I was just saying that about you." Her eyelashes fluttered.

"I just had to come by and pass off some materials to Griffin," Corey explained. "He's going to be helping us out with our chaplaincy program."

"Yeah, he wore me down." Griffin laughed. "I can't go back into the prison just yet, but I can help out in the office. That was my compromise until the time is right."

"I think that's great, Griffin." Tess gave him an admiring look. "Good for you."

Sandie managed to pull Corey aside for a chat about the article he was writing for the paper, which left Tess alone with Griffin.

"I'm so proud of you, Griffin. I really am."

"Thank you. That means a lot." He grinned. "Hey, I heard you caught that guy who stole the money. I'm glad."

"We're very relieved."

"I'm sure."

"I think Winnie has a gift for you when you're done with the lawn. You'll need to head inside to the kitchen to fetch it."

His eyes widened. "Really."

"Mm-hmm. Emphasis on *mm*." She laughed.

"This day just keeps getting better and better. You're not going to believe it, Tess, but my wife has agreed to go out on a date with me later this afternoon. We're going to Muskingum Park, right on the river, for a picnic."

"Griffin, that's fantastic news."

"I'm hopeful." He gave Tess an inquisitive look. "You know, I had never really put a lot of stock in this whole prayer thing. I mean, in prison some of the guys get religious. They talk a big game. When Corey and Harrison used to come to the prison, they would preach to us." He smiled. "Well, that's what I called it back then, preaching. They were sharing their stories with us, I guess you'd say."

"Their testimonies."

"Yeah. Testimonies. Back then I just thought they were a couple of religious fanatics."

"I'd say you've figured out by now that it's not about religion."

"Yes." He smiled. "I guess you could say I've witnessed that firsthand. I'm glad Corey caught up with me that day at the Easter egg hunt. I was embarrassed to see him because I thought he might push me into something I wasn't ready for. But it turns out I was ready. So, I decided to let him know that something in me had changed, that his words finally sank in."

"Griffin, from what I can gather, you're a changed man. And your wife sees the difference in you, I'm sure. There's nothing like a changed life to make someone sit up and pay attention. But if you don't mind, can I give you one piece of advice?"

"Sure, Tess."

"I know you're getting your life together for your wife and children, but do it for yourself too. You're worth it, you know."

For a moment he didn't say anything. Then he slowly shook his head. "It might take a while for that to sink in, but I can see how you might be right."

"I am right. You're as valuable to God as they are, even if you can't see it just yet."

He pulled off his hat and raked his fingers through his hair. "Yeah, it might be a while before I make that much progress. For now, I'll just go with the 'You're worth it' line."

"You'll get there."

"Maybe. But thanks again for everything you've done. I don't know that I've ever met anyone like you. The other ladies too, of course, but especially you. You gave me a chance when no one else would. Risky."

"What's life without a little risk?" Even as she spoke the words, Tess thought about Daisy, parasailing high above the earth, free as a bird.

Yes, life was about risks, wasn't it? And maybe—just maybe—it was about time to take a few of her own. She would start by making her very own bucket list.

DAISY CARMICHAEL'S BUCKET LIST

(What's on yours?)

1. Visit Playa Del Carmen, Mexico, with Tori and other grand-children. (Check!)

2. Trip to Paris with Tori. (Check!)

3. Caribbean cruise with Mandy. (Check!)

4. Parachute out of airplane with handsome stranger as copilot. (Check! Don't let Tori know!)

5. Sing a solo in front of the church. (Check!)

6. Visit Marietta, home of my great-great-grandmother, Adeline Lee. (Check!)

7. Visit library for the blind in Ohio to see the fruit of Adeline's labors. (Check!)

8. Parasail over the Ohio River so I can see the route many of the travelers took as they escaped slavery. (Check!)

9. Present Mandy with the fleur-de-lis. (Check!)

10. ~~Visit the Seven Wonders of the World.~~ (With all I have seen and experienced thus far, this will no longer be necessary.)

AUTHOR LETTER

Oh, how I loved writing this story! The idea of putting together a "bucket list" tale (carefully woven around a mystery at Wayfarers, no less) was pure delight. And boy, did I ever fall in love with Daisy and Miranda. (I want to be Daisy when I grow up!)

Now, I have a few years to go before I hit Daisy's age, but I'm already giving thought to my bucket list. I've been blessed to enjoy so many adventures in my life already (a trip to the Holy Land, for instance, and multiple Caribbean cruises). But there are still adventures to be had, and I'd better set some plans in motion now so that they can become a reality. I've promised one granddaughter a trip to Paris for her thirteenth birthday, and that date is rapidly approaching! I'm also longing to go to Italy and Greece. (Hello, Mediterranean cruise!) That's definitely on my bucket list. To see Santorini would be a dream.

What about you? What items would you add to your list? Sure, some might seem unrealistic, but, remember...God gives us dreams for a reason. They really do keep us alive and looking forward instead of backward. As we age, that's so important.

No matter where you are, you can still enjoy some fun bucket list items (even if your trips are virtual, via the internet). Get creative and come up with a list that makes sense to your situation. But don't be afraid to think outside the box! Do something extraordinary. You'll be so glad you did.

ABOUT THE AUTHOR

Award-winning author Janice Thompson got her start in the industry writing screenplays and musical comedies for the stage. Janice has published 130 books for the Christian market, crossing genre lines to write cozy mysteries, historicals, romances, nonfiction books, devotionals, children's books, and more. She particularly enjoys writing light-hearted, comedic tales because she enjoys making readers laugh. Janice is passionate about her faith and does all she can to share the joy of the Lord with others, which is why she particularly enjoys writing. Her tagline, "Love, Laughter, and Happily Ever Afters!" sums up her take on life. She lives in Spring, Texas, where she leads a rich life with her family, a host of writing friends, and three rambunctious canines. When she's not busy writing or playing with her nine grandchildren, Janice can be found in the kitchen, baking specialty cakes and cookies for friends and loved ones. No matter what she's cooking up—books, cakes, cookies, or mischief—she does her best to keep the Lord at the center of it all.

PARASAILING IN OHIO

If you've ever longed to fly above your circumstances, maybe you should consider parasailing or hang gliding. If you're visiting the great state of Ohio, opportunities abound. Many people enjoy taking to the skies in this beautiful state. And why not? Southwestern Ohio is, after all, home to two of the most well-known flight-loving daredevils of all times, the Wright Brothers.

Whether you're hang gliding or paragliding or parasailing, you will find a plethora of locations, ready to serve you. Climb aboard and soar above your circumstances. You'll feel like an eagle as you take to flight, soaring up to two thousand feet above the ground.

The Ohio countryside is especially pretty in the fall and the spring, so consider a trip during that time of year. Views are breathtaking from up above, where you can embrace freedom as you float along on the morning breeze. No effort required! Just settle in and enjoy this serene experience, one with a stellar bird's-eye view. And who knows? You might just catch a glimpse of Adeline and Shepherd, walking hand in hand along the river's edge below.

Disclaimer: Fly at your own risk!

Winnie's Strawberry Lemonade Cake

Cake Ingredients:

6 large eggs

2 white cake mixes

1 cup lemon juice

1 cup water

1 cup vegetable oil

Yellow food coloring (dash)

1 10-oz jar lemon curd

2 cups fresh strawberries

¼ cup powdered sugar

1 pint heavy whipping cream

¼ cup granulated sugar

1 package instant lemon pudding

Instructions:

- Mix first six ingredients and bake in three 8-inch pans (lightly greased and floured).

- While the cake is baking, stir lemon curd in a bowl until smooth.

- In a separate bowl, make stabilized whipped cream: Whip one container of whipping cream to soft peaks. Add sugar and instant lemon pudding. Whip until mixture reaches a creamy consistency.

- Now it's time to prepare the fruit. Wash and slice 2 cups of fresh strawberries. Sprinkle with ¼ cup powdered sugar and place in refrigerator.

After the Cake Bakes:

- Allow the layers to cool completely. Level, if necessary. Now it's time to stack! Start with the first layer of cake. Spread top with lemon curd, then add berries. Top it off with lemon-flavored whipped cream.
- Add the next cake layer, top with lemon curd, add berries, whipped cream, and so on, until you complete assembly. It's always a lot of fun to figure out how to make the sides look pretty. Choose from any number of frosting bag tips so the whipped cream looks like the star of the show. Top off the whole thing with some fresh berries and just wait for the *oohing* and *aahing* to begin.

Read on for a sneak peek of another exciting book
in the Secrets of Wayfarers Inn series!

TRUE NORTH
by Leslie Gould

Janice stood at the counter of Wayfarers Inn, hardly able to contain her excitement. Not only was it her favorite time of the day—check-in time—but her childhood friend Anthony Herres was coming to town for the Surveyors Historical Society conference. He'd contacted her, after over thirty-five years, saying he'd like to stay at the inn. Thankfully there was a room available.

And now he was here. He'd sent a text a few minutes ago, saying he'd just arrived.

The front door opened, letting in a welcome wave of mid-afternoon sunshine. The late April weather had just started to turn warm in the last couple of days and was predicted to continue through the next week. She squinted. A man with short gray hair and a goatee carefully closed the door behind him. He carried a leather messenger bag strapped over his shoulder and a small suitcase in his hand. He wore a jacket and faded jeans.

The man turned toward the counter. "Janice?"

"Anthony?" she replied.

He nodded.

She hurried around the counter. He put down his suitcase and extended his hand, but she ignored it and gave him a hug.

He chuckled as he hugged her back. "You haven't changed a bit."

She let him go and stepped back.

He chuckled again. "Don't try to say I haven't changed. I have."

"Well, of course you have," she said. "You were still a boy the last time I saw you." He had changed quite a bit, actually. He appeared weathered and worn down, as if life hadn't been kind to him. "What's kept you away from Marietta all these years?"

"Lots of things. My job. Life's twists and turns." He shrugged. "Bad memories."

Janice tilted her head, ready to listen. She knew Anthony's childhood hadn't been easy.

He smiled a little and said, "When I left Marietta, I tried to put it all behind me. And I thought I had. But in the last few years I've found myself thinking about my childhood more and more. When I found out the Surveyors Historical Society conference was here this year, I knew I had to come back." He shrugged. "Anyway, enough of that." He smiled more broadly. "An extra bonus is to get to see you and stay in this lovely inn. When I was a child I was fascinated by Underground Railroad stories. You know, I worked at the Kellen mansion as a teenager."

The mansion had been rumored to be on the Underground Railroad, but no definitive documentation existed. "I do remember you worked there," Janice said. "I've been assigned to host the property for a special Marietta Home Tour this Sunday." It was an annual fundraiser event that featured a different Marietta home each year and raised money for the Washington County Community Foundation.

"Nice." Anthony's eyes were wistful. "I always loved that place but haven't given it much thought until a few months ago. I left Marietta straight for college and never came back. My parents moved to Indianapolis, so I didn't have any reason to, although I didn't see them much after high school either."

It sounded as if there was a lot she hadn't known about his childhood.

"Well," Anthony said, "I should get checked in."

Janice smiled. "Let's do that." She turned back to the counter and grabbed a registration form along with a pen.

Before turning his attention to the form, he glanced around the lobby again and said, "You've done wonders with this place."

"We have," Janice said. "Lots of blood, sweat, tears, and renovation."

Anthony sighed happily. "It has a good feeling to it. I'd say you and your friends have put a lot of love into it too."

"Oh, we have," Janice said. "Love for each other. Love for this town and its people. And love for our guests."

He let out another sigh. "I'm so glad I found you online."

Janice nodded. "So am I."

As he filled out the form, he said, "When can we catch up? I don't have to be at the conference center until after seven tonight, and then only to pick up my registration packet."

"Great!" Janice said. "How about if we get dinner together? We can talk then."

Two hours later Anthony followed Janice into the Galley at the Hackett Hotel. He'd chosen the restaurant and insisted it was his treat. Janice believed it might be more than he could afford, but didn't say anything. Then again, perhaps she was remembering that he grew up poor, or so it seemed to her looking back. As a child she hadn't given it much thought.

She wasn't sure what to order. The teriyaki salmon? Or the coconut lime chicken with basil sauce? She decided on the salmon, and Anthony said he'd have the same.

After the waiter left Janice said, "Tell me what you've been up to the last thirty-five years."

"Thirty-five?" he said with a smile. "It's closer to forty."

She laughed. "That long? It's so easy to lose track."

He leaned forward. "I'm sorry about your husband. When I googled you, I found his obituary."

"Thank you," Janice said. "His death shook my world, but I've found my way again. The inn. Friends. My kids and grand-children." She smiled. "Life goes on."

"It certainly does." He took a sip of his water. "So you were a pastor's wife?"

Janice nodded.

"I bet you were really good at that."

She shrugged. "I don't know about that. But I did enjoy it. And I'm finding that being an innkeeper is its own kind of ministry. I treat our guests the same way I used to treat our church members."

Anthony's eyes glistened. "Back in high school, you had those same gifts, including a tender heart. Do you remember inviting me to your church youth group?"

"I do," she said. "I was so thrilled that you came and then kept attending."

"It was a highlight of my school years, honestly," Anthony said. "Remember the retreat we went on? Up by Jackson?"

Janice frowned, remembering. "Hmm, was that the one where the van broke down and we were stuck alongside the road for half the night?"

Anthony chuckled. "And we stayed awake and played charades and sang songs."

Janice barely remembered the details, but she did remember wondering if Anthony had regretted she'd ever invited him to join the youth group. "I'm glad it's a pleasant memory."

"Are you kidding? It's my favorite high school memory."

Janice couldn't help but smile. She met Anthony's gaze. "Tell me about yourself. All I know is that you live in Maine. What have you been up to all these years?"

"Well, most recently, getting and staying sober."

"Oh?"

He nodded. "I don't know if you remember this, but my dad was a mean drunk. I swore I'd never have a drinking problem, but about five years ago, I finally admitted I did. I've been sober for a while now."

"Excellent," Janice said. "What about family?"

"No kids," he answered. "I was married for nearly twenty years, but we divorced five years ago. That loss actually made me wake up to my drinking problem. However, my ex-wife and I have stayed friends, so that's been a good thing. Her name is Barb—I don't know where I'd be without her."

She wasn't sure how to respond. There was a lot of heartache, along with some positives, all wrapped up together. "What about your work?" she asked. "What do you do?"

"I've worked for the Maine Department of Transportation since I graduated from college."

"As?"

"A surveyor."

"Ah," Janice said. "Thus the convention."

He nodded as he took a small box out of his messenger bag. "Do you remember when I used to do yardwork for Dennis Kellen? He gave me a compass that belonged to George Washington."

Janice almost choked on her sip of tea. "*The* George Washington?"

"The one and only," Anthony said as he opened the box. Inside was an antique silver compass with a floating dial. He flipped it to show *Geo. Washington, 1746* engraved on the back.

"Wow." Janice was dumbfounded. She remembered that Anthony worked on the Kellen estate, but she was shocked that Dennis Kellen would have parted with such a valuable item.

"May I take a photo of it?"

"Sure." Anthony held it up, and Janice took a picture. Then she zoomed in and took a photo of just the face of the compass.

"Take a photo of the back too." Anthony flipped it around, and as Janice took the photo, he said, "George Washington was fourteen in 1746."

"Any idea who gave it to him? Since it's engraved, it seems like it might be special."

Anthony shook his head. "But he used it when he explored the Ohio Country back in 1753. I guessed that was so, but finally had it authenticated through a historian who does consultation work at Mount Vernon. She couldn't confirm who would have given it to him and declined to speculate, but she did mention a journal entry from during his time surveying the Ohio Country. He said he was using a compass he had since he was fourteen. Anyway, I've treasured it all these years, but at the end of the conference, I'm going to donate it to the Washington County Historical Museum."

Janice tilted her head. "Why here and not Mount Vernon?"

He wrapped his hand around the compass. "For a couple of reasons. First of all because George Washington surveyed this area, with this compass. The other reason I want to donate it is because I don't know how long the Kellen family owned the compass or how they got it in the first place, but they must have had some connection to George Washington."

Janice had a vague memory of Prudence Willard mentioning the Kellen name in her diary, from the mid-1800s. She needed to go back and check in what context.

Anthony continued. "When I spoke with the historian and we went through all of the history of the compass, he thought it fitting that it should be donated to the museum here in Marietta. One of Washington's compasses is already on display at Mt. Vernon, and there aren't any items here from Washington's survey crew."

"Well," Janice said, "it will be a really lovely piece for the historical society to have."

"I thought about giving the compass to my ex," Anthony said. "Barb has a sailboat and sails out of Portland all over Casco Bay, and has always admired it. She even asked me for it when I told her I was going to donate it to the museum here. She really does deserve it for staying my friend, for being my biggest supporter through my recovery." He unwrapped his silverware and put his napkin in his lap. "She's a life coach and often uses compasses as a metaphor when she teaches about taking charge of one's life. That was another reason she wanted the compass. But, in the end, I thought it belonged back here in Marietta."

Janice nodded to encourage him to keep speaking.

Anthony smiled. "I spoke with the curator at the museum—"

"Margaret Ashworth."

"Yes, that's her name. I'll present the compass to her on the last day of the conference."

"She must be thrilled," Janice said.

He returned the compass to the box. "She could hardly contain her excitement over the phone. I'll meet with her tomorrow." He closed the box and slipped it back into his bag.

Janice took a sip of her water and then said, "Will it be sad for you to give the compass up?"

He shook his head. "It belongs here in Marietta. It helped me find my way—to college, to my job as a surveyor. It's hard to explain, but I believe it even led me to sobriety."

"Any idea how the Kellen family came into possession of it?"

"I have no idea," Anthony said.

The two continued to chat about Marietta history. Just as they finished eating, Margaret entered the restaurant. She waved when she saw Janice and headed toward the table. "Tess told me I'd find you two here." She turned toward Anthony. "I'm Margaret Ashworth."

Anthony stood and extended his hand. "I'm so pleased to meet you in person."

In a high-pitched voice, Margaret said, "I'm afraid I have something rather important I need to discuss with you."

"Oh."

Margaret cleared her throat.

Janice asked, "Do you need me to leave?"

"No," Anthony said. "It's nothing you can't hear, I'm sure." He turned his attention back to Margaret. "Go ahead."

Margaret sat down in the chair next to Janice. Her eyebrows shot up as she glared at Anthony. "I just got off the phone with LaDonna Kellen Williamson, Dennis Kellen's daughter. She lives in Richmond but is in town for the conference. She saw the item in the program about you donating the compass to the museum."

Anthony smiled. "That's wonderful. Perhaps we can include her in the ceremony."

"Oh, I doubt that," Margaret said as the waiter approached the table with the check. "She claims her father left her the compass in his will, but you stole it before she could claim it." Margaret pursed her lips together. "She's at the college right now, and she wants it back."

A Note from the Editors

We hope you enjoy Secrets of Wayfarers Inn, created by the Books and Inspirational Media Division of Guideposts, a nonprofit organization that touches millions of lives every day through products and services that inspire, encourage, help you grow in your faith, and celebrate God's love in every aspect of your daily life.

Thank you for making a difference with your purchase of this book, which helps fund our many outreach programs to military personnel, prisons, hospitals, nursing homes, and educational institutions. To learn more, visit Guideposts Foundation.org.

We also maintain many useful and uplifting online resources. Visit Guideposts.org to read true stories of hope and inspiration, access OurPrayer network, sign up for free newsletters, download free e-books, join our Facebook community, and follow our stimulating blogs.

To learn about other Guideposts publications, including the best-selling devotional *Daily Guideposts*, go to ShopGuideposts .org, call (800) 932-2145, or write to Guideposts, PO Box 5815, Harlan, Iowa 51593.

Sign up for the Guideposts Fiction Newsletter

and stay up to date on the books you love!

You'll get sneak peeks of new releases, recommendations from other Guideposts readers, and special offers just for you . . . **and it's FREE!**

Just go to Guideposts.org/Newsletters today to sign up.

Guideposts®

Visit Guideposts.org/Shop or call (800) 932-2145

Find more inspiring fiction in these best-loved Guideposts series!

Tearoom Mysteries Series

Mix one stately Victorian home, a charming lakeside town in Maine, and two adventurous cousins with a passion for tea and hospitality. Add a large scoop of intriguing mystery and sprinkle generously with faith, family, and friends, and you have the recipe for *Tearoom Mysteries*.

Sugarcreek Amish Mysteries

Be intrigued by the suspense and joyful "aha" moments in these delightful stories. Each book in the series brings together two women of vastly different backgrounds and traditions, who realize there's much more to the "simple life" than meets the eye.

Mysteries of Martha's Vineyard

What does Priscilla Latham Grant, a Kansas farm girl know about hidden treasure and rising tides, maritime history and local isle lore? Not much—but to save her lighthouse and family reputation, she better learn quickly!

Mysteries of Silver Peak

Escape to the historic mining town of Silver Peak, Colorado, and discover how one woman's love of antiques helps her solve mysteries buried deep in the town's checkered past.

**To learn more about these books,
visit Guideposts.org/Shop**